HELL ON HIGH

"Clark's much-anticipated follow-up to his **Dead Man** series sweeps readers into the tumultuous path of Juliana, a tough-as-nails heroine for the ages. Spanning multiple countries and all terrains, Juliana's journey takes the reader to the mouth of madness, and the furthest reaches of human endurance. A thrilling story of heart, horror and perseverance – not to be missed."

—Laurel Hightower, author of **Every Woman Knows This: A Horror Collection** and **Crossroads**

"Michael Clark returns with his best book to date. An adventurous novel of human horror, Clark has crafted a gripping novel that you won't be able to put down."

—John Lynch, author of **The Warrior Retreat**

HELL ON HIGH

by Michael Clark

Hell on High

Copyright 2023 © Michael Clark

This book is a work of fiction. All of the characters, organizations, and events portrayed in this story are either products of the author's imagination or are used fictitiously. Any resemblance to actual events or locales or persons, living or dead, is entirely coincidental.

All rights reserved. No part of this publication may be reproduced in any form or by any means without the express written permission of the publisher, except in the case of brief excerpts in critical reviews or articles.

Edited by MJ Pankey
Formatted by Stephanie Ellis

Cover illustration and design by Mateus Roberts
First Edition: March 2023

ISBN (paperback): 978-1-957537-54-2
ISBN (ebook): 978-1-957537-53-5

Library of Congress Control Number: 2023932787

BRIGIDS GATE PRESS

Overland Park, Kansas

www.brigidsgatepress.com

Printed in the United States of America

Content warnings are provided at the end of this book

Why Brazil?

In the age of the controversy surrounding "American Dirt" by Jeanine Cummins, I thought I might write a few words about why I chose to start my book in the country of Brazil—a country I wasn't born in.

Back in 1998, I showed up for work as a restaurant manager in Nashua, New Hampshire, and was surprised to discover that the entire kitchen was Brazilian. Back then, New Hampshire was ninety-six percent Caucasian. Nashua, closer to Boston than my hometown of Dover, was slightly more diverse.

I soon learned that Brazilians came to the United States to work hard, sometimes as many as eighty hours per week, to send money home to their families and provide as they could not back home. I admired their spirit and strength. This group of warm souls was quick to drop their native Portuguese around me, which, while unnecessary, was extremely kind, and I was touched; they didn't want to exclude me from their conversations.

Many were here illegally, and that didn't bother me. They weren't stealing anyone's jobs—take my word for it (this is still true today, post-COVID-19. Businesses of all types are woefully short-staffed). They paid taxes too. Some think all undocumented workers are paid under the table, but this is largely untrue. Taxes are taken directly from their paychecks, just like American citizens. I was so appreciative of this crew that I signed sponsorship papers for three of them to be put on the path to citizenship.

Two years later, in the year 2000, after the end of my first marriage, I met a Brazilian woman named Josilene. Josi was here *legally*, first on a travel visa, then transferring to a student visa. As the years went by and our relationship progressed, she made plans to stay, and we attempted to have her family come and visit, but very soon, I learned our system was broken.

At the time (approximately 2005), applying for a tourist visa cost one hundred US dollars—and to my surprise, an almost guaranteed waste of money. I'm not sure if the consulates have daily quotas, but a typical appointment resulted in a two-minute dismissal with no reason for rejection. *Why are you here? Why do you want to go to the United States? No.* The argument to "get in line" to enter legally is a fallacy; *there's no line to get in.*

This happened three times to my mother-in-law, three times to my sister-in-law, and once to my cousin-in-law's mother. A hundred dollars goes a long way in Brazil, and absolutely no one wants to pay to be treated like dirt. Most of these sham appointments ended in tears. Embarrassed by how my in-laws were treated, I realized that if I were a hopeful immigrant, hungry or in peril, I would have no choice but try to cross the border illegally too.

Luckily, my in-laws were not desperate, so we hired a *forwarding agent* (I had no idea the service existed) who knew a way through the wall of red tape. Thankfully, those days are behind us. For the past twenty-two years, I've visited Brazil annually. I've spent more than a year there when I add up all the time. Josi and I have shared cultures for nearly forty percent of my life, so naturally, Brazil is now like a second home.

Why did I use Brazil for a part of this book? The answer is that I was interested in writing about black magick and wanted a fresh setting for the reader—something other than Salem, Massachusetts (not really witches) or New Orleans (voodoo). While Brazil is predominantly Christian, I have seen the Afro-Brazilian religion *Macumba* in practice—in the form of despachos (portable altars) left at crossroads, statues of orixás (gods) in city parks, and flowers tossed in the ocean on New Year's Eve for Yemanja, the goddess of the sea.

This book is not a commentary on the politics of Brazil or the practice of Macumba. My villain is as atypical to Brazil as Hannibal Lecter is to the United States. I do not teach, preach, or condescend but rather launch my story with love and respect for a place I know a great deal about.

The first act is based on real-life border crossings by people with no choice but to leave their countries. My wife, a teacher in Massachusetts, has had dozens, if not hundreds, of undocumented children in her classroom over the years, some sharing stories of crossing rivers to get here. I've driven from Phoenix down through Sonoyta, Mexico, and back, and that stretch of land is in these pages. To round things out, I read *The Devil's Highway* by Luis Alberto Urrea and gave myself a YouTube education on some of the most perilous parts, most importantly, *CBS Reports | Darien Gap: Desperate Journey to America.*

My closing comments on our immigration problem: Diversity is our strength. We always have and always should welcome good people regardless of race or nationality. Aside from love, brotherhood, and sisterhood, immigration keeps America young. Japan and Germany face aging populations that threaten the solvency of their social security programs. We never want that problem.

Of course, we don't want to welcome terrorists or drug and human traffickers either, which leads me to believe the answer lies in an international record-keeping system. It won't be perfect, but it's something we haven't yet tried—and what we have now finances evil and costs good people their lives.

Chapter 1

Boa Vista, Brazil 1970

Carlos DaSilva died on the table, yet another case of septic shock. Dr. José Machado, DaSilva's captor, bellowed in frustration as the soul left the remains. Dr. Zé (as his legitimate patients called him) shook his head. No one was here to help, no assistants, nurses, or other doctors of any kind. Patients did not last long here, especially after they'd lost hope, and hope was the one thing Dr. Zé couldn't sell them. Agitated, Zé stepped back from the operating table and let DaSilva's body slump.

The environment here was not sterile enough and never would be. This barn was wrong for his purposes. It was too close to the livestock and only separated by an unsealed wall. A new facility would have to be built from scratch, but not here, for the new construction would be noticed. Zé pulled off his gloves and cursed. Donors were hard to come by. This one had not made it seventeen days. The body was only suitable for rituals now, which did little for black magick and even less for business. Zé stared at the body, then picked up a scalpel and stabbed it twice. The gods were not helping.

Chapter 2

Heading to the beach, Northern Brazil, 1970

The good news about the family road trip was they were halfway through their seven-hour trip to Parnaíba and its beautiful beaches, but the bad news was their father still had several stops to make along the way. Naturally, the two girls wanted to see the ocean—it had been more than a year since the last trip, and they were beginning to get antsy. Still, Juliana knew that upsetting him would ruin the day. Their father, Dr. Zé, could be, at best, 'unpredictable,' especially when he was in a mood.

Juliana, nineteen, and Vilma, ten, sat on their hands, each trying to be the first to spot an orange car. Twenty minutes later, Juliana sighed as they stopped again at another warehouse while they, along with their stepmother Aparecida, waited in the car as their father conducted business. At some stops, he would be in there for as long as forty-five minutes, and the heat could be unbearable. Why they could not go inside, she didn't dare ask, but every time Vilma complained, Aparecida spun her girthy neck and shushed the little girl. Thirty minutes later, Dr. Zé's gaunt frame returned with three cups of water.

"How much longer, Pai? It is hot. Vilma is getting tired. Can we come inside, out of the sun?" asked Juliana.

"No, men are working in there, and you would be in their way. I am finished. Drink, and we can go." Juliana, meanwhile, wondered what their father, a doctor, might need to do at a warehouse six hours from his office. When everyone finished their drinks, Zé resumed the drive.

***

Juliana ran in the sand, zigging and zagging around Vilma, who was trying to jump on her big sister's shadow.

"Got you!" exclaimed Vilma, but Juliana dodged at the last second.

"No, that was only one foot. Try again!" Vilma giggled and doubled her efforts. They had gotten too far ahead of Zé and Aparecida, who were lost in the crowd somewhere behind them. Juliana turned to look, and as she did, Vilma landed hard, digging both heels into Juliana's shadow.

"Got you that time!" the little girl proclaimed.

"That one doesn't count. I was looking for Papai! Time out, we have to go back."

"No fair," said Vilma. "That should count. You said 'time out' after I scored."

"Okay, whatever. Come on, let's go get Papai." As young as she was, Juliana was like a mother to Vilma. Their birth mother, Beatriz, had left the family unexpectedly and unannounced six years previous.

Juliana found her father two hundred yards down the beach, staring at the ocean. Aparecida, in her hideous one-piece, looked on helplessly, concern written all over her face. It was not the first time one of his episodes had ruined what should have been a fun family day. Dazed, Zé continued to stare at the sea, refusing to acknowledge their presence.

Another trance, thought Juliana.

"Papai. Papai, wake up," Juliana whispered. She had learned, as had they all, that shouting didn't help. "Vilma, I need to help Papai. Find me some pretty shells." Dr. Zé blinked twice, and Juliana spoke in a soothing tone. "Papai, are you all right? What did you see?" Dr. Zé's eyes focused, and after a moment, he remembered where he was. Vilma, meanwhile, splashed in the surf twenty feet away. Aparecida, helpless, did nothing but fret.

"Juliana."

"Yes, Papai. What did you feel? Could you tell?" Juliana knew it was much better for the family when he understood the message, but this was not one of those times. Zé struggled to grasp what he had seen. His very first clairvoyant incident had been at the age of eighteen when he foresaw his own father's death, but having a vision did not always mean bad news. Sometimes, the occurrences were helpful and warned him of danger.

Zé had seen a police officer in the trance, but that was no surprise; he'd been dodging them for years. At the last second, however, had come the real shock. The vision had shifted to Juliana riding a bicycle, and the meaning escaped him. Although it was not guaranteed she would inherit his talent, it would make perfect sense, and having another seer in the house would be a tricky situation.

"I'm not sure, Juliana; I can't see everything. Tell me, did you see anything?"

"No, Papai, I told you a hundred times, I don't have—"

"Then make it a hundred and one! Have you felt anything?" He was not smiling, and his temper was taking off. "Have you ever sensed anything, whether you understood it or not? I was around your age the first time it happened."

"Papai, no. I promise I've never *seen* anything or whatever it is you're talking about." Zé dropped his eyes; she was not lying. Unfortunately, the vision's meaning was a mystery for now, and he had no choice but to wait to figure it out. Whatever it was, he hoped to learn before the vision became reality, but that was not guaranteed either. Suddenly, Zé was very tired.

"Your mother couldn't handle my episodes. They were too much for her, and you know how that ended. You do a much better job, Juliana."

"I know. Let's not talk about our mother. Vilma is right over there."

"You may never have them, Juliana, but you'll let me know the minute you do, won't you?" Aparecida, meanwhile, glared at her stepdaughter as if Juliana were the one to blame.

"Papai, don't you trust me?"

Dr. Zé hesitated before answering. "I'm sorry. I'm just frustrated."

CHAPTER 3

SANTORINI, GREECE, 1970

Patrick Brennan wiped his brow, unable to enjoy the view. He and Peggy fought every time they went on vacation, and this was no different. He was already miserable and counting the days until the end of the trip.

Peggy always chose the destination; somehow, she trained him to be passive. Giving in was easier than fighting. She was of the type to hang a map of the world on the wall with dozens of ball head pins poking out, one for every place they had visited. It annoyed him that many destinations were "checked off" forever just because they had been there once. The country of Switzerland, for example, was eliminated due to a train ride from Paris to Milan, even though they had never set foot outside the vehicle, and it sickened him that he might never lay eyes on the Matterhorn.

Italy was another sin. They had spent a weekend in Rome, and she'd chosen the restaurants, all tourist traps near the Vatican. Patrick didn't know at the time, but that was it for Italy too—they were never going back; he found out the bad news during a dinner conversation.

"I was thinking about the south of France next time," she said.

"I thought we were going to take a deeper dive into Italy? Florence, Venice, the Italian Alps? The Dolomites. Italy has beautiful mountains!"

Sadly, he could hear the desperation in his own voice. She was a *summer person*, something he'd failed to realize early on—his opposite. Patrick loved winter and climbing snow-capped mountains. The view of Switzerland from the train, so close and yet so far, haunted his dreams. In his opinion, cities were overcrowded and overrated. Dear God, why hadn't he noticed this clash of personalities at the beginning of the relationship?

They'd dated for eight long years before the proposal, and he was coming to accept that popping the question had been a mistake. With dental school over, it had been time to get serious, at least according to their families, and as soon as he'd proposed, she seemed to change. Suddenly, there was an attitude, a sense of ownership that wasn't there before. Overnight, she stopped laughing at his jokes and began talking down to him in front of others.

Now they were in Greece, and it was as hot, touristy, and as miserable as he'd feared. To Patrick, Athens was "Rome but older," and Mykonos was just another sunburn. Finally, Peggy became agitated by Patrick's whining and consented to hike the caldera in Santorini.

Patrick had to admit the view of the ocean was spectacular but purposely avoided thanking her. Today was day four of the vacation, and she was jet-lagged and grouchy. He chose to hike in silence, as any conversation had the potential for a blowout. They had the trail to themselves, and anything was better than another museum.

Peggy and Patrick began their hike in the village of Imerovigli and headed for Oia at the island's tip. They walked the spine of the caldera most of the way, a nine-hundred-foot drop off the inside lip. The back half of the ancient cone was to the right, developed for agriculture—a gradual slope to the sea.

Peggy broke the silence. "How far away do you think that is—from here across the way to our hotel—as the crow flies?"

Patrick studied the distance. He knew that the hike was around eight kilometers, but straight across was, of course, shorter. "I don't know, maybe five kilometers?"

"No, I mean in miles. How many is that in miles? I don't know kilometers!"

Patrick's jaw clenched. "Three. Three miles," he said, with his last ounce of patience.

"I think it's more than that. I bet that's four miles. Come take a picture of me on those rocks and try to get our hotel in the background."

The village of Imerovigli looked like a city made of chalk from this distance, bright as can be in the afternoon sun; it was impossible to determine which building was their hotel, but he consented, nonetheless.

"All right, where do you want to be?"

"Right there, on those rocks."

From Patrick's view, it looked as if the boulders were the cliff's edge. To be sure, he walked up and peered over the ledge. It was not the infinite drop he'd imagined, but it was still a dangerous grade that led to one. Another fifty to eighty feet, and it dropped out of sight to the water below. As a climbing enthusiast, heights didn't bother him, but Peggy's sudden bravery was a bit of a surprise.

"Are you sure? *You* are going to sit on this rock right here?"

"Yes, Patrick, I am. But, please, when I get up there, be ready. I don't want to be there long." Her voice was tense, and he sensed that there would be another fight if he didn't take the perfect picture. The two fought dirty, at times embarrassing themselves in public.

If this goes south, I'll fly home, he thought.

"I'm ready, Patrick. Go ahead."

Patrick backed away, lining up the shot, viewfinder to eyeball, and Peggy continued to direct while climbing the boulder of choice. As he tried to locate her in the viewfinder, her scream pierced the air, followed by a shower of stones scattering down the slope. Patrick lowered the camera and looked.

Peggy was gone.

Sense of duty sprung him to action, and he sprinted, looking down the caldera—and she was there, staring back, wide-eyed, thirty feet below; her fingers dug into the dirt, clutching at whatever held. Several knuckles were bleeding, and her arms were beginning to shake.

"Patrick, help! I can't hold on! Get me! Use your belt!"

Stepping back, Patrick did as he was told, whipping off both his shirt and belt in a blur, quickly working to tie the two together through the buckle. He was good with ropes but had doubts the Izod shirt she'd bought him would be strong enough to hold her weight.

"Patrick, hurry!"

Much to his surprise, Patrick found himself purposefully slowing his pace. He'd had enough; he was tired of putting out her fires; maybe an extra minute on the embankment would teach her a lesson. For the first time in as long as he could remember, she was the disadvantaged one.

"I'm tying the knot. Hold tight! I'm coming. Be right there." Meanwhile, he counted slowly: 1, 2, 3, 4, as if willing his pulse down.

"I can't. I'm slipping. I'm slipping. I'm slipping!"

"Here I come," he replied matter-of-factly.

Patrick stepped nimbly past the wall of boulders, making sure to kick up as much loose gravel as possible. He eyed a baseball-sized stone a few feet lower and made his way closer, taking care not to do any slipping of his own.

"You're getting dirt in my eyes!" she complained.

"Sorry, I'm coming. Get ready to catch my shirt."

"Hurry!"

Patrick kicked the stone and watched as it bounced once before connecting high on her cheekbone. Peggy's right hand let go of the cliffside, and she cried out again, her left hand the only thing between her and death. Patrick galloped down the slope like a mountain goat, kicking as much dirt as he could without being obvious.

"What are you doing?!" Peggy cried with one final shriek, sliding another ten feet and hitting an outcropping that spun her over the edge and out of sight. Patrick listened carefully, but the impact never came. Instead, he reached down and rubbed his shirt in soil, then took five more steps for evidence.

He couldn't see over, but that was all right; he wouldn't be calling for help anytime soon—after all, he couldn't—the closest phone was halfway back to the hotel. As he climbed onto the path, Patrick checked for fellow hikers. Thankfully, the trail was empty due to the intense midday sun. It was too damn hot even for the locals, yet he had to smirk; for the first time, the heat felt good.

Chapter 4

The outskirts of Codó, Brazil, 1970

Eight-year-old Diego Santos kicked the ball to his friend, Miguel, on the vacant soccer field. Miguel ran after the ball and returned the kick, shanking the ball over Diego's head and down a steep embankment known to the entire neighborhood as "Loser Valley." Diego arrived at the edge just in time to see the ball bounce one last time before disappearing into the jungle, and a chill ran down his spine. *O meu Deus,* thought Diego who could not afford to lose another soccer ball. *This field is dangerous. No wonder no one plays here.*

"Go get it," said Diego.

"No way! Marcio Bragos says he thinks the *Monster of Codó* lives down there! Better to lose a ball than your life," replied Miguel.

"I don't have another ball, and neither do you! You kicked it!"

"I can't. Sorry, Diego. I'd rather quit than go down there."

"You're the worst," said Diego, while cursing Miguel's foot skills under his breath. It was left up to him; either suck it up and go looking or go back to dribbling coconut shells with his feet to pass the time. Holding one hand out straight, Diego lined up the spot where the ball had entered the woods before he started down the slope, loose gravel filling his shoes. No sooner did he reach the jungle floor than the odor of rot filled his nostrils.

"No, it went in further that way," said Miguel from above, motioning with his hands.

"No, it didn't. I know where it went. Just be quiet, coward!" Diego gagged. *Something down here is dead,* but he parted the bushes anyway, hoping to get this over with sooner than later; he'd seen a tarantula in the bushes at home once and nearly had a heart attack.

The smell intensified as he searched through knee-high ferns tall enough to hide just about anything. A fallen tree divided the clearing. His ball might have ended up somewhere around that tree unless it hit a random trunk, but if that was the case, the ball could be anywhere. Diego bent at the waist and peered under a bough. The tree was a haven for spider-webs. If the ball was under there, he just might leave it. Stepping carefully, Diego looked for recently flattened ferns and, thankfully, spotted one. There, between two fronds, gleamed the white surface of his ball.

Diego rerouted, excited that he could begin thinking about his escape, yet found himself curling his nose more and more. The 'Monster of Codó' was not just the stuff of urban legend after all. People were losing their lives to an unseen predator, and his mother would spank him for even coming here, lost soccer ball or not.

Five yards further in came the droning of flies. Hopefully, the dead animal was further ahead, beyond the ball—but his mind wandered, and he began to imagine stepping right into the lifeless thing, and if that happened, he would lose his mind. *It's very close*, he thought, *but where?* His final step provided the answer.

The body of Carlos DaSilva lay in a state of active decay, the ground around him slick with a viscous fluid that could only come from a dead body. Voracious maggots writhed in his eye sockets as Diego gasped and buried his nose in the crook of his elbow. He'd seen a dead chicken like this once, but this unmoving man would haunt his dreams forever. DaSilva's shirt was torn open at the belly where an animal had feasted, and smack dab in the middle of his blown-out guts was Diego's ball.

Diego sprinted up the hill, and Miguel followed. Diego's ashen face was the only reason he needed. The Monster of Codó *was* there or, at least, had been recently, and three hours of sitting with the police to tell and retell the horrible story was confirmation enough it wasn't safe to play outside anymore.

Chapter 5

The city of Codó, Northern Brazil, 1970

Juliana and her friend, Fernanda, walked home from school on high alert. Both young women were students at Instituto Federal Maranhão studying biology; Fernanda hoped to find a job in the agriculture field, and Juliana considered following in her father's footsteps and becoming a doctor. They checked behind for strangers constantly, and much to Fernanda's chagrin, Juliana mentioned the murders again.

"Stop, Juliana. You're scaring me! We're safe. It's broad daylight!" Fernanda was born and raised in the city of Codó and was still unwilling to accept what was happening to her hometown. At nineteen, she would much prefer to talk about boys. The cover of her notebook was adorned with hand-drawn hearts, all crossed out, but one: *Lucas*. As the words left Fernanda's lips, a page from a discarded newspaper curled through the air and wrapped itself around Juliana's calf. Reaching down to remove it, Juliana read the headline out loud:

Monster of Codó Update:
Body of DaSilva missing kidney, hand, say officials

"You see? It's real! You can never let your guard down." Fernanda, spooked by the timing, bit her lip.

Suddenly, a young boy rounded the corner and began to shout. "Ai! Não! Your father is Macumbeiro!"

Juliana's eyes widened in shock as she anticipated the boy's next move, but Fernanda spoke up. "What are you doing out by yourself? Get home! You shouldn't be out!" The boy turned, frightened, and disappeared down a side street.

Fernanda turned to Juliana. "Do you know that boy?"

"I'm not sure," said Juliana. "There are a lot of boys like him on the streets. But how did he know? He looked me right in the eyes and said my father was a *Macumbeiro.*"

"I don't know, but Macumba freaks some people out. The fact your family practices is not my favorite thing either. If my parents knew, I'd be in big trouble. Let's get to your house."

Chapter 6

———

They arrived at Juliana's apartment building twenty minutes later; the security guard recognized her and buzzed them in. Eighteen floors up, they exited the elevator and approached the apartment door. "Remember, don't say anything about sleeping over."

Fernanda swallowed hard and nodded once again.

"Let me do the talking," said Juliana. "She's weird, and we don't always get along. I'm going to have to read her mood. She's unpredictable. I never know what she'll say."

Juliana was old enough to remember the family before her mother left, but Vilma was not. All Vilma could remember were a few mental snapshots, so Juliana periodically produced a photograph of Beatriz to keep her memory alive. Juliana knew that Aparecida had thrown out most of Beatriz's belongings, pictures, and kitchen tools. It was a real struggle to keep their mother in the family history.

Aparecida was in the kitchen as the girls walked in; the same place she always was when school let out. Candles burned on the pantry shelf, and she was already working on dinner. The woman was almost always there, and she was not an easy presence. Juliana compared it to living with a spy, and she was all but sure her bedroom was searched periodically. Her teenage years had not afforded much in the way of privacy.

"Good afternoon, Dona Aparecida." Juliana used the formal "Dona" title at her stepmother's request. The reason given was "it's a sign of respect," yet Juliana took it as a stipulation.

"Hello, girls! How was school? I'm so glad you're home. I know you take the safest streets, but I can't help but worry."

Juliana knew Aparecida was putting on a public face for Fernanda's benefit.

"Thank you, Dona Aparecida; yes, we stayed safe and didn't stop for anything." Juliana paused for a moment and decided to ask right away.

"Dona Aparecida, how is father doing? Did you have a chance to talk to him?" Aparecida shook her head to imply that Juliana should already know the answer.

"No, child. He's a busy man; you know that. Today is no different."

"Dona Aparecida, Fernanda and I are going to do our homework and chat. I was wondering if perhaps she could have dinner with us, then have a sleepover?" Aparecida stopped peeling carrots and looked up with a smile, and Juliana wondered for a moment when the last time was she'd seen Aparecida's teeth.

"Well, of course she can! I was about to invite her! Call your mother, Fernanda. We're having moqueca. The telephone is right there." Aparecida pointed to the adjacent room, and Fernanda excused herself. Juliana felt the vacuum and followed.

That was too easy, she thought.

Chapter 7

Santorini, Greece 1970

Patrick heard the door open at the end of the hallway and perked up; help had arrived. He stood up to try and look, but the angle was wrong; the bars were in the way. Anxious, Patrick sat back on the bed … thank God he didn't have a cellmate. Finally, two familiar faces approached, accompanied by a police officer, who unlocked the cell and let them in. When the police escort left, Patrick began to whine.

"What took you so long? I've been here three days!" Patrick's father and patriarch of the family dental practice, Dr. Joe Brennan, spoke first.

"Hey, hey, you can stop crying; I've brought Angus! He was busy in California and needed the extra day to come East. Angus, give the boy some good news."

Angus Addison, an influential businessman and family friend, wasn't quite as coddling as Dr. Joe. He'd dropped everything for this emergency and left a deal on the table that immediately fell through.

"Let's not get him excited yet, Joe. The police have questions they need answers to. Let's make sure we have all our ducks in a row."

"Ah, don't scare him, Angus! I mean, you're going to get him out of here, right?"

"As I said on the plane, Joe, it depends on how fast you want it and how much money you want to spend. I have connections, but when the police are involved, it's—complicated, to say the least. So, Patrick…" Angus stuck his head in the hallway to make sure the policeman was far enough away. "… what the fuck happened?"

"I told you on the phone. Peggy slipped and fell while I was taking a picture; I tried to save her but couldn't. The police won't even say why I'm here. So why can't I leave?"

"I've got a lawyer on it, but what can you tell me about trying to save her, Patrick? Tell me everything." Angus rechecked the hallway.

"I tied my shirt to my belt and threw it to her. I saved her life, or at least I had at that point. She would have gone right over if it wasn't for me, but she held on for a good five minutes, and I couldn't get any closer to the edge, or I'd be dead too. Eventually, she just couldn't hold on anymore."

"All right, well, here's their problem, and I have to say, I have the same question: Patrick, why wasn't your shirt ripped or stretched?" Patrick's face froze; he'd rubbed it in the dirt but didn't think to rip the damned thing.

Angus witnessed Patrick's reaction. "Wow, Patrick."

"Hey, wait, Angus, uh … it's not like that proves anything. We can still get him home, can't we?" asked Dr. Joe.

"Quiet, Joe. We can't be sure they're not listening."

"I didn't say anything. You can't convict someone just because..."

"Let's leave that to the lawyer. This is not the States, Joe. Laws are different, so don't say a word."

Chapter 8

Boa Vista, Brazil, 1970

Luiz Oliveira woke on an operating table, his right hand in pain. Fourteen years old and alone, he had no memory of how he'd gotten here. How long was he unconscious? The last thing he remembered; he'd been on the side of a dirt road about to eat a mango.

"Hey, kid, you look hungry. Give me two centavos, and this juicy number is yours."

"I don't have any money," said Luiz.

"Ah, well. Did you go to school today?"

Luiz nodded.

"Well then, I suppose you deserve a free mango. Go ahead; it's on me."

Luiz hadn't believed his ears; he hadn't had more than one meal a day in over two weeks.

"You want coconut water to go with that?" From his left hand, the man tossed a fresh coconut and pulled out his machete.

"Yes," said Luiz, forgetting his manners.

"Do you know how to split one?"

"No. My mom says I'm too young, and I'll hurt myself."

"Oh, nonsense. A man needs to be able to feed himself, and you look old enough to me. Here, hold this machete, and I'll show you how."

Luiz hefted the blade, enthralled.

"Okay, put it down, hold it with your left hand, and come straight down with the knife like this." The man made a chopping motion with his hand. *"Good, now you try."*

As soon as Luiz turned away to attack the coconut, a wet rag was cupped over his mouth, and then, everything went black.

Now, here he was, on some stainless-steel table in an empty hospital, if that's what this place was. Panic struck as reality hit home: this was all wrong. He turned his head and examined the leather straps over his chest and arms, then tried to move his legs, but they were also bound. A white gauze bandage covered his hand, but there was no blood. The room was tiled and clean but strange; a hose hung coiled over a stainless-steel sink. Cleaning chemicals did a poor job of masking the off-sweet scent of cow manure. A minute later, a man wearing a surgical mask entered the room.

"Where am I?" asked Luiz. "I want to go home!"

"Yes, we'll get you back home, but we didn't get your name. From what we were told, you passed out on the side of the road."

"My name is Luiz, and I didn't pass out! The man put a cloth over my mouth, and it knocked me out!"

"Luiz, what is your last name?"

"Oliveira."

"Luiz, you wouldn't happen to know if you've had hepatitis or jaundice, would you?"

"I don't think so. What's jaundice? Are you a doctor?"

"Yes, I'm a doctor. Jaundice is a disease. You don't have any diseases, do you? Have you been to your doctor in the last year or two?"

"I don't have a doctor."

"Luiz, we have a sick boy here who could use your help, and if you're sick, you wouldn't be able to help him."

"Who is it?"

"You don't know him, but thank you, Luiz; I'm going to step out now and work on tracking your mother down. Sit tight."

"Wait! Why am I tied to the table?"

"We didn't want you to hurt yourself. I'll be back."

"Wait, what happened to my hand?"

The door clicked shut. Nothing made sense. Luiz tested the strap, but it wouldn't budge. As soon as he tried, another man wearing a medical robe came in and began to wheel Luiz and the table out into the hallway. The smell of manure was more pungent out here, and the walls were no longer tile but cement; this could not be a hospital.

"Where am I? Where are you taking me?"

"To your cell," replied the man.

"Cell?" said Luiz in shock.

"Room. It's down the hall just a little further." As they arrived at the end of the hallway, the man stopped outside a closed door and began unfastening the straps.

"Are we in a cow barn?" Luiz asked, feeling panicky. "What happened to my hand? It hurts."

"There are no cows here. That's the anesthesia. You're in good hands. All right, we're going to stand you up now, ready? One, two, three."
On three, Luiz stood, and the blood rushed to his head while his hand pulsed in pain. As he struggled to remain upright, the man unlocked the cell door and opened it. Inside was another boy who did nothing but cower. Before Luiz realized what was happening, the man hip-checked him into the room, sending him to the floor, and the door slammed shut, the sound of the locking bolt confirming his living nightmare..

CHAPTER 9

CODÓ, BRAZIL, 1970

When their homework was finished, Juliana lit candles of her own and sat back on the bed. Fernanda stared at the flames. "Fernanda, what happened today with Lucas? Did you get a chance to talk?"

Fernanda frowned. "No, he wasn't in class. A lot of people are skipping because of "the Monster." I hope that's not why he wasn't there, though. I'll never get to date him until the killer is caught!"

"Does he know you like him?"

"I'm not sure. I haven't said anything." Fernanda, in Juliana's opinion, was immature for her years. Juliana, who was used to meeting new people, was more confident socially.

"Do you want me to show him your notebook? He might be flattered to see his name all over it."

"Don't you dare! I cover it up every time he walks by. I would die."

"Well, you have to let him know. It'll help your chances." Juliana lit another candle.

"What's with all these candles?" asked Fernanda.

"I like to light candles in the evening. It's my way of saying 'thanks' at the end of the day."

"Uh-oh. Here we go with the Macumba," said Fernanda, suddenly nervous.

"Macumba," Juliana scoffed. "It's so misunderstood. People that don't know call it 'Macumba.' Black Magick! Ahhhh!" Juliana raised her hands in mock fright. "Everyone is confused. There are many different types, and they all get lumped together as 'Macumba.' 'Quimbanda' is the one you're thinking of. 'Candomblé' has been misunderstood. My religion, 'Umbanda', doesn't sacrifice anything. Umbanda is actually white magic."

"But what about all the red and black? That's bad, right?"

"Not necessarily. The color of the candles doesn't matter."

Fernanda was dubious. "The black and red *beads* are evil, right? That signifies 'Pomba Gira'! She's a witch!"

Juliana sighed. Fernanda knew more about the broad term 'Macumba' than she had let on, and it made for a complex explanation.

"Well, yes, but not everyone goes that route—there's more to it than that. Macumba is about balances. 'Orixás' are gods, and the 'Exus' are their earthly spirit counterparts. We pray to both," said Juliana.

Fernanda stared at the dancing light of the candles, feeling blasphemous. The part about the beads went against everything she'd been taught, but she didn't want to argue. "But—you can cast spells, right?"

"Well, kind of. If you got your hands on a pair of Lucas's underwear, I might be able to make him love you." Juliana burst into laughter.

"That's not funny!" But soon Fernanda was laughing too, then suddenly, they noticed an eyeball peeking through the crack of the door.

Juliana erupted. "Vilma, we're talking!" She lowered her voice, "Don't make me call Aparecida." Quickly, the eyeball disappeared.

"Juliana, I have to pee. Where's the bathroom?"

"Down the hall on the right."

Chapter 10

Fernanda left the bedroom and mistakenly took the first right, directly into the master bedroom. Not four feet away stood Aparecida, folding laundry.

"Oh! I'm so sorry! Juliana said the bathroom was down the hall, and I must not have been paying attention."

Aparecida held her tongue to appear calm but stiffened when she smiled. "No worry, my dear. It's the next room down."

"Thank you—so sorry once again!"

Aparecida's eyes never left Fernanda's as the girl backed away. Hanging off the closet door was a string of black and red porcelain beads. Fernanda's pulse quickened and confusion set in. *Had Juliana lied?* Aparecida glared, having witnessed the shock on Fernanda's face. Fernanda closed the bedroom door and returned to Juliana's bedroom, forgetting to pee.

Chapter 11

Dinnertime came, and the table was set. Aparecida served the moqueca, but Fernanda picked at her food, intimidated, despite it being the best meal she'd had in quite some time. Vilma did her best to win Fernanda's attention, and Juliana kept one eye on her stepmother, all the while counting the minutes until dinner was over.

When the formalities were over, Aparecida shooed them away, which was a break from the norm. Usually, Juliana was responsible for doing the dishes and putting away leftovers, but Fernanda's presence had changed everything. Juliana also knew her father should be arriving, and there was no doubt Aparecida craved his undivided attention. The girls returned to their bedroom, inviting Vilma along.

At 10 pm, everyone prepared for bed, and after her shower, Juliana noticed a glow in the dining room. The same candles Aparecida had burned in the kitchen were now on the table, the room's only light source. Aparecida sat with Dr. Zé as he finished his dinner and noticed the doctor's distraction. In her nightwear, Juliana remained in the shadows.

Dr. Zé spoke. "Juliana. How was your day?"

"Hello, Father. Good, thank you. I brought a friend home to sleep over. How was your day? Why are you so late?"

Dr. Zé shifted slightly, and Juliana felt something, a pressure building behind her eyes. Instantly, the room turned pink, as if she'd put on a pair of rose-colored glasses. The candle flames burned black in the strange illumination. She blinked twice, but nothing changed, and Zé began to speak. *Didn't they see this too?* Juliana thought.

"We had an unfortunate case today—a terminal one. The woman hung on as long as she could, but in the end, it was simply her time."

The glowing walls pulsed in time with her heart. *He's lying. This must be the sensation he keeps asking me about.* It took all her concentration to hide her shock.

"I don't want to sadden you both with the details; why don't you go back with your friend? We can catch up tomorrow."

It was more a dismissal than a conversation, but Juliana didn't care; she only wanted to get back to the bedroom and collect her thoughts. Suddenly, three pictures flashed in her mind: her father's downtown office with a 'closed' sign in the window, a padlocked shed, and a Styrofoam cooler. Juliana blinked twice and managed to blow a nervous kiss before retreating to the bedroom.

Chapter 12

Aparecida cleaned up after dinner while Zé showered. His long day wasn't over yet; of that, she was sure. She hadn't told him yet about Fernanda barging into their bedroom and seeing his beads. Fernanda's parents were Catholic, and if they heard about what Fernanda had seen, it would not be good. Rumors were dangerous. Every town had its share of 'sensitives,' and it only took one to ruin everything. On her way to the bedroom, Aparecida listened carefully at Juliana's door. It was well after midnight, and the girls were asleep.

She would ask Zé to perform a short ritual to keep their enemies at bay; five minutes and no more, and then he could sleep, for he'd be up early again the next day to run his empire. Tomorrow, Aparecida would even contribute.

She whispered as she shut the bedroom door. "Fernanda saw your beads."

"What?"

"She saw your beads. I was doing the laundry, putting clothes in the closet, and she thought this was the bathroom."

Zé shook his head. "You're certain?"

"Yes, but I have a plan. First, a quick despacho."

Zé shook his head again, looking twice as tired. "It won't help. It's late. It's a waste of time."

"No need for you to sacrifice anything this time. I've already killed a bird." Aparecida referred to the cage of canaries they kept for such purposes. They had to lie periodically, telling the girls the birds kept escaping. "I have the blood right here. We're half-done already."

Zé consented to appease her. It was too late for debate.

Chapter 13

Santorini, Greece

Patrick woke on the seventh day of his incarceration to a guard at his cell door. The officer gestured and spoke Greek even though Patrick had heard him speak perfect English to Angus and his father. The police didn't like him, and neither did the Greeks in general. The Associated Press had picked up the story of Peggy's death, and although it wasn't front-page news, it was an embarrassment for Santorini. Eyes, from as far up as the Prime Minister, had checked in, putting pressure on all involved. On this morning, Patrick was led down the hallway to a conference room where Dr. Joe, Angus, and a lawyer sat opposite three government officials. No one in the room was smiling.

"Dad, what's happening?"

"Not now, son. You're here to listen."

"To what? Am I getting out?"

Angus stirred. "For God's sake, Patrick, sit down. These three gentlemen have flown here from Athens, and you'd be wise to keep your mouth closed."

Patrick did as he was told.

"This is Mr. Papantonakis, the Mayor of Santorini, this is Mr. Stamos from the Hellenic Parliament, and this is Mr. Pappas, who assists the Prime Minister. They'd like to say a few words before we depart."

Patrick, taken aback, bowed his head. Much to his surprise and chagrin, Peggy's death had attracted a lot of attention—too much. But Patrick caught Angus's cue and decided he should listen to whatever these three had to say.

Papantonakis spoke, "You have brought shame and unwanted attention to Santorini and all of Greece. If it weren't for your connections and their generous donations to make our island safer, you would be sitting in a cell in Athens. We have come today to tell you that you are banned from visiting Greece. Mr. Pappas, Mr. Stamos, is there anything you would like to add?"

Both men declined, and with that, the three stood and filed out of the room.

Patrick smiled. "That's it? Did you have to pay them?"

Dr. Joe smiled back, half-heartedly, bursting to confirm the good news, but Angus cut him off, whispering through clenched teeth, "Don't say a word until we're on the plane."

CHAPTER 14

CODÓ, BRAZIL

The girls woke up together and left for school. Then, in the afternoon, each went their separate ways. Fernanda knew her way home but felt unusually anxious. The blowing newspaper and the little boy on the street yesterday had gotten under her skin. A knot in the pit of her stomach intensified her discomfort when suddenly, she heard a familiar voice behind her.

"Fernanda, is that you? I was hoping I'd find you. I was on my way to your house to drop this off. These are yours, right? I don't think they're Juliana's." A car was parked at the side of the road, and the trunk was open. Aparecida, standing next to it, waved her over. "I think you forgot them this morning."

Fernanda looked down at her knapsack as if to imagine the contents. She hadn't brought much for the sleepover. What might she have forgotten?

Meanwhile, Aparecida gestured.

Puzzled, Fernanda started across.

"They must be yours. Juliana doesn't wear this type of thing, and it certainly wouldn't fit Vilma."

Fernanda circled around to the trunk. Inside was a tall duffle, deep enough so she couldn't see the bottom.

"I would have dropped it off at your house, but I have to get home for Vilma. It'll save me time if I can give them to you here. Do you mind?"

Fernanda peered into the bag, but it was empty—then she gagged as an oily cloth closed over her face, causing her knees to buckle and her vision to fade. Aparecida held her firm until Fernanda's muscles relaxed, then bumped her into the trunk with a burly hip.

CHAPTER 15

The following day, Fernanda didn't show up at school, and Juliana felt the pressure in her head begin to build again. At 2 pm, the students were dismissed, and a policeman entered the classroom to talk to the professor. Juliana, eyeballs pulsing steadily to the beat of her heart, heard Fernanda's name mentioned and asked to speak to the policeman in private.

"Fernanda stayed at my house the night before last. How long has she been missing?"

"Since yesterday. Her parents say she never came home from school."

Juliana ran home crying and broke the news. Aparecida played along, joining in with a measure of crocodile tears. Juliana had never seen Aparecida cry before and was taken aback, as her stepmother, for the first time ever, picked up the phone and called Dr. Zé home from work. Twenty minutes later, the three of them were on the couch, commiserating.

Juliana realized she hadn't been this physically close to Aparecida since the day they were introduced. Her father's presence, however, offered no comfort. He was odd and disjointed, a distraction more than anything, as if he had better things to do and more important places to be.

"What's the matter, Juliana?" asked Vilma. She'd been playing in her room and missed the commotion. At the same time, she noticed her father was not at work. "Papai! Why are you home?"

Aparecida interrupted. "Juliana's not feeling well, sweetheart. She's going to lie down. Why don't you give her some space?"

"But why's she crying? Are you okay, Juliana?" Vilma attempted to sidestep Aparecida.

Juliana wiped her eyes and tried to put on a brave face. She was in no mood to explain—at least not yet. "I'm okay. My stomach hurts, that's all. Thank you, Vilma."

Dr. Zé stood. "Vilma, go to your room until we can get Juliana to bed. We don't want you sick as well." Dr. Zé put his arm around his younger daughter and shuffled her down the hallway. Everyone agreed that Juliana should stay home from school the next day.

Alone with her thoughts, Juliana stared at the ceiling, wondering why her body was trying to tell her something—something much more than Fernanda going missing.

Chapter 16

Juliana awoke to the sweet scent of mint toothpaste.

"Juliana. Juliana, are you sleeping?"

What time is it? Juliana slept later than usual, but seconds after her eyes opened, the memory came roaring back. Yesterday was no dream. Fernanda was missing.

"Yes, Vilma. I'm sorry, honey. I'm so tired." *What a love.* In many ways, Vilma reminded her of their mother, who had been so caring and sweet.

"Please get up, Juliana. I don't like it when you're down."

"It's only for a little while, Vilma. I just need time to gather my thoughts. After that, I'll pray, and I'll feel much stronger. Then we can be happy again."

"I still think you should get up. You know I need you." Vilma bent down and kissed Juliana's cheek while stroking her hair. It felt good. Vilma was the only thing that reminded Juliana of happier times when their mother was still in their lives. A tear dripped from Juliana's cheek and disappeared into her pillow.

"You won't be hurting much longer," said Vilma. "You'll be back stronger than ever." Juliana smiled at how motherly the ten-year-old could be. Then, suddenly, the bedroom door opened, and Aparecida peeked in, speaking in a hurried whisper.

"Vilma! I told you to let your sister sleep! Come out of there. Be quick and quiet!"

Vilma caressed Juliana's cheek one more time before obeying. Juliana closed her eyes to avoid conversation, and the door shut with a click.

Chapter 17

Juliana tried for forty minutes to go back to sleep but couldn't, so she got out of bed then wandered from the bedroom to the living room and finally to the kitchen, seeking conversation, even if it had to be with her stepmother. Aparecida should have been the only one home for Vilma was at school, and her father was working. Perhaps there was some news about Fernanda?

But the kitchen was empty, and it wasn't long before she figured out she was home alone. Aparecida's purse was gone, so she was probably at the market. Anxious and lonely, Juliana searched for her set of keys, but they were nowhere to be found, and no key on the hallway rack fit the front door. However, her father's desk was a catch-all full of miscellaneous things, so she decided to check there. Sure enough, she found a ring with four keys, including one to the apartment. Juliana took it and let herself out.

She stayed on the busier stretches to be safe. The sun was shining, and people were out, which comforted her somewhat. Life went on for the rest of the world. Some laughed, some talked, and others were deep in thought, but all of them helped take her mind off the last forty-eight hours.

Juliana walked past the corner market where Aparecida frequently shopped but didn't see her inside and, all at once, remembered she'd forgotten to leave a note. After a moment of deliberation, she decided it was too soon to return and continued walking; she might not even be missed.

Two meandering miles later, Juliana realized she had reached her hair salon, which meant her father's office was just around the corner. Dr. Zé ran a small office, as they'd all been in every town he'd worked. Suddenly, Juliana stopped dead; the CLOSED sign from her pink-visioned hallucination from the night before was there. Her heart pounded as she pondered what to do, finally tugging the door handle, which was locked. She checked her watch: 11:04 am; *An early lunch?*

Juliana stuck her hands in her pockets and felt the keyring, then pulled it out and examined them; one had *197* engraved on it—the same as the street number. Perhaps she could wait for him inside? The latch slipped, and she went in. The office consisted of an entryway and a small waiting room with a reception window to the left, while a door led to four examination rooms straight ahead.

The lights were off, but the picture windows on the street provided all the light she needed. The front desk had a cup of pens and a block calendar by the slider window; the date read *10 Nov 1970*—three days ago, but nothing made sense. Suddenly, the memory of the padlocked shed flashed before her eyes.

"Papai?" she called out, but no one answered. No one moved in the back rooms either. There was an appointment book on the desk behind the glass, so she made her way around. Juliana worked fast; for now, she was blatantly snooping. *When's the next appointment?*

November 13 was a blank page, as were November 12 and November 11. November 10 had only four appointments listed. Looking back through the months, she found several more "blackout" days in the schedule. Her father was not scheduled to return. *What does he do with his time?* Acting fast, Juliana locked the front door and closed the blinds; she had to know.

Daylight from the street couldn't reach the back hallway, so she closed the door behind her and flicked on the lights. She knew from previous visits that the examination rooms were on both sides of the hall, and at the end was a bathroom and a back entrance. As she walked, the excuses ran like a river of deceit.

Maybe he has another office I don't know about.

Maybe I'm just paranoid because Fernanda is missing.

Maybe this sixth sense thing can be wrong.

Juliana wasn't sure what she was looking for, but anything that might explain what he did with his time would help, or any sign at all that the office was legitimate. Hopefully, there was a simple explanation.

What was it he'd said? *"We had an unfortunate case today—a terminal one. The woman hung on as long as she could, but in the end, it was simply her time."*

Perhaps he'd treated the woman in the city hospital? Might that be possible? Suddenly, a vision of the Styrofoam cooler as clear as day interrupted the thought, then faded. She hadn't conjured it, that much was sure. Still fighting her better instincts, she pressed on.

Juliana stuck her head in the first examination room and turned on the light, listening carefully for the front door. The fluorescent lighting was blinding, but her eyes adjusted. The room was clean, but a stack of books on the examination table and a mop bucket in the corner were strange things to see in a sterile room.

The second and third examination rooms were much cleaner and prepped for business. A wide strip of table paper was pulled and draped across both benches, ready for the next patient. A smidgen of confidence in her father returned. The bathroom was just that—a bathroom. The fourth exam room was padlocked.

Thankfully, there was still no sound from the front door, for she was in the belly of the beast, and it would be awkward to explain what she was doing back here. Juliana tried another key, and the padlock sprung open. The fourth exam room was dark, so she hit the switch and waited as the fluorescents blinked on. This room was nothing like the others; inside was an angled stainless-steel table against a wall sink. Anything spilled would flow directly down the drain. She recognized it from a television *novella* a few years back—an embalming table.

Juliana backed out of the room, trying to convince herself the table could be left over from the previous business, but deep down, teenager or not, she knew better. Her eyes began to throb. For a moment, she considered leaving before seeing something truly unforgivable, but she knew she would never trust her father if she didn't see this through. There was one thing she hadn't explored—the back door. Juliana turned the knob and pushed, and it creaked open into an alleyway.

Buildings surrounded her, two or more stories high, a single window behind her the only witness to whatever went on in this dim passage. A narrow driveway ran for thirty yards to the next street with barely enough clearance for a car, the paint from many a fender marring the walls.

On the street side of the alley, power lines crisscrossed overhead, and a puddle the size of a small pond made the cul-de-sac impassable to anyone not wearing boots. Street-blown trash had gathered along the brick to rot along the foundations. No one had cared for this filthy cavity in eons.

To her left was a stack of dirty milk crates and the utility shed from the vision, a padlock hanging from the handle. The Styrofoam cooler flashed in her head again, leaving little doubt of what was to come. *What might that keep cold?* She wondered, knowing nothing meant to be kept sanitary should be out here. Juliana looked back into the office one last time. Still nothing.

Wedging the door open with a milk crate, Juliana started her final approach. Her gut told her to leave, but her head demanded answers; she tried the fourth key, and the lock popped open. The door creaked as she pulled, allowing a cluster of flies to escape. As they passed, she brushed wildly at her face, sickened by the filthy tickle. The room smelled of bleach, disguising something. What was it? *Blood?*

The shed was narrow, barely wide enough to fit a ladder and some paint cans. On the nearside wall was a small workbench, and on it—was the cooler. Hanging from a thin wire was a lightbulb. Reaching up, she pulled the chain.

Juliana swallowed hard and checked the back door again to ensure the milk crate was still in place. She hesitated, dreading the next step, carefully placing a hand on each side of the Styrofoam and pulling evenly, praying it wouldn't squeal. Just as the lid began to shriek, the inner lip cleared, and she peered in.

Half-buried in fresh ice was an organ, a kidney, or a liver; she couldn't tell which. Juliana gasped and stepped back, mind whirring. Denial concerning her father's character still lived in her mind, but it was on life support.

One of the employees must be doing this. Father must have moved offices and forgotten to turn in the keys.

Juliana's vision turned pink, and some of the noise in her mind went silent. Time slowed. There were facts to consider. The nearest doctor's office, complete with an embalming table, left little room for doubt. No liver, whether for transplanting or someone's dinner, should be locked in an unrefrigerated shed for any length of time. Juliana then dropped the lid, which bounced off the table onto the floor.

Bending to retrieve it, she found something else: a notebook with hearts drawn on it, the name *Lucas* emblazoned in the one heart not scribbled out. Whose liver was it? A cow's? A patient's? She stared down at the notebook, her hands shaking. *Fernanda's?* The throb behind her eyes pulsed as if to answer. *But how?* And—*why?*

To the best of Juliana's knowledge, Fernanda didn't even know where Juliana's father's office was. Suddenly, the image of someone inserting a key into a lock flashed up. Styrofoam coolers were meant to keep things cold, but only until the ice melted. Of course, they'd be coming for it.

Juliana bolted, splashing through the great puddle to the adjacent street, looking back only once. Thankfully, no one followed, and the water would hide her footsteps—but whoever was coming for the organ would find the open shed, and there was no way she would risk returning to cover her tracks. The Monster of Codó would know someone had been in there and had seen the unholy package.

Juliana recalled the warehouses the family had stopped at on the drive to the beach and shivered. *What went on in there?* Tears ran down her cheeks as life as she knew it faded away. She couldn't even risk going *home*. If Dr. José Machado, Dr. Zé—*Papai*—was indeed the *Monster*, he would kill her too, daughter or not. There might be some bargaining at first, but she could never forgive him for Fernanda, not ever. Fumbling, she checked her purse, praying to find enough money for a bus ticket.

As Juliana ran, thoughts raced through her mind. Where was her father? *Aparecida must know, too. She must know everything.* Whether or not she took part—she *knew*, and one last pulse behind Juliana's eyes was all she needed for confirmation—*a sign.* Aparecida had always disturbed her *normal* intuition, never mind this new-found sixth sense.

Suddenly, Juliana stopped. *What about Vilma?* Her sister would still be in school right now. Vilma's teachers had never met Juliana. They would insist on calling Aparecida for permission to allow Vilma to be picked up. Tears continued to stream as she came to terms with who her family really was. Real-life monsters had custody of her sister, and there was nothing she could do about it—at least for the time being.

CHAPTER 18

FROM SANTORINI TO MASSACHUSETTS

By the time they made their connection in London, Patrick had realized there would be no welcome home.

"We're just glad to have you back, son," said Dr. Joe.

Angus glared at the aging dentist; after eight days and more than twenty-five thousand dollars in fees and pay-offs, these were the first words chosen by the old man for this born-lucky brat.

Angus exploded. "Are you fucking kidding me, Joe? After all the money you just put up, that's what you come up with? A girl—" Angus lowered his voice— "a girl lost her life, and no one's talking about her. People will notice. Peggy Smith was not just a … a … placeholder. She was a person, and she will be missed. Remember that. Do you realize what just happened? Patrick, you were one lawyer's rejection away from spending months in a Greek prison, and that's if you were found 'not guilty,' mind you. Be thankful you're on this plane because I'll tell you, for a while there, it was up in the air, my friend."

"Angus, we haven't discussed money yet. Sarah wants to be involved," said Dr. Joe. Patrick winced; Dad was easy. His mother was another story.

"I'll tell you this, gentlemen, I've lost eight days to this debacle, and I'm pissed off and don't want to discuss it anymore. Patrick, I don't know where to begin. Frankly, I'm embarrassed. To say I'm disappointed would be an understatement. Now, if you'll excuse me, I'll see if I can find a different seat because I need a break and a good stiff drink. Have a nice flight." With that, Angus Addison stormed off.

Chapter 19

———

Beverly, Massachusetts

As they pulled up the Brennan driveway, Patrick's palms began to sweat. He'd not spoken to his mother since before Greece, including absolutely zero correspondence or communication during incarceration. She was angry, of that he could be sure.

The house was dark as they entered, but there was a light still on in the dining room. Sarah had set up a sort of war room to deal with Patrick's problem. Piles of papers and scratch pads littered the table, and there was no telling how many hours she'd spent taking phone calls, transferring money, and worrying about her son and the family's reputation. There were no pleasantries of any kind as Patrick walked in.

"Sit down. We've got a lot to talk about, and don't you dare say you're tired."

Patrick sat without a word.

"Twenty-seven thousand dollars, Patrick. Twenty-seven thousand! It's a good thing you're a dentist now. If you were still in college, I …" she let the thought hang in the air. "You're paying us back; that's a given. We'll put that on the tab with your student loans. You've mortgaged your future. I hope you realize that?"

Patrick nodded.

"Honey, maybe we should—" Dr. Joe interjected.

"Not yet, Joe. I'm not finished. You don't know the whole story. A reporter from the *Salem Evening News* printed an article that came out today. Does the name 'Nichi Tiffin' ring a bell?" Patrick had dated Nichi Tiffin in high school, and the relationship hadn't ended well.

"Well, you know she hates me," offered Patrick.

Sarah pulled a newspaper from her stack of papers and slid it across the table.

"One of your 'burned bridges' has come back to haunt you, Patrick. It's all about Peggy and what happened in Greece."

"Bitch. What's it say?"

"She interviewed Peggy's parents, who are, of course, beside themselves. It's all factual, every word, and she mentioned the Brennan practice, which stands to hurt everything we've ever worked for, including your inheritance. This grinds me like you wouldn't believe, Patrick."

"We could sue her!"

"We're not suing anyone! It's classless and bad for business. Nichi was careful to leave her opinions out of it. She's a brilliant girl. I always liked her. I bet you wish you hadn't smashed her windshield now!"

"I didn't smash her windshield!"

"Who do you think you're talking to, the Greek police? Sorry, but I'm your mother. I know a hell of a lot better, and I can't be bought."

CHAPTER 20

CODÓ, BRAZIL

Aparecida unlocked the office door, and as soon as she entered and saw the back door wide open, her heart sank. If it was the police, they were all going to jail. She listened carefully and, after a minute, decided it was safe to investigate the alley. To her dismay, the shed door was also wide open; the padlock was on the ground. She took two steps back to listen again, but all was quiet. If there was someone in there, surely, they would be making some noise.

Aparecida worried about the package. Organs were their bread and butter and were hard to come by. Surprisingly, the cooler was still there, but the lid was on the floor.

Merda, she mouthed, but there was still plenty of ice—it might still be salvageable. Maybe someone had heard her coming, and it scared them away: a street urchin looking for scraps or something to sell. Moving quickly, Aparecida grabbed the cooler, resolving to figure the rest out later. The organ was precious cargo and would spoil before too long.

Chapter 21

Boa Vista, Brazil

After a very guarded drop, Aparecida drove a tense hour and ten minutes to the farm, her mind racing. If the police had been there, they would not have left. She couldn't wait to tell Zé, but he would no doubt be livid. The city of Codó had been good for them thus far— much better hidden than the previous facility in Mantena, and the money was finally pouring in. It would be a shame to have to leave so soon.

The farm in Boa Vista was their most advanced to date. The main barn was immense and home to a legitimate slaughterhouse. There were hundreds of cows, and the money-making operation beneath the barn was impossible to find if you didn't know what you were looking for. Even if the police showed up, they would be hard-pressed to find anything. All but three of the ranch hands were unaware of what went on below ground.

The guard opened the gate and waved Aparecida in, where she parked by the house and walked to the barn, palms beginning to sweat. Not only was this a hectic day, but it would soon get ugly. Thankfully, she wouldn't be able to stay long; Juliana was home and would wonder where she'd been. Vilma, too, was due to be picked up from school.

Aparecida knocked on the hidden panel, and Zé opened it. It was cold and dark downstairs for bacteria control, and she shivered, cursing herself for forgetting to bring a sweater. The basement was multi-purpose: part-office, part-operating room, and part-jail. As soon as she saw him, she knew Zé had already sensed something was wrong.

"What is it? Tell me," he said, veins bulging in his neck.

"I'm not sure. The back door and the shed were both wide open, but nothing was missing." Aparecida purposely left out the lid being taken off the cooler. The transfer was over, and the money had been received and counted.

"Did anyone follow you?"

The final half-hour's drive was very rural, and she'd been the only car on the road for most of the trip. Aparecida tried to read his eyes, but all she could make out was his silhouette.

"No, no helicopters either. I looked several times."

"If you were followed, all this would disappear!"

"I had nothing to do with what happened," she insisted. "And you know that."

Chapter 22

Codó, Brazil

Aparecida picked up Vilma from school and took two cautionary circles around the block before entering the apartment. Thankfully, there were no police in the area. When she opened the apartment door, Vilma ran to Juliana's bedroom to check on her distressed sister as Aparecida's brain worked in a frenzy.

Vilma returned immediately. "Juliana isn't here. She must be feeling better."

Like the dawn of a new morning, it was all evident, and Aparecida's purse fell from her arm to the kitchen floor. *Of course.* Quickly, she ran to Zé's desk, confirmed the missing keyring, and picked up the telephone.

CHAPTER 23

SALEM, MASSACHUSETTS

Salem Evening News reporter Nichi Tiffin sat at her desk, proud that the Patrick Brennan article was finally out in the wild. It was cathartic in many ways, both for herself and Peggy's parents, but the whole story, to her mind, was far from over. There was more. She knew it, and she felt it. Patrick had always been an asshole, well, almost always.

Nichi considered herself Patrick's first victim. They'd dated for a year and a half in High school. He was her first love, for crying out loud—but as soon as Patrick was accepted to Tufts University School of Dental Medicine in the second quarter of their senior year, something changed. His ego had swelled, and he'd developed an arrogance about him. He began taking her for granted and spending more time with his friends—so Nichi, a free-thinking, confident, attractive woman, broke up with him— and Patrick didn't like that.

A month later, she was in a restaurant enjoying a first date when her windshield was smashed. Insurance paid for most of it, and she'd thought it a random act until a week later when her windshield was broken a second time while hiking in the White Mountains.

Nichi knew of only one person who spent time in Beverly, Massachusetts, and Ossipee, New Hampshire, two towns nearly a hundred miles apart. His disdain was telling. Patrick was the type to think he would never get caught. Two weeks later, Nichi's windshield was smashed again in a supermarket parking lot, and enough was enough.

Nichi called the Beverly Police and reported her thoughts. The cops followed up by visiting the Brennan residence, and after questioning, Patrick dared to pick up the phone and lecture her. Although never proven to have broken the windshields, Nichi filed a restraining order. Patrick didn't like that either, but he could do nothing about it. Finally, he left her alone.

Poor Peggy Smith was dead, and Patrick was the only witness. The Greek police thought it fishy, as did Peggy's parents; Nichi found validation in that. The Greeks held him until family money came to the rescue. It was even international news, albeit third-page material, but it was all the motivation Nichi needed to pick up where the trail left off. She had some friends who spoke Greek; maybe with their help, she could make some phone calls and learn something from the officials in Santorini.

CHAPTER 24

Patrick arrived at his townhouse, excited to see a package waiting for him on the front step. With great anticipation, he scooped it up and brought it inside, tossing his car keys on the table. Then, grabbing a knife, he cut the tape, peered inside, and couldn't believe his eyes; although the price tag made him wince, he couldn't wait to try it out.

Patrick, forever a lover of buying gadgets, was an avid reader of *Rock Climber* magazine, his favorite section being the classifieds in the back. He combed them monthly, looking for new ideas and new ways to spend money. Then, last month, he stumbled on a rare find, a brand-new revolutionary tool that would up his game and make him the envy of the mountain.

A hippy named Ringo Baker had developed an idea for a device that could be inserted into a crack in a rock face and expand within, creating a secure hold, he claimed, which could support a climber's weight. Patrick lifted the foot-long contraption out of the box and examined it; the "cam," as it was called, was a bit heavy but a solid work in progress. Baker himself machined the Cams individually, each unit taking more than two weeks to finish. Each unit consisted of a solid aluminum bar with four oyster-shaped claws on the business end, small enough to fit into a crevasse and expand as the lever was let go.

Genius, thought Patrick. *I'm probably one of the first to own one.*

Chapter 25

São Paulo, Brazil

"Are you all right, Juliana? He's looking for you," said Telma, Juliana's maternal grandmother. Juliana was at a payphone outside a rest stop as the bus from Codó refueled.

"Don't tell him we talked, Vovó. I have terrible news, but it must be in person. I can't believe it myself."

"We've never spoken of your father, you, and I, but I've been waiting for my opportunity. Praying for it, really. I'll explain later, but in the meantime, know you've come to the right place. Where are you?"

"Vovó, it was so horrible." Juliana burst into tears, but Telma interrupted.

"Never mind, Juliana, we can talk soon; just get here safely. There's no way he followed you, is there?"

"Not unless he took a plane. I left yesterday."

"I'll make some phone calls. My friend Guilherme may be able to help; watch yourself until you're safe inside my building."

Chapter 26

Juliana stepped off the bus and noticed a huge, bearded man staring.

"Juliana?" She looked around, panicked. São Paulo was a city of six million people, eight of whom would be eyewitnesses if he tried anything.

"Yes," she said, prepared to run.

"Your grandmother sent me. Let's get you there." His name was Guilherme, and he seemed kind. Exhausted from the dirty bus trip, she couldn't help but let her guard down. Once past security, up the elevator, and locked safely within the apartment, Grandma Telma insisted Juliana shower and lay down before they talked. "Laying down" turned into two hours.

Juliana awakened to the pleasant smell of Grandma's rice and beans. Grandma managed a comforting smile as soon as she saw her in the doorway, but behind her eyes was a mountain of concern. They hugged without words. Finally, Telma spoke, "You don't have to worry. Guilherme lives across the hall, and I've told security to be on the lookout. Let's eat and talk while the arrangements are made. Are you hungry?"

Juliana, despite her grief, was in shock over the discoveries of her beloved father, not to mention being famished. She'd had nothing to eat in the last twenty-four hours. Before the food could be served, however, the phone interrupted them. Grandma, seemingly ready for the call, put her finger to her lips before picking up. "Don't say anything. It could be your father. Hello?" Telma stared into Juliana's eyes and nodded.

"No, I haven't heard from or seen her, José, and now you've got me worried. Are the police any help? Have you thought of a private investigator? Things move a little too slow for my liking up North. Everything is backward. They take their sweet time. Didn't they mess up an autopsy in Belém a couple of years ago? Remember that? It made the national news! They're inept! Yes, I know Belém is fifteen hours away, but it's still the North. What? Well, if you say so. I will be here—anything I can do to help, yes, of course. Tchau."

"Is he in Codó?" asked Juliana.

"I'm not sure, but my guess is he's on his way, coming back to be sure, no doubt. Give me two minutes. I need to talk with Guilherme. I'll be right back." Grandma opened the door and crossed the hallway. Juliana heard rapping on the door, followed by excited murmuring. Ten minutes later, Telma returned. "It pains me to say this, Juliana, but you're going to have to eat while I talk, and then—" Telma teared up.

"Vovó, what is it? You want me to hide?"

Telma pulled a shrimp pie from the oven and gestured for Juliana to sit. She cut the pie and wiped her cheek with her sleeve. "Juliana, years back, your father told me your mother had abandoned you for the United States, and I couldn't believe it, so I told him exactly how I felt—about everything. Then, after I'd accused him of murder and a host of horrible things, he produced a letter in her handwriting—a goodbye letter—and I couldn't believe my eyes.

"I was so overwhelmed with guilt for having accused him that I apologized, but something still didn't sit right in the days and weeks that followed. Even though you haven't told me what you saw, I can't help but imagine that I was right all along. You look like her, you know."

"Do you think he … killed her?"

Telma sidestepped the question. "Tell me what you saw."

Juliana's mind flashed to the organ in the Styrofoam cooler. The shed was still vivid, and the memory of Fernanda's notebook made her shiver. "I went to my father's office, and nobody was there, so I let myself in with some keys I found, and—I saw—" she hesitated— "signs that he killed my friend. Her notebook was there." The thought brought tears, and Telma stroked her back.

"That's enough, dear. You don't have to say anymore. We must move you. I think your father is well on his way to São Paulo if he hasn't already arrived, and it wouldn't surprise me if he shows up downstairs."

A lump formed in Juliana's throat. "Where am I going?"

"Sweetheart, I put Guilherme to work as soon as you called from the bus station. He's a good boy with a troubled past, but he knows you're in danger and can help. He thinks you should leave the country, at least for a while. You should go to the United States; you can hide there and find work. Then, you can come back when it's safe."

Juliana sat up in shock. "But I don't know anyone there!"

"I know, my dear. And on top of that, you'll be illegal. It will be difficult, no doubt, but I have friends of friends who have made it there and lead very productive lives. They even send money home, but I suggest you save yours for your sister." Juliana choked up at the thought of little Vilma, still in Codó, living with the Monster.

"I never liked that you were brought up to practice Macumba," said Grandma. "I nearly died when your mother told me your father was into it. I was raised to believe Macumba was Black Magick, nothing more. All those gifts and sacrifices to an *Exu*— Do you know my family equated *Exu* with the Devil?"

Juliana's mind drifted. The evening news programs were never watched in their home, nor had the family subscribed to a local newspaper. Anything she'd learned current events-wise her entire life had been via word of mouth, in school hallways, and such. What else had been hidden from her? Then, suddenly, there was a knock, and Juliana looked down at her plate—she'd yet to take a bite.

"Eat quickly. That's Guilherme. Sweetheart, we must get you out of here. When you need money, I can wire some a little at a time, and you can pay me back when you're settled. You'll call Guilherme's phone number but not mine—I have no idea what your father knows or how he knows it, but I suspect he has a lot of help. Take this. You'll need it." Grandma handed over two hundred cruzeiros. "Guilherme has more money for you later—remind him at the airport if he forgets."

Everything was happening so fast. Reality came crashing down on Juliana as she gulped the pie, and Guilherme rapped again. Whatever fragment of Juliana's childhood remained ended then and there, and she swallowed her tears as Grandma answered the door. Guilherme entered, holding a packet of papers and a set of car keys.

"You two should go," said Grandma. "Your father might be here any minute. I love you, Juliana, be safe!" Grandma hugged her tight, and she returned the love, but sorrow and anger roiled beneath the surface.

Chapter 27

Guilherme drove without speaking for twenty minutes. During that time, Juliana's fear turned to anger, and she broke the silence. "Where are we going?" Her voice was different, the tone of a woman twice her age.

"Congonhas. We must get you on a domestic flight to Acre. From there, you enter Peru."

"Where is Congonhas?"

"Congonhas is the name of the São Paulo airport."

"And after Peru?" Guilherme looked into the rearview mirror.

"Ecuador, but I suggest you take it one country at a time. It's a long journey. It's too much to think about all at once."

Juliana reached over the passenger seat for his folder, and he let her take it. Most of it was handwritten notes, along with some names and phone numbers. There was also a list of countries: Brazil, Peru, Ecuador, Colombia, Panama, Costa Rica, Nicaragua, Honduras, Guatemala, Mexico, and the United States.

Eleven countries—and Juliana had never set foot outside Brazil. She would have to say goodbye to her native Portuguese. From here on out, it was Spanish or English unless she got lucky along the route and met another Brazilian. "Are you a coyote?" she asked.

"I was, but not anymore. Your coyote is my brother. You will refer to him as Gambá. You'll meet him when you get to Acre. I only work in the background now. I've seen enough of that jungle."

Juliana found it mildly humorous that Gambá meant skunk, but she was in no mood for laughter. "It will be dangerous?"

Guilherme met her eyes in the mirror. "It is. You will have to be very careful. Many people die—or worse."

"What's the worst part? The desert?"

"No. This time of year, the desert is one of the easiest."

Chapter 28

Boa Vista, Brazil

Fernanda opened her eyes only to be reminded of the hell she was in. It was dark and always too cold, a place of suffering. Aparecida was the reason she was here, that she remembered, and that sinister surprise would never leave her, but did Juliana know?

Her cell was ten-by-six with nothing but a cot and bucket. The walls were made of cement, and the only light came from a bulb high overhead. Fernanda blinked twice in great pain and assessed her ailments; of utmost concern was her wrist. She reached to massage it—and found her hand missing. *Dear God!*

Clumsily, she explored the nub wrapped in gauze and taped neatly. Her back hurt too—a throbbing agony—and as she tried to move, she could not. She'd been in denial for the first week or so, but ever since, she'd accepted the hard truth: she would die here.

Occasionally, Juliana's evil father would deliver two pills at a time. She couldn't stand him, the wolf in sheep's clothing, the damned Monster of Codó. Fernanda also hated that she needed him and even looked forward to his visits.

Tragically, she'd become addicted to whatever it was he gave her, one problem she couldn't afford to worry about. Suddenly, the door opened at the end of the hallway, and her heart rate increased. She attempted to stand, but a back spasm collapsed her to the cot.

"Don't try to get up, Fernanda—you're weak. I have your pills, as many as you need. I want you to be healthy."

"What did you do? My hand! Why, why?!" Tears fell like rain.

"Let me have a look. I'm going to roll you over, but first, here's something for the pain." Zé put the pills in his pocket and instead pulled out a syringe. The fact that she was in so much pain was not good. Other business had pulled him away from her for too long, and her condition had worsened. Dr. Zé watched as Fernanda's face relaxed, and the drug entered her bloodstream. Her body, hot to the touch, settled visibly, and her eyes went glassy. Now, he could position her as he needed. Very carefully, so as not to pull the stitches, Zé rolled her over.

The back of her gown had a fist-sized pus stain over the incision, a foul smell coming from it. Zé lifted the dress and found her back covered in red blotches. He cursed, aware that even though she was drugged, she could still hear. Fernanda wouldn't last much longer.

CHAPTER 29

Zé stepped into the night and walked behind the barn to his usual thinking spot. The farm was built for eight prisoners, most of whom would be sold as slaves, but some were reserved for organ harvest. Zé threw Fernanda's hand on the fire and cursed his gods; her organs were tainted due to infection and could no longer be sold. Stepping back from the smoke, he gazed at the stars and contemplated. Burnt offerings were all she was good for now, and Zé wasn't sure if they even meant anything.

He tried his best to keep the donors alive, taking them piece by surgically removed piece, but so far, none had lasted a year. He expected help in return, yet the gods continued to disappoint. 'Quimbanda' was his first and only religion, and although he'd met Aparecida through it, he'd always been disappointed by its limitations. Additionally, it attracted unwanted attention. There must be something else. His enhanced intuition told him so. The world was full of magick, and the Federal Police here in Brazil would catch up sooner or later. Until that day, he'd save all the money he could to disappear.

Alternate avenues of darkness beckoned, leading Zé to believe his destiny lay elsewhere. Voodoo and Santeria caught his eye, and he read whatever he could about them. Peru, Africa, India, and the Caribbean were also hotbeds of Black Magick. He studied Allan Kardec's *Le Livre des Esprits*, Aleister Crowley's *Book of Law*, and another magick man named Claude Allemand, who was rumored to have found a way to cheat death.

CHAPTER 30

SALEM, MASSACHUSETTS

Despite help from her good friend Zina, Nichi Tiffin ran into a stone wall. The Greek police had washed their hands of the matter.

"I'm sure they want that story to go away. Santorini is a tranquil island and relies on tourism," said Zina, which made perfect sense. At an impasse, Nichi moved on, and two days had passed when she bumped into an old classmate who worked downstairs.

"Nichi, I loved that article you wrote on Peggy Smith. My mother knows her folks. They're really broken up about her death."

"Thanks, Brad. I tried checking with the Greek police, too, but they aren't talking."

"Forgive me for asking, Nichi, but didn't you have a restraining order on Patrick when you two broke up?"

Nichi searched for words. "I did. Not amongst my fondest memories."

"Sorry. I only ask because I can't stand the guy, either. A buddy of mine who went to college with him said he was always freeloading. Stupid stuff, like saying he'd pay you back after a bar tab, then never coming through. He even got drunk one night and drove into my friend's parked car. It was no huge deal, but the quarter panel was shot. Patrick begged him not to call the cops because he was drunk, so he didn't, yet Patrick never paid him for the damage."

"He couldn't sue?"

"Well, he didn't report the accident and didn't want to get in trouble, plus he had friendly connections with an auto body shop. The bottom line is that Patrick stiffed him. So, my advice is, keep watching. That's three strikes if you ask me: your history, my friend's history, and now Peggy. Patrick Brennan is bad news."

Chapter 31

São Paulo, Brazil

Guilherme pulled into the airport terminal, got out, opened the trunk, and removed a small bag containing five hundred Brazilian cruzeiros, fifty American dollars, and a strange pair of neoprene socks with stiff felt soles. He also took the travel folder from Juliana, put it in her bag, and handed her a business card with nothing on it but a phone number.

"This is my number. Memorize it because it will get wet. You will need me to wire you money several times throughout the trip. Without it, you will be stuck."

"Why can't I just have it all now?"

"Because you stand a good chance of being robbed. The cruzeiros are to purchase your plane ticket, and the dollars are for the rest of the journey."

"What are these?" said Juliana, gesturing to the sock boots.

"Those are for the jungle. You will need them, believe me. Those shoes could be the difference between life and death. They're perfect for walking on slippery rocks. Discard them after the jungle. And one more thing: try to dress like a man. Do anything to blend in and avoid attention. Buy something baggy at the airport. Many women are raped, or worse. Wear a hat, pull out your shirt, and cover your tits and ass. Your flight information to Acre is written on the inside of the folder. The ticket is the only documented part of your itinerary. The rest is in the folder, and you must find your way. I'm sorry, but there was so little time."

Chapter 32

The state of Acre, Brazil

Gambá lifted the bottle to his lips as a hard slap landed on his shoulder, spilling his beer. Wiping the foam from his chin as he turned, it was no surprise to find Urso's gap-toothed grin smiling back. Being a coyote was a dangerous job, and Urso loved to brag about how much better his job was than everyone else's. The rumor, however, was Urso was unpredictable on the trail, and that made things more dangerous for everyone. For this, Gambá despised him.

"Como vai, puto, I'm back," said Urso. "Twelve more happy customers delivered and only slightly damaged. Now, I have ten days off. I'm telling you, I can get you a job. Even the FARC won't fuck with us."

"Congratulations, but I'll pass," said Gambá. "The money's good because you don't know who you work for. I need to know who I'm dealing with, so I work for myself."

"You're going to get yourself killed, my friend. When's your next trip?"

"Tomorrow. This beer is my last until Mexico."

Urso took the opportunity to rub it in. "Sorry about that, man. I'll drink for both of us!"

"Fuck off, Urso."

"Ah, I'm just riding you, Gambá. The fact is, I could be called back in. They're looking for somebody."

"Who?" asked Gambá, ears perked up.

"I don't know yet. Why?"

"Because maybe I'll find them first and collect the reward."

"No chance, meu amigo. When you hit that jungle, you're like a sloth, and I'm like a jaguar."

CHAPTER 33

CODÓ, BRAZIL

"I miss Juliana. Where is she?"

"We aren't sure, Vilma. She might have run away. Remember how sad she was the last time you saw her?" replied Aparecida.

"Did she run away like my mom did?"

"I don't know, dear. Nobody knows until we find her. Only then can we ask her."

"I'm going to look in her room," said Vilma.

Aparecida lurched forward in her chair. "You can't do that!"

"Why not? I miss her. I want to smell her clothes. I want to look for clues, and maybe she left me a note."

"You wouldn't want Juliana going through your things, would you? It's not nice. She could be back home tomorrow. You never know."

"I wouldn't care," said Vilma. "Besides, what if she ... What if it's the only way we might figure out where she went?"

"Your father was in Juliana's room the other day doing just that. He didn't find anything."

Vilma dropped her head the tiniest bit but maintained eye contact with Aparecida. "When was that? I haven't seen Pai since she disappeared."

Aparecida's tone went from scrambling to make up an answer to authoritative stepmother. "He did it when you were asleep."

Little Vilma, ten years old but nobody's fool, knew better. *No, he didn't,* she thought. Not twenty minutes after their suspicious conversation about Juliana, Vilma heard Aparecida tiptoe down the hallway, enter Juliana's room, and close the door. Vilma listened and watched through her bedroom door keyhole, waiting for Aparecida to return, which she did ten minutes later.

In her stepmother's hands were a few notebooks, some envelopes, and a jewelry box.

You said it wasn't nice to go through someone's things, Vilma thought to herself.

Chapter 34

Acre, Brazil

Juliana passed through the airport, watching for her father or anyone who looked suspicious, and used some money to buy the most nondescript men's T-shirt she could find. When the time came, she boarded her plane and tried to sleep but couldn't because of a connection in Brasília. Nine hours later, she was in Acre, Brazil, a five-hour bus ride from the Peru border. A large, unsmiling man greeted her as she exited the plane.

"Are you Gambá?" asked Juliana.

"Yes. Come this way."

"Not yet. First, tell me your brother's name."

"His name is Guilherme. Have you memorized his phone number? You have five hours to do just that. I'm your guide, but I don't have money for you—that is between you, Guilherme, and your grandmother. You will need that number burned into your memory."

Gambá was all business, but she was relieved she'd found the right person.

"Gambá, how much is this costing my grandmother to send me to the U.S.?"

"Why? Are you going to do the right thing and pay her back?"

"Yes, because I want to pay for my sister someday. I need to know how much to save."

Gambá stopped to calculate. "For most people, it costs $1,500 American. But for you, the price was more than six times that. Come, let's get you to the bus."

"Six times? Why is that?" whispered Juliana, astonished.

Gambá scoffed but kept his voice low as they exited the airport and walked around the building to a waiting bus. "Ah, Guilherme didn't tell you everything, did he? That's just like my brother, leaving me with the dirty work. Come on, keep moving."

"What do you mean?" she asked.

"Querida, your father is maybe the largest trafficker in South America. He knows this business better than anyone. He knows the cops and the border guards, and worst of all, I think they're already looking for you."

Juliana's eyes popped. "How do you know?"

"Word travels fast. Everyone stays away from his business, or they end up dead."

"What kind of trafficking," asked Juliana, fishing for information.

"Drugs, slaves, organs, you name it. If a rich guy needs to cut the line for a heart transplant, your dad is the guy they go to. Some of it is probably far-fetched, but I can't tell you how many coyotes like me have disappeared, and we all think he's the reason. He's known by a few names. *The Farmer* is one. *O Monstro* is another. The rumors say he's into Macumba, and not just the casual kind."

"The Farmer? But my father is a doctor."

"Of course, that makes sense, but harvesting crops is not his moneymaker. I have a pilot friend involved with black-market shipping, although he's never seen him. Your father would *have* to be a doctor or at least have one on staff to do what he does. That's why you're so expensive, querida—bodies are turning up missing parts. Some parts you can sell, but sometimes the bodies are missing hands or eyes. You can't transplant hands or eyes. What's he doing with *them?* Nobody knows."

Juliana shook her head, debating whether she wanted to hear more. Up ahead of them was the nondescript bus parked at the back of the lot. "What about my sister? I need to save nine thousand dollars?"

"The little girl? Her passage will be nearly impossible because of her age. I don't want to tell you what can happen to kids. Don't forget your father will watch her much closer than he watched you. I'm not in the kidnapping business; I'd have to find somebody good *and* stupid."

"Give me a number. I'll figure out the rest later. First, I need an idea of how much to save."

Gambá frowned and looked to the sky. As he calculated, he wondered if he would live to see the money. "Twenty thousand, and I can't guarantee when the time comes that will still be the price. I hope you turn me down, to be honest. After this trip, I hope I never hear your voice again."

Twenty thousand dollars sounded like a million to Juliana, as it was nearly enough to buy an entire Codó neighborhood. Overwhelmed, she boarded the bus. During the drive, she had an epiphany—she would have to change her name. There was no good reason to remain Juliana. In fact, it was foolish. She needed every bit of invisibility she could conjure. Within ten minutes, she thought of the perfect pseudonym, choosing *Renata* for its meaning: Reborn.

Chapter 35

Codó, Brazil

"She wanted to go through Juliana's room before we had a chance," said Aparecida. "Watch out for her, Zé. She's as smart as Juliana and twice as adventurous. The second child is almost always braver than the first. If you want to keep Vilma here long-term, I say we start the process."

Zé put his head down as he finished the thought. "I'm too busy for that, Aparecida. The rituals take time, and she will have plenty of questions. Besides, she's too young. And if I'm honest, my faith has been slipping of late. We've strayed, gotten away from the basics. We don't practice the same thing anymore, and our gods aren't helping as I'd hoped—after all the risks we take."

"I'll help. I'll get the ball rolling, and you fill in where I can't. We'll start over. You can't quit now, Zé. We've come so far. You're wrong about the gods."

Once again, Zé elected to pick his battles and let Aparecida win. Tomorrow was another busy day. Juliana was out there somewhere, and she knew far too much.

CHAPTER 36

____

The following day, Vilma woke up, brushed her teeth, and went to the kitchen for breakfast. On her way by Juliana's room, she stopped, made sure no one was coming, and turned the doorknob. What she saw made her heart sink. In shock, Vilma walked back to her bedroom, emotions churning. Juliana's bedroom was empty: no furniture, curtains, or rug. Beneath her sadness was anger—anger for Aparecida and her father, who were purging the house of Juliana the same way they purged her mother.

They want me to forget her, thought Vilma, *but I won't.*

CHAPTER 37

That evening at the dinner table, Vilma sat across from Dr. Zé and Aparecida. She'd kept her mouth shut about Juliana's empty bedroom. The door had been closed for a reason. To say she'd gone in and looked after being told not to would invite punishment. The parents sat at the table talking, not nearly as mournful as they should be. Something was wrong. She picked up her cup and took a sip.

"Ugh! This isn't Graviola!" Vilma had been expecting the flavor of her favorite fruit juice.

"That's herbal tea, dear. Your father and I have a bit of an announcement to make, and it's all good news. I'll let your father do the talking."

Dr. Zé cleared his throat. "Vilma, your stepmother, and I have decided you're ready for indoctrination."

"What's in-doc-trin—"

"It's a welcoming to our religion. A confirmation that you belong. It's a big deal, and you should be excited. We waited too long with Juliana, and we're kicking ourselves for it. Perhaps she wouldn't have gotten so lost if she'd been part of the faith. Tomorrow, we will begin teaching you the ways of the 'Exus' and 'Pombagiras.' May they serve you as they have served us, and vice versa.

"That tea you're drinking is a special blend, essential to our faith. We'll get into more details about what all this means and what is expected of you later, but for now, we just wanted to congratulate you and tell you how proud we are. The training is intense but well worth the result. And remember that we wouldn't have you do anything that we have not already done."

Vilma looked down into her cup and pretended to take another sip. "Thank you, Pai. Thank you, Aparecida."

***

The following day, Vilma awoke, fully remembering that today was to be the beginning of her indoctrination. After brushing her teeth, she strolled down the hallway to the kitchen, where she found Aparecida washing a dish.

"Good morning. Where—?" asked Vilma.

Aparecida whirled and raised a finger to her lips, gesturing for Vilma to turn around and stay out of the kitchen.

"Where are we—?"

"Shhhh!" said Aparecida as she continued to herd Vilma down the hallway to Juliana's room, where she grabbed Vilma by the arm, opened the door, and pushed her in.

The door clicked shut before Vilma could figure out what happened. It took a moment for her eyes to adjust. The window was painted black, and a lit candle sat on the sill. The only other thing in Juliana's bedroom was a mattress.

CHAPTER 38

TURBO, COLOMBIA

It took nearly a week from Brazil to Peru to Ecuador via buses, automobiles, and sneaking miles on foot. She was tired and dirty, and the trip had barely started. By the time she, Gambá, and a host of other hopefuls arrived in Colombia, Renata had begun to notice recurring faces: people like her on the same itinerary—the same man on two different buses and a woman walking with a young boy in consecutive airports.

Then, as they drove deeper into Western Colombia, a woman tapped her on the shoulder, whispering. "My name is Maria. I've seen you several times since we left Brazil. Are you going to the United States, too?"

Renata estimated Maria's age to be mid-thirties. She wore a long dress and flat shoes, ill-prepared for a grassy field, let alone a jungle. She answered cautiously. "I think so. Are you prepared?"

"I'd better be. It's too late to turn back." Maria seemed pleased that Renata had engaged. It was her first conversation in two days. "I'm nervous. They say the worst is coming, and there are still seven more countries even if we make it through the jungle. I didn't sleep last night."

"We're all nervous. If you lose your cool, it'll be worse." Renata already pitied Maria, who seemed even more naïve than she. "We'll make it, don't worry." Neither said another word until they arrived in Turbo, Colombia, the last stop before the stretch of jungle known as the Darien Gap.

***

After a poor night's sleep on a bus seat, Renata awakened to someone shaking her shoulder—Gambá.

"Let's go! It's time for the boat."

Moving quickly, Renata grabbed her bag and followed him off the bus and onto the pier. They walked along the docks on the river, and Maria was there too, bleary-eyed. Renata took note of the now-familiar faces. In total, there were eight travelers. Old, dented canteens of different shapes and sizes were passed out, along with a warning to conserve the precious liquid. Then, carefully, the band of migrants boarded two rickety canoe-like boats fitted with motors, and they were off.

The man Renata had noticed on the bus was named Hector. The woman and her young son from the airport were Yara and João. There was also a husband and wife named Francisco and Rosa and another man named Carlos.

Hours passed as the canoes powered on, and the river eventually narrowed to a dirty stream that snaked beneath low-hanging branches. Several times, they had to stop and get out through shallower passages. Renata was glad to have the felt-bottomed boots. They were made to be wet and grabbed the slippery rocks better than her companions' shoes. Once on land, she removed them and switched to her dry pair. Some looked on with envy, so Renata tucked them away.

***

Eventually, the river became too shallow for the boats to pass, so the pilots let everyone off, turned around, and headed back. The eight migrants stood in a grassy clearing with Gambá and a second coyote Renata had yet to speak to.

As the sounds of the motors turned into the buzzing of cicadas, Maria turned to Renata. "You've been so nice. What's your name?"

"Ju—" she almost slipped. "I'm Renata. Are you ready?"

"I'm not sure. I wonder if I might be in trouble with all this mud and these terrible shoes. You seem prepared. It's sixty miles through, isn't it?"

"I don't know, but you'll be fine. One step at a time."

Suddenly, Gambá was ready to speak. "Okay, listen up. I am Gambá, and this is Rato. The Darien Gap is a deadly place. There are poisonous snakes and spiders. There are also jaguars and crocodiles, but most of all, we worry about the guerillas, known as FARC, who call this jungle home. They run drugs and guns and consider themselves an independent nation. In short, they make the rules.

"Hopefully, we will not run into them, but there is more, so listen closely - the greatest danger of the jungle is what it does to your body. There are long stretches without clean water, and you will become dizzy and delirious if you do not manage your intake. We will walk the river for most of the trip. There is also a lot of rain, so listen up: your feet will be wet the entire time. The skin will weaken and blister if you don't care for them, and we cannot wait for you. If you can't keep up, you will get lost; if you get lost, you will die."

No one spoke.

"The only good news is that jaguar and crocodile attacks are rare, and we have paid the FARC a modest fee with some of your money. However, there are no guarantees. The jungle is littered with the bodies of people looking for a better life just like you. Vamos." Gambá ended his speech and turned into the tall brush. Everyone scrambled to gather their gear and keep up.

Chapter 39

Beverly, Massachusetts

"Mr. Melvin Watkins, how are you today, sir? Are there any problems to report? Any tooth pain?" Patrick stepped into the room, sporting his friendly, fake business voice. Olivia, the hygienist, handed him the X-rays.

"Nope, no problems to report, Dr. Brennan." Patrick perused the photos and set them aside.

"All right, well, I'm just going to look at your second molar, and we'll get you out of here. Sound good?"

Mr. Watkins nodded. "Say, Dr. Brennan, I wanted to offer my condolences. I saw the story in *The Evening News* about your fiancée and couldn't believe it. That must have been terrible."

Patrick hesitated. His first patient since the article appeared had read the damned thing. "Thanks, Mel. I appreciate that. Yeah, it's hard to talk about. Sorry, I get emotional."

"What was that like? I mean, you must have felt so helpless. How close were you to her?"

Patrick clenched his teeth. "Open, please, Mel." Patrick inserted the mirror and probe into Watkins' mouth. "As I said, it's hard to talk about, but to answer your questions, the gravel was very loose, and I couldn't get closer than ten feet from the edge. I hate thinking about it."

Mr. Watkins waited until the tools were out of his mouth for his next question. "And she was holding onto something?"

"Mel, you're killing me. She was holding onto a stone, her hand slipped, and she fell. It will haunt my dreams forever."

"Have you spoken with her folks? How are they doing?"

"They're dealing with it, Mel. And you're all set. No cavities. See you in six months."

Chapter 40

Acre, Brazil

Urso unlocked the door to his apartment and flicked on the lights. He was drunk, taking full advantage of his ten days off, but the vacation was more than halfway over, and he'd begun to anticipate the return to work. Soon, he'd be back in the jungle, wading through rivers and slapping mosquitos. Urso blinked twice. Across the room was a man pointing a pistol at him.

"Who are you? I don't have anything, and you don't know who you're fucking with."

"Relax, Urso. I don't want your belongings. I'm here for information. You've been on the trail recently, and I need to know if you've seen this girl." Dr. Zé lowered the pistol and held up a photograph of Juliana.

Urso stepped forward to look, never taking his eyes from the gun. "I haven't seen her. Who is she? And who the hell are you?"

"This is my daughter, Juliana. She's run away, and I want her back."

"You still haven't told me who you are. I work for dangerous people, puto."

"You were recently seen talking with a man called Gambá. What was that about?"

"How did you know that?" Urso reassessed the man, who seemingly wasn't here to rob him and had no fear. "Wait, are—you—him?"

"Yes." Zé lowered his gun, and Urso stood tall, addressing the stranger with renewed respect.

"You want to know about Gambá? That was nothing. I tried recruiting him, but he said he likes to know who he's working for."

"Think hard. Was there anything Gambá said that might lead you to believe he would know something about my daughter?"

Urso strained his boozed brain to recall the conversation. "Come to think of it, yes, he did seem to get a lot more interested when I told him

The Farmer—um, you—the company—was looking for someone. He wanted to know who it was."

Dr. Zé nodded. "Urso, I'm going to need you to find Gambá."

Chapter 41

Codó, Brazil

Vilma got used to her dark surroundings but still couldn't understand why she was locked in Juliana's bedroom. Despite banging on the door, no one answered. Eventually, she gave up and slept.

Later, she woke to the same darkness, and it was impossible to tell how long she'd been sleeping. Vilma crawled in the darkness, hoping to find food. Maybe they'd left her something to eat while she was unconscious. The door, including the cracks, was as black as the rest of the room. Why would her father allow this to happen?

She felt for her bedpan, and it was empty—proof that they'd been here. Her hopes lifted. Surely, they'd left some food, too? A half-minute of careful searching later, she found it, and, as meager as it was, it was delicious.

Chapter 42

The Darian Gap, Colombia

The hopeful migrants hiked a well-worn trail for over an hour before crossing the river on foot. The water was over three feet at its deepest point, and the current was enough to pull Renata off her feet on two occasions. Finally, she climbed out, working quickly to pull the wet clothing from her curves, but Rato noticed, or at least she thought he did.

Maria fell prey to the same current. One of her shoes popped to the surface as she drifted, but luckily, she retrieved it before it washed away. As Maria climbed onto the bank, Renata helped her needy companion dry everything off for the same leering reason. Muddy water squished from Maria's shoes as she took her first step, reminding Renata to change her wet boots. Renata examined Maria's feet, which were already pale and pruny. Then, a mile downriver, they crossed again.

At noon, the group stopped in a clearing. Rato produced a large pot and a bag of rice, built a fire, and began cooking. The jungle was, as always, hot and humid. Maria started to remove her damp overshirt, but Renata stopped her. Appreciative, Maria corrected herself and worked to dry her shoes instead.

After eating, they continued up a steep incline. The jungle was hilly, a river winding between six-thousand-foot mountains. Both Gambá and Rato were surprised to see Renata beat them up most of the slopes. She even turned back to help the struggling Maria several times.

During their twelfth hour, the sun went down, and the tired travelers trudged their way up what they hoped would be the last hill of the day. The ferns were thick on either side, the trail under their feet packed hard by years of travelers, when it began to pour. Renata, leading the group, saw something ahead in the middle of the trail. It wasn't a person, but it had been left by one. It was a warning.

A human skull on a pike looked down on her, rainwater pouring through broken teeth. No doubt the FARC had left it. Pulse racing, Renata backed down the incline and waited for Gambá. Finally, he came shuffling up the rainwater-carved trench, with Rato close behind him, followed by Carlos and Hector. The jungle hid the rest of the group.

The two coyotes considered the skull whispering heatedly. Renata tried to listen in but only heard "FARC." The two coyotes disagreed, and as the rain soaked everyone to the bone, Renata noticed Maria was missing.

Renata ran down the hill more than a hundred yards before she found her, crying, one shoe missing. Renata took out her dry pair and examined Maria's feet. The skin was milk-white and spongy, with a puncture wound that bled as fast as the rain could wash it away. Both women knew that Maria might not make it out of Colombia.

Renata assisted, consoling as they went, motivating when she could, attempting to convince the poor woman tomorrow would be a better day. Ten minutes later, they arrived at the skull. Gambá and Rato were still arguing. At that moment, the rain intensified, and Rato gave in. Not even the FARC would be out tonight. With the matter settled, they began pitching tents.

***

Four hours later, when the rain stopped, thousands of mosquitos descended on the campers. Everyone swatted as if their lives depended on it. Sleep was impossible; their feet stung, bones ached, and skin bled. Renata finally closed her eyes an hour before dawn.

CHAPTER 43

Codó, Brazil

Zé sat up in bed, sweating after another nightmare, and Aparecida attempted to settle his nerves.

"Dream or premonition?" she asked.

"I saw the police again," said Zé.

Aparecida sighed. "Relax, darling, we have more resources than they do, we're smarter than they are, and we own whom we need to own." Aparecida stroked his shoulder, but he shrugged her away.

"Our business can't last forever. Nothing does. Eventually, we will have to leave Brazil."

Aparecida didn't want to hear those words. Brazil and Quimbanda were her life, despite Zé's recent indifference. "You thought they'd find our previous facility in Mantena, so we moved, and to this day, it remains undiscovered. Sleep," she said. "We'll talk in the morning."

Chapter 44

The town of Mantena, Brazil

Detective Olival Freitas of the Federal Police arrived at the Mantena farm and walked to the back of the barn. Luckily for Freitas, the owner, who had purchased the farm two years prior, had noticed his barn was larger on the outside than it was on the inside. When he decided to investigate, he pulled back some boards and found three jail cells and a tiled room.

"You were right to call us," Freitas said to the farmer. "We might have something here. The first three rooms lock from the outside. The tiled room looks like an operating room. We will need to look at the deeds and any other papers related to the purchase."

Whoever was committing the murders had lived here, and the tiled room led him to believe a doctor might be the culprit. Now, there was a growing body count two thousand kilometers to the north, which told him a newer, better facility existed somewhere in the northeast. The big problem, however, was that there were hundreds of thousands of farms up there.

Chapter 45

The Darian Gap, Colombia

Gambá woke the travelers just after 5 am. The bugs had feasted on Little João, who had gotten more sleep than anyone, but the mosquitos made him pay. When he woke crying, Rato was instantly in Yara's face, threatening her to quiet him.

"Cala boca!" he whispered through bared teeth.

Yara panicked and continued to quiet her son. Renata recalled the skull-on-a-pike, not twenty feet away. They were all at risk; she could see it in the coyote's eyes. Paid off or not, the FARC was best avoided. As soon as João stopped crying, it was Hector's turn.

"Cobra!" he yelled as he burst from the bushes, still tying his pants. Rato ran to Hector, tackled him to the ground, then pulled out his machete and went behind the tree. They all heard him curse.

"Porra! Fer-de-lance. Pit viper. Venomous." Rato looked to Hector, who had been hoping for good news. "You will die." Everyone gasped.

"No! Cut above the wound and suck out the poison!" cried Hector.

Gambá shook his head. "I'm sorry, but that is only in the movies. Let me see your hands." Hector, confused, held both palms up.

"Take off your ring, and if you have a necklace, take that off too. I don't want your jewelry. I'm telling you because you will want them off before the swelling begins." Hector obeyed, then turned to the snake bite, squeezing and wiping frantically. "Gather your things, everyone. You too, Hector; you're welcome to follow as long as you are able."

Hector shook his head as if he didn't believe a word.

"Vamos!" barked Gambá.

Chapter 46

Hector feigned strength as if to convince himself he would make it. *A desperate man will believe anything*, Renata thought, and within twenty minutes, Hector began to limp, and Renata got her first good look at the bite. A softball-sized blood blister had spread across his calf, surrounded by a deep red ring. The calf was swollen, stretching the skin tight, and clear liquid oozed rivers from the two punctures. His body hitched with every step.

As the two women overtook him, their eyes met as they passed, and Renata saw a man who knew he would soon die. Hector looked away. Less than an hour later, the jungle swallowed him up.

***

Renata followed Rato close, wanting to overtake him, holding back only because she didn't know where the trail went. She could burn through this jungle in two days if she only knew the way, but she didn't. At midday, she was surprised to feel a tap on her shoulder.

"Hey." It was Gambá.

"Hey." Renata was surprised to be approached by the man who had so far seemed apathetic to her presence.

"You're fast. Are you a hiker or something?" said Gambá.

"No. Why?"

"Look behind you. Everyone is sucking wind, trying to keep up, myself included."

Renata smiled, albeit briefly. "I just want to get this over with."

"Your grandmother is friends with my brother, right?" said Gambá.

"They're neighbors. Guilherme lives across the hall from her."

"Yeah, I heard that. Hey, listen. You have something about you these other people do not. And any friend of your grandmother's is a friend of mine. You have a real chance to make it, and it would be a shame if you didn't. The longer it takes to travel, the less chance you have, and you move fast."

"Thanks," said Renata.

"Jul—Renata, let me give you a number. In case something happens. For your sister, if nothing else."

"What do you mean?"

"I mean, nothing is for sure on this journey. You can die of dehydration, and you can die with a gun to your head. Remember, your father is a mighty man. He has eyes and ears everywhere."

"Go ahead then."

"I know a man in Mexico. He knows the route as well as anyone, but he's an expert at crossing the final border. If something happens to me, give him a call." Slowly and carefully, Gambá read off the number.

Chapter 47

Salem, Massachusetts

Patrick did some calculations, then screamed aloud in his empty townhouse. "Fuck it!" Forty-five minutes later, a deal was struck; he was buying the Porsche, his mother be damned. Of course, he would hide the purchase for as long as possible.

***

Patrick drove to work but parked on the street. Now, at least, the new car wouldn't be immediately noticed. He hoped to have a week or so of fun before someone saw it and the fireworks began.

"Wow, new wheels?" Patrick jumped. He hadn't seen Olivia getting out of her car. *Shit.*

"Yeah, I'm trying it out. We'll see. It's a lease."

"Super snazzy!" Olivia flirted, but only because he was the boss.

***

The office was abuzz by lunch, and finally, Dr. Joe heard the gossip. Olivia led him to the front window and pointed to the Porsche on the street, and as soon as Patrick finished with his next patient, Dr. Joe knocked. "Patrick, can I come in?"

"Sure, Dad, what's up?"

"Uh, is that your car out on the street? The Porsche?"

"Yeah, Dad. I did the math, and I'll still be able to pay my debts to you and Mom."

"Nice wheels, but did you clear that purchase with your mother first?"

"No. I've been busy. Don't worry, though."

Dr. Joe wiped his palms on his pants. "Well, I'm guessing she's going to say you'd be able to pay your debts quicker without the car."

"I got a great deal. It's not as expensive as you think. And my car was getting old," Patrick lied.

"Well, do me a favor. Please park it on Maple Street, at least on Fridays, when your mother stops by with payroll."

"Great, thanks, Dad."

Chapter 48

Codó, Brazil

Vilma was hungry again. *Why can't there be light? Why can't I talk to anybody?* With nothing better to do, she crawled on her hands and knees, searching for missed crumbs. The first thing her fingers found, however, was a pack of matches with one remaining. She struck it, blinded by the first light she'd seen in—how long?

Vilma knew the match had a short life, so she looked for something else to burn and found the stub of a candle. In the flickering light, Vilma saw a three-foot-tall, devil-man statue painted red from head to toe, complete with horns and a goatee. At his feet was her food dish. Confused, Vilma stared until the candle burned out.

CHAPTER 49

THE DARIAN GAP, ALMOST IN PANAMA

With Hector still in their thoughts, Renata and Maria were startled to hear voices for the first time all day, which was a racket compared to the gag order they'd been under. The two women were last in line, forty foliated yards behind Yara and little João. Renata grabbed Maria's arm and made her stop. The voices were speaking Spanish, not Portuguese, as the coyotes had been the entire trip.

Renata pulled Maria into the brush, where they hid behind a massive Ceiba tree, the trunk teeming with leafcutter ants. Maria began to cry, scared of the intruders, but managed to stifle her tears. Together, they listened. There was nothing but murmuring for several minutes, and finally, they saw what they had been dreading: FARC soldiers combing the bushes.

***

Urso estimated where Gambá and his group should be on the morning of day two. The Farmer had arranged things so that six FARC guerrillas would accompany him, and since they had no migrants to transfer, they caught up in no time. As Gambá and Rato crested the hill, Urso drew his gun.

"Hola, amigos. ¿Como te va?" Urso spoke Spanish so the FARC would understand.

Gambá recognized his rival, as did Rato, and their hearts began to pound. "Hola, Urso. I see they called you back from your vacation. Are you after the missing person?"

"Yes, my brother, but listen. If we find her, we all go home, and everyone is happy, including you. Her name is Juliana, and she looks like this." Urso reached into his pocket and produced a photograph, and Gambá stepped forward and took it. Rato looked, too, and after a moment of deliberation, both shook their heads. Just then, Francisco and Rosa emerged from between two ferns and gasped.

Urso switched to Portuguese. "For those just arriving, we're looking for a woman named Juliana, and she looks like this. Have you seen her? Is she part of this group?" Luckily, the picture looked almost nothing like the dirty woman in their group wearing the oversized men's t-shirt. Both shook their heads no.

"How many more in this group, Gambá?" said Urso.

Gambá lied. "We lost one to a snakebite, or, at least, I think he's gone. We have six left, not including me and Rato." As soon as he finished the sentence, Carlos arrived, followed by Yara and little João. Urso repeated his spiel and showed the photo again. Carlos and Yara lied, too, and João didn't even recognize the woman in the photograph.

"Where's the sixth, my brother?" said Urso. "You said there were six. Don't tell me you've lost two travelers already. It's only been two days." Urso shook his head.

Gambá looked down the path and shrugged. "She's not going to make it. She only has one shoe. We couldn't wait." Two FARC soldiers peeled off and disappeared into the ferns to search.

"I'm having a hard time believing you, amigo. You aren't this bad at your job, are you? Two in two days? That can't be good for business," said Urso.

"You know how it is. Bad shoes mean death in here, and she was wearing flats. Let us go, brother before we lose more. We don't have this woman you're looking for."

"Not so fast, my friend. How about we say this bitch with one shoe shows up in three minutes, or I shoot you?"

***

Suddenly, the distant conversation escalated to shouting. Maria searched Renata's face for answers, but there were none. A moment later, the crack of a rifle followed by a chorus of screams ended the wondering. The two women crouched behind the tree as shouting in Spanish gave way to silence.

Renata let twenty minutes pass before giving the okay. "I'm going to go look." The path was deserted, but she continued with caution. Forty yards later, Renata heard sobbing. A minute later, she came to a clearing and a man was lying dead. There were no strangers and no FARC, so she stepped over him.

Renata knelt. The dead man was Gambá, their reliable guide, and Vilma's savior-to-be. Carlos sat with his hands on his knees. Rosa wept as Francisco attempted to console her. Yara held João's head in her lap, still shielding his eyes from a sight she could never unsee.

"They killed him, and they robbed us!" cried Rosa, as if Renata could do something about it. They didn't have much money, but everyone carried some, and now it was gone. All they possessed was the water in their canteens and clothes on their backs.

***

Carlos talked with Renata as the group hiked on. "The coyotes covered for you, and when Maria didn't show up, they shot Gambá. The FARC was looking for someone named Juliana."

"Oh?" Renata shuddered.

"Yes. The FARC had a picture of *you*, though."

Renata shrugged her shoulders. The cat was out of the bag. "I guess I'm like you. I'm running away from my former life." Not a single person pointed a finger for the unwanted FARC attention. If anything, it felt as if they'd rallied around her.

Rato marched them five more miles before Yara asked for assistance with João. The boy was overtired, had fallen three times in the last mile, and had scratched his mosquito bites bloody. Agitated, Rato yielded. It had been an insane first two days, and already, this trip had become his worst nightmare.

***

Renata couldn't sleep, hiding beneath a muddy T-shirt from the mosquitoes. There was no shortage of discarded clothing along the trail, shed by the many tortured travelers before them, too hot and tired to care. She couldn't get the sound of the gunshot out of her head. Her father was looking for her and was willing to kill. What would happen to her if he found her?

Renata rolled over to stare at the tarp ceiling when the sky opened again, huge drops drumming the rotting canvas. As she listened to the violence and the rhythm, she wondered about the monster Dr. Zé had always been, yet she'd never realized.

The deluge intensified, making it too loud to think. They were all awake now, and someone in the darkness began to cry.

Chapter 50

Codó, Brazil

"I want her out of there," said Zé.

"Vilma's not ready yet," replied Aparecida. "I went much longer, didn't you?"

"I did, but I'm not sure this is necessary anymore."

"What do you mean it isn't necessary? We pray to the Orixás and Exus, and they have given us all that we have!"

"I'm not so sure anymore," said Zé. "Another week, and she's done."

Aparecida, disappointed, surrendered. "All right. One more week."

Chapter 51

Boa Vista, Brazil

Zé, working alone, made the incision and reached inside the body cavity. Suddenly, his eyes rolled back, everything went red, and his knees buckled as the liver slipped from his grasp, falling to the floor with a wet slap.

The next thing he knew, he was sitting in an octagonal room overlooking a meadow and a pond. He didn't recognize the spot, so he stood, and to his left was something special. Sitting on a table was a thin, black book that seemed to breathe. With caution, Zé ran his finger across the cover. It was an ordinary book by most accounts, old, not unlike an antique ledger or Bible. The tickle on the tips of his fingers was intense. He *had* to read this book—but as soon as he lifted the cover, the scene flickered and faded to black.

***

Zé's eyes fluttered open, and he found himself sitting against the wall, his victim long since expired on the table above. A darkened puddle of blood surrounded the tainted liver, a sure sign he'd been out for a while. Surprisingly, he wasn't angry. He'd been looking for direction, and his sixth sense had come through. The place in his vision was real. It had to be! Now, all he had to do was find it.

Chapter 52

The Darian Gap, Panama

No one had gotten any sleep at all, including Rato, who was especially gruff while folding tarps. Carlos attempted to help but was shooed away, and when Yara didn't have little João ready, Rato exploded.

"Get him up, woman, or so help me, I'll leave you in the jungle!" Rato poked João with his boot. Yara protested and tried to push him away, and Rato clamped his hand over her mouth, pressed his nose to hers, and whispered with intensity. Carlos grabbed Rato from behind and pulled him back, and Renata intervened.

"Stop!" she yelled. Rato looked up at her in shock. "Listen to Yara."

Yara saw her opportunity and spoke. "He has a fever. He can't leave yet. Give him an hour. Give him some food and water, and he'll be better in an hour!"

Rato went to the boy and pulled his shirt up. João's torso was covered in red dots. Rato sighed, shaking his head. "Chikungunya. Mosquito virus. I know an outpost, but first, I must take everyone else out of FARC territory. I'll return with medicine in two hours."

Yara consented, and Renata frowned. João needed much more than an hour to recover if that were even possible. Rato was up to something. Quietly, Renata removed twenty American dollars from her pocket and tucked the bill into the doubled section of Yara's canteen strap when she wasn't looking. Yara would find it the first time she picked it up. Perhaps it would give them something to bargain with, but perhaps not. It was all Renata could offer.

Renata realized that the FARC was Yara and João's best chance of survival. She touched Yara's arm as she got up and turned her head to hide the tear running down her cheek.

Chapter 53

————————

Boa Vista, Brazil

Fernanda wanted to die, but Zé wouldn't allow it. Her infection had healed, and she was still of value. He would harvest as long as she lasted. After almost a month of torture, Fernanda awoke, unable to see. Near panic, she touched the gauze taped over her face. *What do they want with my eyes?*

Despite Zé's wishes to keep her alive, Fernanda felt her strength ebb, and her dying thought brought her an ounce of joy. She'd had time to search her soul and knew in her heart that, despite the Macumba, there was no way Juliana knew all this was happening.

Juliana was sweet. There were so many details that proved she'd had no idea of the horrible truth. Fernanda said a prayer they would meet again one day so she could apologize for ever doubting her. When the prayer was finished, her chest hitched three times and came to rest.

Chapter 54

The Darian Gap, Panama

There was a river crossing on the third day, and, unfortunately, the river had risen overnight. What had been a manageable expanse the day before was now a white-water nightmare. Rato brought a rope with him as he crossed and tied it to a tree on the other side. Now, there was at least something for the rest of the group to hold onto.

Maria went first, followed closely by Renata, who did not trust her friend to make it alone. There was a stumble or two, but Maria held on, and with Renata's helping hand, they made it safely. Rosa went next, followed by Francisco. Surprisingly, Rosa did very well after observing Maria and Renata for the best footholds, but Francisco hadn't paid close attention and slipped.

What might have been an easy recovery went awry as he attempted to stand with nothing to hold onto. Everyone gasped as Francisco was swept back into a roaring pool. When the cross-current caught him, he hit his head and lost all sense of equilibrium. The entire group watched in horror as Francisco tumbled, bouncing off rocks, unconscious and unable to fight.

Rosa stood, about to scream, but Renata held her, talking, persuading her to be silent. There was no saving him. Rato, meanwhile, knew he would be ridiculed until the end of his days. This crossing would go down in coyote circles as one of the worst in history. With approximately two days left in the jungle, Rato went quiet.

***

Rato broke his silence the following day with the last words they would hear him say. "If we get to Panama, do not get stopped by the border patrol. If you see them, run."

"Why? Will they throw us in jail?" asked Maria.

"Sometimes. They put you in jail for a night and then give you twenty-four hours to leave the country. If that's the case, you're lucky. Be sure you cross at the *northern* border. But other times, it's much worse. They turn you around, sending you back into the jungle, which is a death sentence. None of you would survive one night without a tent." Maria was upset, and Renata did her best to soothe her.

***

An hour later, the smell of death hit their nostrils. The odor of rotting meat wafted across the path. Twenty yards later, they heard the buzz of swarming flies. Renata pinched her nose, and the droning became a dull roar. Finally, just off the path through a thin wall of bamboo, they came upon the bloated corpse of a fellow traveler who'd fallen short in his quest for a better life.

The whites of the man's eyes were jaundice-orange, and his tongue had been pushed from his mouth by expanding gases within. Blood ran from his nose and cheek, a single bullet hole in the center of his forehead. His left arm was damaged, as if torn by teeth. The flies erupted as they passed. Renata pulled her shirt over her head and ran.

An hour later, Rato disappeared for good.

***

"Where did he go?" asked Maria. The four remaining migrants stood together in the path, looking lost.

"I don't know. Rato rounded the bend, and when I came around the corner, he was gone. I think he's ditched us," said Renata. Together, they stood in stunned silence.

"We must be near the end of the jungle. Are we in Panama yet?" asked Rosa. No one knew, but they had been in the forest for over a week and had been on any-time-now mode for nearly two days.

"Let's keep going," said Renata, "and be on the lookout for border police. Don't follow too close. We'll be able to hear more with space between us. Watch where the sun is and keep heading north." Everyone agreed. Carlos took the lead, followed by Rosa and Maria, with Renata bringing up the rear.

Six miles later, the rapid rhythm of Spanish disturbed their silence, and Renata took cover in the ferns. She listened, choking back tears as Carlos,

Rosa, and Maria were apprehended by the Panamanian Border Guard. Renata said a prayer for them all, especially Maria. Their journey together was over, and most likely, Renata would never see them again.

Six hours later, she came upon the first signs of civilization in over a week. The jungle was behind her, but the journey was still young.

Chapter 55

Codó, Brazil

Vilma picked herself up off the mattress and crawled, looking for food as she had so many times before. Hopefully, there would be more than a morsel this time, and without any theatricals, like the matches and the statue. *Just give me some food*, she thought, as she felt carefully along the floorboards, being sure not to knock over anything in the dark.

Finally, there it was, at her fingertips—her glass. Most likely the same glass she'd been gulping from for as long as she'd been in the room. Without tasting or smelling, Vilma drank. She'd been expecting their bitter tea again, but this time, it was thicker, more viscous. Despite the warning bells, her body wouldn't stop, and she chugged on. At the last gulp, her stomach lurched, threatening to expel her only sustenance.

Concentrating, she willed her nausea away, measuring breaths until her stomach obeyed. Still hungry, she fumbled for more and found another match. Prepared for the blinding light, she struck it, eyes darting around the room for anything that might prolong the flame. She'd already tried the mattress and found it flame-retardant.

There was a candle nub on the floor, so she lit it, but all it did was buy her time to inspect the dirty drinking glass. There were dark streaks inside. Was that blood? Then, Vilma saw the dead pigeon. Her stomach gurgled. It was disgusting, but it was even more repulsive that she thought of eating it. She began to cry. Why did *indoctrination* feel like punishment?

With a belly full of blood, Vilma crawled onto her mattress and cried until the candle nub burned out. When the room was dark again, she did what she always did to get to sleep. She thought of Juliana.

CHAPTER 56

Zé dreamed. This time, he was buried alive, but it went further than that. He wasn't suffocating despite the dirt holding him captive. His arms couldn't move, but he was progressing, one wriggle at a time. Finally, his hand broke through, then an arm, his head, then the other arm, into a forest. Zé looked around, determined to know where he was. He walked until he found a road.

He already knew that this was not Brazil. Pine trees. Cool weather. Judging by the vegetation and Juliana's presumed path, he guessed it was somewhere in the United States. Finally, he saw some buildings on the far side of a field—a barn with a house next to it. Now he had a reference, and his heartbeat intensified as Aparecida shook him awake.

"Zé, you're dreaming."

"It was more than a dream. What time is it?"

"Nearly eight."

Zé shrugged her off and stood. "I'm going to the library."

"What for? What did you see?"

"I'll tell you when I know."

With that, Zé dressed and drove to the most extensive library he knew of and went straight for the encyclopedias, searching for American architecture. Within an hour, he'd identified the barn as New England style. *New England:* the collective name for six of the most northeastern United States. His instincts told him he was onto something.

After a half-hour of closer looks at the individual states, he noticed that the pictures appeared more rural in the northern three. To save time, he put Connecticut, Rhode Island, and Massachusetts on the back burner. Maine, New Hampshire, and Vermont had far more pictures of barns, fields, and farms. As he thumbed the pages, he recalled another guru of black magick, Aleister Crowley, had spent time in New England. Come to think of it, so had Claude Allemand. *Ah, to walk in their footsteps!*

Pushing the books aside, Zé browsed for in-depth information on these two iconoclasts, most specifically, where they were when they'd had their darkest breakthroughs. Unfortunately, Crowley had only spent a summer in New Hampshire. As much as Zé wanted his vision to involve Crowley, the odds weren't good.

Next, he researched Allemand, born in France and a world traveler, killed in Salem, Massachusetts, by a mob of townspeople who went so far as to remove his heart and burn it to ash. Some suggested he'd become something inhuman, the leader of a race immune to death, although his demise disproved that. His followers were said to have fled Salem for a more reclusive life.

As soon as he finished the paragraph, Zé's eyes began to pulse, and the lights overhead turned blood red. His heart pounded as he put the book down, and he smiled. It was as if Allemand himself had tapped him on the shoulder.

***

Zé arrived at the barn in Boa Vista to prep for surgery. His head was elsewhere—on another continent, to be more specific, but money was needed. Today's patient was a prostitute, as so many were. People who would not be missed made perfect victims as long as they hadn't poisoned their organs with too many drugs.

Thiago, one of three employees aware of the underground operation, greeted him as he stepped in. "Have you heard? The Federal Police are checking farms."

"Yes, I know. They've found the old facility, but it took them three years. Don't worry, my friend. Nothing can be traced through the paperwork, and our new facility is practically invisible. They'll never find us."

CHAPTER 57

SALEM, MASSACHUSETTS

"Charlie wants to see you." Nichi Tiffin stopped typing and looked up at her co-worker Neil Harrington. "He's not in a good mood either. Bring whatever you're working on." Nichi shrugged and pulled the paper from the carriage. This story wasn't flowing, and her editor would see it right away. *Shit.*

***

"Where's your column?" said Charlie.

"I need an hour. Sorry, Charlie, I know it's late, but ..."

"A whole day late. What's the deal? Are you still trying to find a way to send Patrick Brennan to jail?"

Nichi stared back in surprise. She'd bent over backward to strip her personal feelings from the Peggy Smith story. "I have remained impartial."

"I wasn't born yesterday, Tiffin. Sarah Brennan called me this morning. She told me all about you two. She said you even had a restraining order on Patrick back in the day."

"I did, but you didn't know that until—"

"Brad Proctor told me you both hate Patrick Brennan."

"I don't hate Patrick Brennan. I just know there's more to the story."

"Like what?" Charlie hadn't dropped his eyes once. He was mad.

Nichi's shoulders slumped. "I don't have anything solid if that's what you're asking. It's more of a feeling than anything."

"Well, until you have something, I want your column on my desk every Wednesday without delay."

"Will do, Charlie. Sorry about that."

"Sarah Brennan wants me to fire you, and I don't care to be sued for libel. Watch yourself. Whatever you write had best be true."

***

Nichi sat in her car and waited to see Patrick and his date come out of the restaurant. Her friend Mark had tipped her off with the gossip, and she had to see it to believe it. Peggy Smith, Patrick's fiancée, hadn't been dead for two months, and he was already dating. *'Slipped and fell' my ass.*

CHAPTER 58

PANAMA

When Renata arrived in the small town of Torti, Panama, the first thing she did was find a store with money transfer capabilities. After that, she called São Paulo. Guilherme answered, surprised to hear her voice. Renata's heart sank. His brother Gambá was dead, and she would have to break the bad news.

"We thought you were dead."

"Yes, it was terrible, Guilherme. I—don't know how to tell you this, but Gambá was shot. It was a man named Urso with the FARC. We had no warning. I'm so sorry."

There was silence on the other end, then finally, "It's to be expected. My brother chose a difficult life. I tried to get him to leave with me. We all knew he was living on borrowed time. I appreciate that you lived to tell me."

Renata counted the coins in her hand. As uncomfortable as it was to ask to speak to her grandmother, she would run out of coins soon. "How is Vovó?"

"She's fine. Your father never showed, but she is nervous about you. Hold on." Guilherme put the phone down and ran across the hall. Less than a minute later, her grandmother picked up.

"I'm so glad you made it! Guilherme just told me the dreadful news. Oh dear, it must have been horrible, but I'm so glad you're all right! How long until you reach the United States?"

"It is horrible, but I don't want you to worry. I don't know what to say about Guilherme's brother, Vovó, except I'm glad the jungle is behind me. I think there are six or seven more countries to go through, but I don't know how long it will take. They say the jungle is one of the worst parts of the trip, and I hope they're right."

"How will you get there with no guide?"

"Gambá gave me the phone number of a man in Mexico, but I'm not going to call yet. I'm going to find my way further north first."

The call lasted another sixty seconds. Renata promised to call from every country if possible. They both hung up crying.

****

It took Renata a week to cross Panama. She didn't dare hitchhike but instead waited in parking lots for lone travelers and offered money. She crossed into Costa Rica in a woman's trunk but was apprehended in Nicaragua and spent a week in jail. Finally, she had her day in court and was released with the provision she leave the country immediately which she did via the northern border.

Crossing into Mexico was easy, as was most everything compared to the stint in the jungle. Once in the country, Renata purchased a bus ticket to Mexico City, which was the reprieve her body needed. Over twenty hours on a bus was a bug-free nap, and as she traveled, she dreamt of Maria, praying her unlucky friend was safe.

Brazil was a million years ago, nine countries behind, but the thoughts pushing her forward were angry ones. "The Farmer," aka "The Monster," was more than a bad dream. He was the devil responsible for all this pain.

CHAPTER 59

The day before she crossed the United States border, Renata entered the town of Nogales and called the number Gambá had given her. An aging coyote by the name of Lencho answered and told her it was safer to sneak across the border from the town of Sonoyta. An hour later, she was in the back of his pickup truck, along with four other immigrants, driving to a motel a half-mile from the crossing point.

The day was warm, and the desert was dotted with saguaro cacti and creosote brush. Renata was anxious but couldn't tell why. Even though she was near the United States border, it was far too early to celebrate, much less think about life on the other side. It was dark when they arrived at the motel, and Renata was plastered with red dust.

Although she'd slept well the past two days, Renata couldn't wait for her first hot shower in over a month. The motel was constructed of cinder blocks, no-frills, to be sure, but the first disappointment came when her room was already occupied by eight other migrants packed in like sardines. There was even a ninth pasajero in the bathroom, and by the smell of things, they'd been in there awhile.

"What's this?" Renata protested. There wasn't even floor space to sleep.

"This is your room. We have a big group crossing tomorrow. Get to know one another before we start," said Lencho.

Disappointed, Renata called Lencho into the hallway. "All right, how much for a private room?"

Lencho played as if embarrassed before getting down to business. "I can put you in with my niece for only three hundred more pesos. Nobody gets their own room, querida. There is not enough space."

Renata considered before agreeing. "Can I see the room before I pay?"

"Of course." Lencho led her down a long hallway to another wing, then down another hallway with half the light fixtures missing. Finally, they stopped outside a paint-chipped door, where Lencho produced a key and opened it.

Renata looked in. A man sat on the bed, smoking a cigarette. Before Renata could protest, Lencho shoved her into the room, where she fell hard, scrambling to get up as he stepped in and closed the door.

"Sorry, querida, I lied. Why don't you stay and party with us? We'll have a drink and relax, and tomorrow, we take you over the border. What do you say? Give us an hour of your time." Lencho's friend Tavito smiled, revealing his wretched dental history.

"This is not happening," said Renata.

"We do this for a living. You're illegal, and you aren't going anywhere without Tavito and me. So, make it easy on yourself. Don't fight."

Renata made one move for the door but found herself no match for Lencho's bulk. One quick elbow caught him on the cheek, and she raked his face with her nails, but Tavito rushed over, wrapping his arm around her neck, and dragged her toward the bed. Lencho touched his face, peeved by the claw marks, and began removing his belt.

In less than three minutes, Renata was bound to the bed by two belts and two sets of handcuffs they had hidden under the mattress. She never stood a chance, ambushed by career criminals, but even though she refused to cry.

They took turns while the idle man periodically reminded her they could just as easily find a hole for her in the Sonoran Desert. Fetid breath, poor hygiene, and the reek of mildewed clothing filled Renata's nostrils as whiskers scratched her neck and chest. She tried to pretend she was somewhere else, even the jungle, anywhere but here. When Lencho was done, Tavito climbed on without a care for Lencho's mess.

***

Forty minutes later, they kicked her out with a final reminder that if she tried to cause trouble, their police chief friend would be happy to take a turn. But Renata didn't go back to the overcrowded room. Instead, she walked into town wiping away her tears, wondering if she should try and find another way across the border. Lencho had already been paid, and it wasn't cheap. She had five hours to decide.

***

At 5 am, Renata swallowed her fear and boarded the bus. Lencho was half awake before he noticed, and when he did, he smirked. Tavito saw her two minutes later, and the men exchanged winks. Renata found a spot in the last seat and kept tabs on the two coyotes as twelve more travelers boarded. Her hands were shaking, and it took all of her strength to stay there.

As the last passenger sat, a pickup truck barreled into the parking lot, kicking up dust, and a third coyote got out, gesturing wildly. Renata lowered her window to listen to the rhythm of their Spanish flying thick and fast. Although she couldn't understand everything, she heard the word *monstruo* several times, which was similar to *monstro* in Portuguese. They were talking about her father.

Renata's pulse quickened as Lencho turned and searched the bus windows until he found her, then dropped his gaze. Lencho kept talking as the other two men looked. All three were whispering. The third coyote shook his head, and Lencho tried to calm him down. For a moment, no one moved. Lencho and Tavito seemed to be waiting for him to decide. Finally, the man cursed and waved them away, then got back in his truck and sped away.

Renata understood. They knew who she was, and now they were afraid her father would find out what they did to her. It was safer for them to get her over the border and pretend she was never here. Renata breathed a sigh of relief. Lencho wanted her out of Mexico as much as she did.

***

The bus drove ten minutes to a parking lot, from which they crossed the border into the United States on foot and began hiking to a town with the odd name of *Why, Arizona*. The trek was thirty-two miles as the crow flies, but they would be zigging and zagging up and down mountains to avoid the authorities. Thankfully, this was not July. If the two coyotes had any luck, the migrants would be handed off in three days. Renata, however, had other plans.

***

Lencho made his bed in the sand and tried to find a comfortable position, finally settling on his belly. He was tired, mostly from nerves and the late night of tequila after fucking the *Monstruo's* daughter. As he closed his eyes, Tavito groaned, and one of the migrants screamed. Startled, Lencho lifted his head.

As soon as he did, something bit him in the small of his back. His first thought was a scorpion had crawled under the blanket, but he'd been stung before. What followed was far more violent. Air escaped his chest as he struggled to draw a breath. Confusion set in as he tried to roll onto his back but couldn't. Something had hold of him.

***

As Lencho struggled to breathe, the migrants stirred, whispering and worried. Renata pulled the knife out of Lencho's back and sunk it again, and the coyote grunted. She looked over at Tavito to be sure he was still down. Slicing his throat had been the right move. He couldn't breathe now and would soon drown in his blood.

With the knife halfway up Lencho's back, she repositioned, planting her other knee in his back, and continued to cut. When she was sure he couldn't stand, she removed the blade and stood tall.

CHAPTER 60

Renata made an announcement. The migrants would be safe because she knew the way. In truth, she only knew the sun rose in the east and set in the west, but she could also read Lencho's map. "These men raped me last night. They do it all the time. They do it for a living."

"You should have killed them after we were all safe!" said one man. "Now we're all dead!"

A woman Renata hadn't met spoke up. "They raped me too. They told me the same thing. They do it for a living. I'm glad they're dead." As soon as the woman was done speaking, she burst into tears.

Another woman spoke up. "She's right. They were pure evil. They almost raped me too, but I got lucky. I thought they would try again tonight!"

"We're not going to die," Renata said. "I can get us to where we want to go."

No one spoke as they moved away from the two corpses. Real coyotes would feast tonight.

***

Two days later, the group waited on top of a hill overlooking a gas station as a van pulled into a fuel stop. The town of Why, Arizona, was little more than a water tower with a gas pump, and Renata climbed down to tell the driver they'd been abandoned. She passed him twenty-seven American dollars as she talked, and the man took it, no questions asked. Exhausted, Renata signaled to the others.

***

Renata had been so nervous hiding her knife the first day that she'd spent zero time getting to know the others. Now that the worst was over, she slept in the van as she had on the bus to Mexico City. Three of the other travelers were also Brazilians and were headed for Massachusetts, where they knew of a sizable Portuguese community. Portugal was not Brazil, but they spoke the same language, and that would make starting over in a strange place much more accessible.

"Are you okay?" a woman named Ana asked.

Renata was half-asleep, her head resting on the back of another traveler. She opened one eye. "I'm okay." Renata recognized her. Ana was the second woman to speak up after she killed Lencho and Tavito.

"He almost raped me, too, until he saw my little girl. Thank God they left us alone. They had guns! My husband was helpless. Imagine the women you've saved."

Renata managed a thin smile and looked at Ana's little girl. "What's her name?"

"Janete."

"How old?"

"Ten. We left Brazil for her sake. It was unsafe where we lived, and the politicians did nothing to fix it. My sister lives in Massachusetts. She says it's safe there, and there are jobs."

"My sister is your daughter's age. I worry about her, too. I'll have to send for her someday."

"Do you have a place to live?" asked Ana.

"Not yet," replied Renata.

"Follow us. We know people who can help you get on your feet."

"Thank you." Renata smiled, laid back down, and closed her eyes.

There were only state borders to cross from here on out, and she had a real bed to look forward to. As she laid back down, her hand found the curve of her stomach and began to rub. Although Lencho and Tavito were dead, they continued to haunt her. Upset, Renata opened her eyes and sat up, suddenly unable to rest.

Chapter 61

Codó, Brazil

Vilma awakened, and for the first time in recent memory, she had to squint. Her door was open, allowing light in from the hallway. At first, she was suspicious, but there was no choice but to escape. As she made it to the doorjamb and peeked around, however, they were waiting for her.

"Congratulations, Vilma, you've made it! Come, eat, and drink, and we will discuss your journey!" Aparecida did all the talking while her father sat stoic.

"Why was I—"

"Hush, child. You've been through a lot, and we have all the answers to your questions, but first, let's eat."

Vilma was ravenous, so there was no argument. As soon as Aparecida finished her sentence, two people Vilma had never seen before came from the kitchen, filling the table with food and drink. Before she knew it, Vilma was seated at the table with a plateful of nearly everything. Close by was a cup of the now familiar tea.

CHAPTER 62

ACRE, BRAZIL

After a month in the jungle, Urso was glad to be back in his bed. Exhausted, he fell right to sleep. Two hours later, he woke, dreaming he was still on the trail. *Relax, hombre, you're home,* he thought to himself. Then, as he turned his pillow over, a voice in the darkness spoke.

"What happened?" it said, and immediately Urso knew who it was.

"She wasn't there, but Gambá was lying about something. He said he had six people but could only produce five, so I killed him. The FARC searched the area for your daughter and found no one, so I let the rest go."

Because Urso couldn't see The Farmer, he began to get nervous.

Finally, The Farmer spoke, "She was there, they just didn't find her. She's further north, but I'm not sure exactly where. Where is Rato now?"

"I don't know."

"Find him and call me. Memorize this number and then destroy it." Zé scribbled on a napkin and left, pondering his next move. It was almost time to leave Brazil.

Chapter 63

Phoenix, Arizona

Renata dialed Guilherme from a pay phone in Phoenix. She didn't need any money yet but wanted her grandmother to know she'd made it to the United States. As the phone rang in São Paulo, a chill washed over her. On the fourth ring, the phone hesitated, then continued in a slightly different tone. Renata considered hanging up, but someone picked up.

She almost said hello, but something was wrong. Renata slammed the phone down, wondering if the call was traceable. She'd be leaving Phoenix within the hour, but if her father could pinpoint her position, it wouldn't be good. Worst of all, she feared for her grandmother.

Chapter 64

Boa Vista, Brazil

Dr. Zé listened from the bunker beneath the barn. When Juliana hung up, he returned the phone to its cradle, far from pleased but at least satisfied with the confirmation. The call was not traceable, but his intuition gave him her general direction. Zé chewed his thumbnail as he considered his options: America was the logical choice, but it was vast. Finding her would not be easy.

In retrospect, kidnapping Fernanda had been a touch on the greedy side. They certainly hadn't anticipated Juliana finding out, but what was done was done. Juliana had gone from being their daughter to a loose end in a business that could not afford loose ends. She would cause attention because she loved her sister, and attention was the last thing they wanted.

Chapter 65

Codó, Brazil

"Dona Aparecida, I'm thirsty. Can I have some more tea?" asked Vilma.

Aparecida, staying home to monitor Vilma's progress, looked at her watch. "Yes, you may. Go sit in your room, and I'll get you some."

Vilma turned, glassy-eyed and lumbered to Juliana's old room. The door was always open now, but she hadn't left the apartment or looked out a window in what seemed like forever. But she was all right with that now. Once clear thinking went away, Aparecida became much nicer, and it was just easier to do as she was told.

CHAPTER 66

PEABODY, MASSACHUSETTS AND ALTON, NEW HAMPSHIRE

Renata and Ana had much in common, including Brazil and similar horrors shared on their paths north. Very quickly they became friends. Two and a half days and multiple hours of swapping stories later, the blue Ford van arrived in Peabody, Massachusetts, and although exhausted, they were hopeful. Ana called her sister Bruna from a road stop in Oklahoma to see if she could find a room for Renata, and Bruna managed to book a shared studio in an apartment building nicknamed the Pombal, or "pigeon coop." Ana, Paulo, and little Janete were just down the hall.

"Rest for now, Renata, but come with us tomorrow, we're going to get papers." Ana referred to a forger on the outskirts of town who produced fake drivers' licenses and Social Security numbers for the undocumented. When the time came, six of them piled into a car and drove across town. Each person chose an American surname, and when it was Renata's turn, she decided on Johnson, after the former U.S. president.

After that Ana helped Renata find work cleaning houses. It was difficult scrubbing tiles and cleaning toilets at six homes per day, but she did it. Renata knew the money was better here than in Brazil, but after she counted her first week's pay (seventy-five dollars), she broke into tears. It would take over twenty years at this rate to save for Vilma's rescue fund. The little girl would be a woman by then, if she made it that long. There must be better ways to make money. Renata vowed to keep her eyes and ears open.

On her third Saturday in America, Renata sat in her room, trying to decide what to do on her first day off, when she heard some excitement down the hallway. Some of her neighbors were carpooling up to New Hampshire's White Mountains to take advantage of a spectacular late-fall day. With nothing better to do, Renata tagged along.

Two hours later, they stopped at a state park overlooking Lake Winnipesaukee. The hike was a two-mile beginner loop up a small mountain that began as a dirt road and became an easy trail to a bald peak. Without realizing, Renata left her companions in the dust as she had in the Colombian jungle. Twenty minutes at the summit passed before boredom kicked in and inspiration struck. Motivated, she leaped to her feet and charged down the backside of the mountain. A half-hour later, she summited again, lapping all but four of her neighbors. For the first time that day, she cracked her canteen and took a drink, realizing she was good at hiking.

That evening, as she undressed to shower, Renata saw her underwear on the floor, a fresh streak of crimson calling her attention. She'd managed to put the rape out of her mind, but it all came rushing back. Thank Oxalá, she wasn't pregnant. Renata cried in the shower for an hour, lonely but grateful.

***

The following week, Renata learned her neighbors did not share her enthusiasm for hiking. Several of them had been sore for more than two days after the previous weekend. Eager for more time in the mountains, she tried to find people who wanted to go, but the response was limited. After six straight weeks of nothing but work, Renata made the tough decision to put off her sister's rescue by two hundred dollars and bought herself a used car.

Chapter 67

Sonoyta, Mexico

It took longer than it should have, but finally, Urso's hard work paid off. The clues led him to Sonoyta, where he began asking questions, and by midday, he knew where to be. At 7 pm, he made his way to Manuel's Cantina and found a seat at the bar, wearing glasses and a bandana. Rato sat across the bar drinking a Tecaté but didn't seem to recognize him. As soon as he was sure, Urso called The Farmer.

***

Rato left Manuel's Cantina good and drunk, washing away the mental abrasions of his former career. Coyote life had been hell, and many men like him died on the job. Once he'd left the jungle for the last time, he knew where he wanted to settle. The beer had always tasted good in Sonoyta, and he'd always longed to settle there. This was that time. Halfway to his hotel, however, a man in a mask stuck a gun in his face.

"I only have a hundred pesos. Take the money, but don't kill me."

"You're coming with me. Let's go."

The voice was familiar, and after a series of misdirections, the man led Rato down a dark side street and into an apartment building. "Who are you? What do you want?"

"We need information. You'll be out of here in ten minutes. Stay cool." Inside, the glow of a dozen candles illuminated the room. Dr. Zé sat in the darkness—three Styrofoam coolers behind him on the floor.

Rato recognized the candles, and his stomach sank. He stammered, "W-What do you want?"

"You're hard to find, Rato. Tell me what I need to know, and you can leave."

"Of course," said Rato, heart pounding.

"Six months ago, you helped my daughter through Panama, isn't that right?"

Rato nodded his head. "I believe so."

"What happened after that?"

"I quit. I abandoned them," Rato replied, hoping that was good enough.

"Not what happened to you, Rato. What happened to my daughter, Juliana."

"We knew her as Renata, and she's the same woman who later killed two coyotes in Sonoyta. People still talk about her."

Zé was silent for a moment. "Renata, how clever. The name means *reborn*."

"Yes, we had Renata, Maria, Yara ..."

"Thank you, Rato. So, she crossed into Arizona? Where to after that? Phoenix?"

"Almost everybody goes through Phoenix, but I don't know anything else. I've only been in Sonoyta a little while."

"I'm disappointed, Rato. She'd be dead already if you'd told the truth in the jungle. Urso, We're finished here."

Urso pulled a knife and perforated Rato's neck, working his way down the body, being careful to avoid the saleable organs. Rato tried to scream but couldn't. His vocal cords were in ribbons. He tried to fight, but it was too late. He'd lost the ability to raise his hands. As soon as the realization of his death hit home, there was nothing he could do.

When Rato's attack was over, Zé delivered final instructions. "Take a week and find out what you can about Juliana, then get back to work. Running migrants will be our only cash flow for a while."

Chapter 68

Peabody, Massachusetts

Christmastime came, and against her better judgment, Renata decided to try and call Vilma. The phone call to grandmother three months back had not gone well, but her father had not come for her; perhaps he wasn't the eye in the sky she'd feared. Renata needed confirmation that Vilma was okay. If something had happened to her, that would change everything.

After a moment of deliberation, Renata sighed, picked up the phone, and dialed Codó. It rang four times as she imagined life inside the apartment. It was just after 7 pm in Brazil, and if the routine hadn't changed, Zé would be "working," and Aparecida would be home with Vilma.

"Alô." It was her father's voice. Renata froze, aware she must say something or hang up, but Zé wasn't finished.

"It's you," he said, a statement rather than a question. "Where are you, Juliana?"

Renata slammed the phone down.

CHAPTER 69

BARTLETT, NEW HAMPSHIRE

Winter passed, and finally, on May 8, Renata put her hiking boots on and chose a climb with a strange name: *Frankenstein Cliff.* It was not one of the White Mountains' four-thousand footers, nor was it named after Frankenstein's monster, but it was rated as *difficult* in the guidebook she purchased. As she pulled into the parking lot, however, it appeared Frankenstein Cliff wasn't a hike or a mountain at all.

The top third of the cliff was a bald strip of granite in the shape of a giant frown. There were several cars parked, and, as Renata got out, she noticed several climbers hanging from the rock with authentic climbing gear: ropes, pitons, the whole works. Tools she'd seen on television but couldn't afford. In short, this was real mountain climbing.

Fascinated, Renata watched as the climbers worked and thought she might like to try it someday. The 48 four-thousand-foot mountains in the White Mountains were numerous but in all honesty, tame. She had a thousand questions and found a good spot to wait as the climbers practiced their techniques. Many wore belts adorned with shiny metal attachments, each with a specific purpose. As the day wore on, she saw most of the gear in action.

Chomping at the bit, Renata found a trail to the top and waited on a steep grade as the climbers neared the top. Because she hadn't spoken much English with Americans yet, the words didn't flow, and she relied on courage to get her through the conversation.

"That's good. How you learn that?" Renata asked the nearest climber from the top of the cliff, looking down on him.

"Oh, jeez, you scared me! I didn't see you up there. Do you mean climbing? I've been doing it my entire life. I love it. My father's friend got me interested."

***

The first thing that struck Patrick was her eyes, dark and piercing. She barely blinked and seemed interested in what he had to say.

"Muito tempo? Sorry. A long time to learn?" The woman stumbled in her excitement, mixing languages.

"You want to learn climbing? Where are you from?"

"Brazil."

"I don't think I've ever met anybody from Brazil before," said Patrick. "You speak Spanish, right? I'm sorry, I don't know anything about Brazil. I've heard of Rio, though—forget it. Can we start over?"

"We speak Português."

"Portuguese, I should have known. So, why did you come to New Hampshire? Don't you folks like the tropical weather?"

"It's cold here, but I like it. I wear extra clothes. My friends, not so much."

Patrick had never had a girlfriend that enjoyed winter, never mind the White Mountains. Surprisingly, he found himself coming up with more questions. "What part of Brazil are you from? The Amazon?"

"Não. I'm from everywhere. Move a lot." Renata's mind whirred as she struggled for words. This was the most extended conversation she'd ever had with a native English speaker—even Professor Smith, the Brit who taught her in Brazil.

"Oh, man. I'd have to look at a map. They don't teach us about Brazil in school."

"A Garota de Ipanema?" she offered, referring to the famous song by Tom Jobim.

"What? Oh, *The Girl from Ipanema,* Yes! But my dumb ass thought Ipanema was in Japan. I need a refresher course. I'm Patrick. What's your name?"

Renata slipped and pronounced her Rs as Brazilians do—like an English H. *Henata.*

"Well, it's nice to meet you, Henata. Hey, would you like to get some coffee? Then we can talk about technical climbing, and you can tell me more about Brazil."

"Yes, I like that."

"Where do you live? I'm only asking because I want to pick a coffee shop that's on your way home."

"I live in Massachusetts."

"Me too, what town? I don't need your street address. I'm not a stalker."

Renata hesitated before answering. "Peabody."

"Peabody? I live in Beverly—we're practically neighbors! Follow me to Conway. I know a lovely little café."

***

It turned out that Patrick knew a café so lovely that Renata would never have picked it. It was French-themed, and the cups were separated from the saucers by doilies. She liked her coffee cheap and robust, not fancy and expensive, and had yet to find good coffee in New England, at least at the local chains.

"What about your family? Are they here with you?" asked Patrick.

Renata hesitated, unprepared to swap personal stories, as she hadn't made up one yet, so she decided to forget some English so they could change the subject. "Is hard for me to say, ah … *abusada*."

"Abusada? Do you mean …" he lowered his voice; "*abused?* I'm so sorry. We don't have to talk about this."

"It's okay. And your family?"

"My family? I recently graduated from dental school and joined my dad's practice. We work together now. It's kinda nice. We're going to rename it Brennan Dental Care. Dad ordered the sign last month. Right now, we're still *Dr. Robert Brennan, DMD*—um—on the sign …" Patrick's eyes darted around the room, having failed to impress. He looked at Renata's cup. "Would you like some more?"

"Não, obrigada—oops, no, thank you. I'm sorry, I speak Português all the time." She smiled, slightly embarrassed.

To Patrick's right was the check. He opened the book it came in and tore off a piece to write his phone number.

"This is my number. If you ever want to try a more technical climb, or if you just want to go on a plain old hike, or whatever, give me a call. I'll find some gear for you."

Renata glanced at the number and left it on the table, untouched.

"Should we go?" he asked, at a loss.

"Yes," she said and stood up to put on her coat.

Patrick wondered for a second if she would leave the number on the table, but at the last second, she picked it up and put it in her pocket. Renata casually nodded as she said goodbye, and Patrick thanked her and waved, confused. He watched her headlights in his rearview mirror for nearly three hours until Renata turned for Peabody. He wondered if she would call.

CHAPTER 70

The following Sunday was Mother's Day, and while most people in her building were calling Brazil or Portugal to send their love, Renata needed time alone. "Can I borrow your bike?" she asked a man on the second floor, and he let her take it. Renata headed toward the water, hoping that the ocean would help clear her mind.

She grieved for her mother, Beatriz, still coming to terms with the probability that her father had killed her. Beatriz hadn't abandoned her and Vilma after all. Renata left Peabody and cruised into Salem and then Beverly, heading north on Route 127, where denser neighborhoods ended and the forest began. In less than half an hour, she'd passed Endicott College, making good time. Her legs were powerful, and she wondered how she'd never realized she loved the outdoors so much.

Ten minutes later, she rode into the village of Beverly Farms when the sky suddenly took on a reddish hue, and her eyes began to pulse. Shaken, she pulled off the road and stood on a beach to look at the ocean. Undoubtedly, this was a *moment*. Renata stared past the houses and into the forest. There was something to see somewhere in the trees.

Spooked, Renata got back on the bike. The last thing she wanted on Mother's Day was to be reminded of her father. Thirty minutes up the coast, she laid eyes on Hammond Castle and tried to forget the vision, but it didn't work, so she headed back, and the sensation returned. After a moment of indecision, Renata decided she had to know.

The chance of it being her father was unlikely. She'd only decided to borrow the bike this morning and could have headed in any direction. *He couldn't know that, could he?* As the sky turned red, she coasted inland, letting her intuition make the decisions: a right, then another right, and finally, a left. It might not be easy to remember the way back, but if she could find her way through ten countries, she could see her way out of Beverly Farms.

Renata smelled smoke and looked up to see a wispy plume over the trees. A minute later, she arrived on the scene: the rubble of a smoldering house in an acre-sized lot. Next to the remains were a barn, a yard, a shed, and the surrounding forest. The fire trucks were gone, and the burn was contained. As Renata dismounted, she felt something. Whatever had called her here was close.

It wasn't the still-burning coals, and it wasn't the house. Something in the vicinity radiated. It wasn't something she could see, but a feeling—a presence. It was so intense that Renata decided it was none of her business. She didn't want to know. Renata said a quick prayer, wishing she'd brought something to offer her gods, then got back on the bike and pedaled away as if her life depended on it.

Chapter 71

Near Codó, Brazil

Zé was driving when his next episode commenced. This time, the sky was not pink but a dark maroon. Wisely, he pulled over when the visions began. *A burned-down house, a clearing, some woods, and a bicycle.* Where was this? He must know. Was that Juliana? He'd seen this before—that time on the beach. It was frustrating then, but it was unbearable now.

Chapter 72

Salem, Massachusetts

By the following Friday, Patrick hadn't heard from Renata and had given up hope. It had been a long and tiresome week at the practice. Dentistry paid the bills but sure as hell didn't light his fire. The good news was that the weekend was here, and first thing in the morning, he would jump in his car and head up Route 93 to burn off steam, doing what he loved the most.

Patrick let himself into his Salem townhouse just before 4 pm. Friday was a half day at the office. It had been Dad's schedule ever since Patrick went to grammar school, and now it was his turn to enjoy long weekends. Patrick had plenty of friends who'd gone on to corporate careers, working much harder for less money. There were benefits to being an SOB—son of the boss—and four-and-half-day work weeks was one of them. As he closed the door, the telephone rang. He put down the bottle of gin he'd purchased and answered.

"Hello?"

"Hello, this is Renata. Will you climb tomorrow?"

"Uh—Hi Henata! How are you? Yes, I'm climbing tomorrow. Do you want to go?" Patrick chided himself for sounding too eager.

"I don't know. Maybe I need shoes?"

"Do you want to use ropes or just hike?"

"Hopes—uh—*ropes.*

Hopes? Patrick noticed that Renata mixed up her Rs and Hs.

"Henata, I have a question. What does R-I-O spell?

"Hee-o."

"Hee-o? So, it's pronounced Hee-o de Janeiro?"

"Almost. *Janeiro* needs more practice."

Patrick smiled. "So, does your name begin with an R?"

"Yes, I always get the R and the H sounds mixed up."

Patrick was giddy. They had a date.

***

Renata hung up the phone, feeling guilty. She was about to have fun, and Vilma was in danger. But she'd worked more than sixty hours per week ever since she'd been in the U.S. and needed a break. *All work and no play* was a recipe for burnout.

***

Patrick picked Renata up the following day, and they drove to the White Mountains to practice technical climbing. Their conversation had its share of misunderstandings, but all in all, they figured things out. Patrick demonstrated rudimentary climbing skills, like hand movements and basic grips, and she took to them like a duck to water. By noon, she was jamming cracks and belaying. Later, she learned to set anchors and rappel. Her coordination was incredible. She was already better than seventy-five percent of his climbing buddies after just one day. He wondered if the boys had been replaced until he showed her his newest toy.

"Check this out. It's called a cam. If there's a crack in the rock, you squeeze here, put it in and let go. It grabs the rock and makes a solid anchor. It's the first of its kind. It's so strong you can hang off it!" Renata looked at the foot-long slab of aluminum with distrust. "Try it out," said Patrick. "Pull the handles back and stick it in that crevasse right there. I'll talk you through it."

Renata did as instructed and pushed the cam into the rock.

"All right, now. Let go." Renata again followed instructions, but instead of grabbing, the cam slipped and tumbled down the mountain to a granite shelf sixty feet below, smashing into pieces. "What the hell!" Patrick screamed. "You have to make sure it's secure before you take your hands off!"

Renata glared, having done as instructed. "I did what you said."

"You should have—ah, never mind. Bye-bye, three hundred dollars. It's only money, I guess."

Renata couldn't believe her ears. Three hundred dollars was more than her car. It would take her a month to earn that much.

"Look, sorry, I lost my temper. Let's call it a day."

Renata said nothing.

CHAPTER 73

____

SONOYTA, MEXICO

Urso spent three days in Sonoyta looking for information on the now-legendary woman who'd killed her coyotes. He caught a break when someone knew the driver who shuttled immigrants from Why to Phoenix, and Urso tracked him down.

"What happened after you dropped them in Phoenix?" he asked, sliding twenty American dollars across the table.

"Someone in the group had a ride waiting. The van had Massachusetts license plates."

"Do you remember the color or the plate number?"

"It was a blue van. A Ford, I think. Light blue, pretty beat up. I didn't get the plate number."

"Anything else you can think of?"

"That's it, man. I turned back around and went straight back to Why."

CHAPTER 74

SALEM, MASSACHUSETTS

May gave way to June, and Patrick, having gotten over the broken cam, looked forward to his Saturdays with Renata. On their fifth date, Renata mentioned she might have to return to Brazil someday, and he realized he'd miss her.

"What's back in Brazil for you? Isn't it dangerous? You said—you said you were …" Renata interrupted. "My sister is there."

"You're working too hard. It would help if you had a better job, maybe a better apartment, like a duplex or something, and then bring your sister here to live. It's safer here, right?"

"She will never get papers."

"Why not? We'll fill out the papers, do it right, and in a couple of years—"

"Patrick, if it were that easy, people wouldn't risk their life. It's not just waiting in line. Most times, they take your application money and tell you no."

"But my father has friends with international connections. Maybe she can claim asylum or something?" Patrick had been doing some homework.

"Patrick, I do not have papers either." Renata wasn't ready to tell him the truth, but he was prying, and his "help" might muck things up. Casually, Patrick reached into his coat pocket and removed a small container. From it, he shook out two capsules and popped them in his mouth.

"What's that?" asked Renata.

"I have a bum knee."

"What does that mean?"

"It means bad knee. I hurt it a couple of years back, hiking Mt. Chocorua. It still hurts sometimes." Patrick changed the subject. "I can get you a better job, you know. Come work for my practice. We can get you trained as a hygienist, and then you can help your sister. No pressure, just friends helping friends."

Renata smiled, but despite the temptation to earn money quicker, it didn't feel right. "Patrick, thank you. Maybe I'm proud. I appreciate it, but I stick to my plan for now."

CHAPTER 75

GORHAM, NEW HAMPSHIRE

Another month passed, and Patrick was more and more impressed with Renata's climbing abilities. She wasn't just good, she was outstanding. Because of her talents, he chose more challenging climbs. Today was Huntington Ravine on Mt. Washington, often called the most difficult trail in the White Mountains.

It didn't require ropes and pitons, but it was a grueling eight-hour climb, ten miles up a rock face. Patrick challenged himself to beat her to the top—without letting her know. Patrick won, but only because she never knew it was a contest. "You're amazing," he said, out of breath.

Renata looked back at him, squinting in the sun. She was breathing hard but not nearly as heavily. "I was trying to win the whole time, but you would have if I'd told you." Renata blushed. "You're a great climber. I busted my ass, and you're barely winded."

"What is busted?" asked Renata.

Patrick smiled and stepped closer, and they kissed for the first time. The day was beautiful, the view was splendid, and he'd been waiting for this moment for too long. Later that night, they relaxed on the couch, talking.

"Will you climb Mt. Rainier with me?" he said, resting his hand on her knee.

"Where is Mt. Rainier?"

"Washington State. It's about a six-hour flight from Boston. It's big and snowy, and I think you can do it." Patrick leaned in close.

"Patrick, no," she said and stood up.

"What, no kiss? Or you can't climb Rainier?" He'd never seen her this nervous. "What's the matter?"

"Sorry, it's not you."

"I wish I could meet whoever did this to you. Please sit down. We can take it slow."

Renata sat back down and exhaled. "I should go."

"No, don't do that. Stay here. Take my bed, and I'll stay on the couch. It's late, and we've had a long day. Besides, you'll wake your roommate."

Patrick was right about that. Katia went to bed early. "Okay," she replied.

Patrick went to his linen closet, grabbed a blanket and pillow, and made his bed on the foldaway couch. At 2 am, he woke to find Renata lying next to him.

Chapter 76

Beverly, Massachusetts

After their first night together, Renata stayed at Patrick's townhouse more often. The Pombal tenants teased her by calling her "Papelzinha" (Little Immigration Papers), but Ana, in private, was kind enough to check on Renata to make sure things were okay.

Two weeks later, Patrick convinced Renata to meet his parents for dinner. He drove his Porsche through Salem and over the bridge into Beverly, knowing that his mother wouldn't make a scene in front of Renata. As they pulled in, Patrick noticed a red sedan in the driveway.

"Mr. Addison is here. He likes climbing. You'll get to meet him." All of a sudden, Patrick started acting ten years younger. Even his tone of voice changed. Renata wondered if Patrick was nervous. The house was beautiful and located on the water, coincidentally not far from the smoldering house she'd seen on her bike ride.

The Brennans sat in the living room chatting with an older gentleman. As everyone exchanged introductions, Renata felt their eyes on her.

"Hello, Henata, it's so nice to meet you." Sarah was the first to get up and greet.

"Oh, Mom, it's Renata with an R. I had to figure that out the hard way. I forgot to tell you. Brazilians pronounce R's like H's. Sorry, my fault."

"Well, if that's how she pronounces it, maybe she wants us to say it that way! So, which is it, dear? Which do you prefer?"

"Renata is fine," she replied. "*When in Rome*, isn't that right? Nice to meet you." Patrick laughed, exaggerated, almost overdoing it.

Dr. Joe introduced himself next. "Renata! So nice to meet you! I have so many questions about Brazil. Oh, and congratulations, by the way. Your third World Cup! That Pelé is amazing."

"Yes, Pelé is very good, but I don't watch futebol much, sorry."

Losing his audience, Dr. Joe changed the subject. "Brazil is a dictatorship, isn't that right?"

"Dad, please." Patrick interrupted.

"What is it, Patrick?"

"Did you study Brazil this week? I didn't know you were such an expert."

"As a matter of fact, I did look into it since you were bringing a special guest. Renata, I'd like you to meet my very dear friend, Angus Addison. He's passing through on his way to Europe." Renata shook his hand. Angus Addison looked every bit an executive of a major corporation, from the three piece suit to the gold cufflinks.

"Pleased to meet you, Renata. Did I hear correctly that you two are going to give Mt. Rainier a try? Have you been to Washington State? That's beautiful country."

"Yes, we will climb Rainier, and no, I haven't been to Washington," replied Renata.

"That's fantastic. Keep me posted. I'd love to hear how that goes," Angus replied.

Dr. Joe interrupted. "What part of Brazil are you from, Renata?" After a moment's hesitation, Renata decided to lie. If Dr. Joe had studied for this little meeting, he might dig deeper next time and want to discuss current events in Codó.

"I'm from São Paulo."

"Dad," said Patrick, "I should have mentioned that Renata came here in an asylum-type situation. It's not the happiest of conversations."

"Oh my goodness, I apologize, Renata. Well, uh, if there's anything we can do, let us know. I'm not sure if Angus is as well-connected in South America as he is in Europe, but we'd be happy to help if we can. We're glad you're safe."

"No problem," said Renata, who, all of a sudden, was having a hard time keeping Vilma out of her thoughts.

Angus continued, "Patrick tells me you are one heck of a climber. Have you always climbed?"

"No, I'd never climbed. But I really like it."

"I never knew that Brazil doesn't have any ten-thousand-footers. All the big mountains in South America are in Argentina, Peru, and Chile," added Dr. Joe.

"Nice one, Dad," said Patrick.

"Renata, did Patrick mention he's not the first of the Brennans to wear crampons? We've been climbing for three generations. A good friend of mine even climbed with Sir Edmund Hillary. Not Everest, mind you, but Cho Oyu.”

Renata struggled with the proper names and micro-terminology but caught the gist. She also recognized the name *Hillary*, even though it was pronounced differently in Brazil.

“Are you talking about Nigel, Dad?”

“That’s right. Nigel Fletcher is that man. He’s twenty years younger than me, but I love him like a brother.”

“You’ve met the right family if you like mountains, Renata,” said Angus.

“Do you climb, Mr. Addison?”

“No, but my company sponsors climbers from time to time. I’ve been waiting for Patrick here to make a move on a big hill, but so far, he’s left me hanging.”

Patrick’s face lit up. “I’m game! I didn’t know you were sponsoring! I just need to get, uh, some things in order.” Patrick’s mother, Sarah, nodded in agreement.

“Well, I’ll be watching. I want to see my *Airventics* flag flying at the top of a major peak. It’s good for business and the sport as a whole. A win/win deal.”

“Did you hear that, Patrick?” said Dr. Joe. “The man wants to give you his money. Why don’t you take it?” Sarah shook her head.

“Well, I …” Patrick glanced at his mother, who glared back.

“Renata, since Patrick is not ready, will you take Angus’s money, for God’s sake?”

“Dad, stop! We’re climbing Rainier in September, and we’ll take it from there.”

Renata, meanwhile, couldn’t help but wonder what a sponsorship would pay. Climbing a prominent peak would be much more than a day hike. They would have to sleep on the mountain and lug their equipment—a climb *and* a camping trip, and a snowy one at that.

“How much does it pay?” she blurted, louder than intended.

“Well done, Renata,” said Angus. “I’ll pay you $1,000 apiece.”

Renata ran the numbers. *A quarter-year’s pay for less than a week of work.*

“I’m in,” she said.

***

By September, it was time to fly to Seattle. The night before the trip, Renata stopped by the Pombal with Patrick to pick up a few things. It was his first time in her tiny apartment and the first time in his life in the minority. The Portuguese language dominated the hallways, and from some of Renata's responses to the giggling going on, he sensed he might be the butt of a few jokes.

The one plus was Renata's roommate was not home. As she packed, Patrick sat on Katia's bed. Her studio consisted of a kitchenette, a table, and a television across from an old couch, followed by two bureaus and two beds.

Renata's bed was covered with clothing and an open duffel bag, so Patrick perused the room. Over Katia's bed was the flag of Portugal, and on her bureau were photos of her family back home. Renata's wall was bare, and instead of photographs on the bureau, there were dozens of candles, primarily red and black.

"Wow, you like candles, huh?" Renata glanced at him and nodded. He wasn't ready to learn about her religion yet.

***

Mt. Rainier was very different from the White Mountains. First, it was colder than anything she'd ever experienced. It wasn't like going from the car to the house in a Massachusetts winter. They were outside all the time, and comfort had to be managed via clothing adjustments. Sweaty clothing would chill you later, and she learned to strip and reapply layers as conditions changed.

Second, she was given her first ice ax. The guides set ropes to clip onto in case of hidden crevasses, and climbers were hooked together. Renata wore a thick parka, gloves, and even a helmet. On her boots were spiky crampons, and goggles were a necessary evil.

Patrick had hired a guide, and it turned out to be a smart move, as it reduced their exposure. The permits were taken care of, and the equipment was double-checked. The air was noticeably thinner, too, but so far, her body had adjusted. But despite all the positives, their overnight was nearly sleepless, even after an exhausting day.

***

They spent two days on the mountain, and Renata found it cold, tiring, and exhilarating. As the group arrived safely back at the bottom, Renata took one last look up at the white peak, proud of herself. Perhaps this talent of hers could help save Vilma's life.

CHAPTER 77

BEVERLY, MASSACHUSETTS

Two weeks later, Angus Addison rearranged his schedule to be in Beverly for dinner. He'd heard the news: Patrick and Renata had conquered Rainier in under two days, very respectable for hobbyists. The question Angus had was, did the mountain chew them up, or was their passion for climbing stronger than ever?

At the dinner table, Patrick told the stories. The boy had been through a rough patch in Greece, but tonight he seemed reborn. On the other side of the table, Renata had the same reserve he remembered from July: an intelligent, calculating aura, confident yet humble.

"Renata, I must say that I'm very impressed that a woman from a tropical country managed to climb more than nine thousand feet in the cold in under two days. How'd you feel?"

Renata's eyes went from neutral to on fire. "I loved it, and I want to go back." Angus Addison collected winners. He looked for winning traits in every job applicant and had a knack for spotting all-stars. In his mind, the woman across the table had the potential to become the premiere woman in her sport.

"Well, I've seen enough, so listen up. I think we're looking at the start of something special. I want to see my company logo on the summit of Mt. McKinley. It's good for business, and it's good for you. $2,000 apiece."

A hush fell over the table. Dr. Brennan broke the silence. "Two thousand bucks to hold a flag at the top of McKinley? That's twice as much as my first car!"

"Hold on, Joe, they might want to think about it," said Angus. "People die up there. It's serious business, and there are risks."

"Well, safety is always a consideration, Angus. People die on Mt. Washington every year, too, and these kids are up there every weekend!

Plus, they've already climbed Rainier. They're naturals! Are there any famous female climbers in the world, Angus? The press would love her! Get her a yellow parka to match the Brazilian soccer jerseys. She'd blow up! What do they have, a hundred million people?"

All eyes turned to Renata, but she wasn't sharing in their excitement. Attention was the last thing in the world she wanted. "You want publicity, Mr. Addison? I would love to climb, but I do not want publicity. I came from Brazil to hide."

"Renata, your safety is of the utmost importance to me," Angus paused, processing the moment. "Let's think our way through this. Joe, please help me out. If Renata becomes a *name*—an up-and-comer in climbing—she might eventually appear in magazines and such. I might be jumping the gun, but my gut says I'm not. Not many women make it up even one of the Seven Summits, and at her age, she has a shot at every damned one of them."

"Is there anything we can do for you, Renata? I mean, back in Brazil? Can we notify the authorities?" said Dr. Joe. "I don't mean to pry, but what kind of problems are we dealing with?"

Before Renata could answer, Angus chimed in. "International dealings are tricky and expensive, Joe. Maybe we can give her a nickname or something? Alter her identity just enough, so her real name doesn't make the wire?"

"Honey, I'm sorry," offered Patrick. He reached over and took her hand.

Angus spoke up, "May I ask you an honest question? Is your name really Renata Johnson? Because if it's not, maybe we don't have to worry about publicity."

"My face will be in the picture. And you will say I'm from Brazil."

"You will wear your goggles at the summit. The UV rays burn the cornea. Some people go blind while still on the mountain. The perfect excuse is built into the sport itself. Wear the goggles, and we'll say you're an American."

Renata wondered for a moment if she might be worrying too much. "Three thousand," she replied.

Angus stared back with a grin. "I'll pay the two of you five thousand dollars, and you can split it as you like."

"I want three thousand, and Patrick can decide if he'll be happy with two."

"Done. Five thousand, and Renata gets three," said Patrick. The room was all smiles.

Chapter 78

Boa Vista, Brazil

Weeks had passed since Zé had learned the Feds were checking farms, but as expected, his turn came. Detective Olival Freitas and three police officers knocked on the front gate, where they were promptly greeted and let in.

"We're investigating the murders in the northeast and have reason to believe the perpetrator has worked on a farm. You're not a suspect, but we're asking for permission to inspect the facilities. President Médici has made a campaign promise to bring the Monster of Codó to justice. If you decline, we'll obtain a warrant and return later."

"You're welcome to take a tour, Inspector," said Dr. Zé. "Take your time. I'll provide the employee records. How far back do you need?"

"Ten years."

"Ten! Well, we've only been here for three, but I'll give you what I have." The two men strolled to the business office, where one of Freitas's men peeled off and began working with Zé's office manager.

"Who owned the property before you?" asked Freitas.

"No one, we built it. It's a second career for me." They walked into the barn and down the line of cows.

"Interesting. How many head of cattle?"

"Two hundred and fifty, give or take," replied Zé. *Go ahead*, he thought. *I know the farming business like the back of my hand.*

Freitas walked to the back wall and knocked on it. "Inspecting farms has been an education for me. I've seen many, and I've learned a lot. Tell me, what challenges you the most on a day-to-day basis?"

"Disease, without question. You have to stay on top of it, or business will suffer. You can't have infection running through the herd."

"That's what I hear," replied Freitas. "It can be an enormous expense, keeping a veterinarian on call. No wonder beef costs so much."

"We check the herd daily. I do much of it myself."

"Are you a veterinarian, Mr. Machado? Forgive me, but you don't look like a farmer."

Zé bristled but kept his cool. "It's Dr. Machado, actually, and I've taught myself a great deal of bovine medicine. It saves on medical expenses, and we see the results on the bottom line. I started as a general practitioner—humans, not animals—and went part-time, hoping to transition. The medical field is a thankless occupation. I can't stand the paperwork. I was born to work on a farm. It's my true calling."

Freitas and his team inspected the farm for nearly two hours, including an intense focus on employee records. As Zé had predicted, they missed the secret door but sensed it was only a matter of time before they came knocking again.

***

Six nights later, after checking sources, Detective Freitas knew a lot more about Dr. José Machado. It was raining in Codó, and the lights were off in the downtown doctor's office. After an hour of surveillance, Freitas walked past the building twice before cupping his hands against the window and peering in. He tried the door, but of course, it was locked. Sensing he was on the right track, Freitas walked around the building and through a gigantic puddle in an alleyway to the back door.

Despite the rain, Freitas kept his trench coat open with his pistol at the ready. He tried the knob, but it was locked. A utility shed in the alley called his attention, but it, too, was padlocked. Unwilling to break in and search without a warrant, Freitas waded back through the alley to the street.

***

Zé knew that the time had come to leave Brazil, even though the arrangements were far from complete, and the journey had to be taken seriously. Finances would be tight, and he would not have control over the business for an undetermined amount of time.

Zé grabbed his keys and drove through the pouring rain to close down the office. There could be no trace of evidence left. He'd park in the back alley, grab any proof, and get the hell out of there. Zé jumped, however, as he drove through the rain. A man emerged from the alley, acting as if he

142

belonged there. Thankfully, Zé's headlights blinded him as he wrestled with his trench coat. *It was Freitas, the cop.*

Without braking, Zé drove by, almost sure he hadn't been spotted. He'd have to forget about cleaning the office. They wouldn't find much, anyway. It wasn't as if he never knew this day would come.

***

The next day, Detective Freitas secured a warrant and prepped his men. Nervous but confident, he'd reviewed his meeting with Zé through his mind a thousand times and was satisfied he hadn't tipped the Monster of Codó off. The plan was to apprehend Zé and then dismantle his farm until they uncovered what was sure to be a smoking gun.

Freitas produced the warrant for the apartment's security guard, and they buzzed him in. The Feds then marched into the elevator and went straight to the eighteenth floor, where everyone took their positions, waiting for Freitas to give the signal. Finally, Freitas stepped to the door and knocked.

Nothing stirred within the apartment. Freitas knocked again, but still nothing. After one more warning, Freitas waved to security, who produced a key. As the apartment door opened, Freitas shook his head. The Monster was already gone.

CHAPTER 79

THE BORDER OF ECUADOR

Urso drove The Farmer and his family to the border in silence. On the one hand, this should be the easiest trip ever. The Farmer and the FARC were partners in crime. On the other hand, if it didn't go smoothly, it might be his last.

Zé arrived with a suitcase of money, a good portion of which was already spoken for. The family would be expedited through the Darien Gap. But there was no way to prepare them for the heat, insects, and multitude of discomforts awaiting. The little girl seemed docile enough, but kids were always a wild card.

The wife would be the most challenging part. He would have to be very careful to keep her happy.

***

Vilma watched in a daze as no fewer than a dozen mosquitos sucked blood from her arm. Then, breaking her trance, came a hand from above, crushing most of them, mashing their swollen bodies against her skin, turning her arm crimson.

"Doctor, she's not swatting the bugs. If we don't watch her, she could get sick and slow us down. We must keep a better eye on her," said Urso.

Zé inspected Vilma's bloody arm, wiping it with a discarded shirt he found on the trail. "Dammit, Aparecida, where are you?"

Aparecida appeared behind them, coming around the bend. "I—I need to rest. I need water. How much longer?"

Urso looked at Zé and shook his head almost imperceptibly. They weren't even close to stopping for the day. Aparecida hadn't even been told how many days it would take to cross into Panama, which was *Zé's idea,* and Urso silently questioned the strategy.

"Just keep walking," said Zé. "At least two days. Longer if you don't pick up the pace."

Urso turned away. It was better for his career if he didn't watch them fight. As Aparecida began her rant, Urso grabbed Vilma's hand and led her down the trail, slapping mosquitoes as they walked, being careful not to leave the VIP travelers behind.

Chapter 80

Beverly, Massachusetts

Dr. Joe answered his home phone after another easy day at the practice. On the other end was his old friend, Nigel Fletcher. It had been nearly two years since they'd last spoken, but it was as if they hadn't missed a day.

"So, how's Patrick?" said Nigel. "I was talking to Angus about him. He's part of the practice now, isn't he? Is he going to take over the practice once you grow tired?"

"Much better now, Nigel. As you know, we had a setback with the Peggy situation, but that's over now, and the practice is in good hands. He's got a new girlfriend, and they're unofficially living together. They climb all the time. Lord knows Peggy wouldn't get within a hundred miles of a mountain. They're training for McKinley, can you believe it?"

"Angus told me! That's amazing news and part of the reason I called."

"Oh?" said Dr. Joe, ears perked.

"I'm excited to announce that I'm planning another shot at the goddess Chomolungma. Spring of '73."

Dr. Joe paused to process the information. Nigel was going to take another crack at Mount Everest. *Chomolungma* was the mountain's Tibetan name. Nigel had tried and failed six years ago, succumbing to altitude sickness. "You can't be serious! They had to carry you down on a stretcher. You're lucky you weren't left behind."

"Oh, rubbish," snapped Nigel. "For the amount of money we pay the Sherpas, they'd bloody well better bring me down."

"You're younger than I am, Nigel, but that doesn't mean you're *young*. Forty-six years at twenty-nine thousand feet is serious, my friend. How many people summited this year out of curiosity?"

"Zero," Nigel stated the word with defiance, and Dr. Joe heard his tenacity clear across the Atlantic.

"And how many have died?"

"Only one."

"All right then, how many people have ever summited? All-time."

"Twenty-eight." Nigel knew all the statistics. When he became inspired, he would read everything he could on the subject while concocting a plan. Dr. Joe had never known Nigel to back away once he'd reached the planning phase.

"Only twenty-eight people have ever summited?"

"Well, nobody can be sure," said Nigel. "Mallory may have, but he disappeared. A Sherpa or two might have snuck up there, but probably not."

"And how many deaths, all-time?"

"Twenty-seven."

"Oh, that's brilliant, Nigel. Twenty-eight made it, but twenty-seven are dead. I bet Gwendolyn loves this idea."

"I was getting to that, old chap. Gwendolyn left last month."

Dr. Joe's jaw dropped. Gwendolyn Fletcher had been Nigel's wife for as long as he'd known him.

"Good Lord, Nigel, I'm sorry."

Nigel cut him off. "She'd had enough of my adventures, leaving her alone with nothing to do but worry. She tried, Joe, but I wasn't there. She's hired a barrister and might have a new bloke as well. She saw me digging out the Everest books last August, and that was the last straw."

"So, you feel you've nothing to lose, then? You're not going to get reckless up there and get yourself killed, are you?"

"Put it out of your mind, Joseph. I feel more alive now than I have in six years—since the first Everest trip. I called you tonight to put a feeler out on Patrick and his girlfriend. What's her name again?"

"You're what?"

"Oh, shush, you heard me. What's her name?"

"Renata!"

"*Renata*. Well, I can't make any promises just yet, but I believe I have room on my team. Tony Baker broke his tibia two weeks ago, and he was rubbish to start. I'm down to myself and the Sherpas, but I'll remind you that you'll have to put all of your dreary thoughts on hold. We can't have a doom-and-gloomer sapping the spirit! Relax for once, and let your boy experience the thrill of a lifetime."

Dr. Joe was speechless, then added: "I'm all for it, but Sarah will want to hear the news. That climb would put them in rare company."

"Don't say anything to them yet. Let's see how they do on McKinley. I need more proof and wouldn't want to have to retract the offer if it's a sub-par trip. Oh, and there are strings attached. Purse strings, to be more specific."

"To pay the Sherpas, of course. How much are we talking?"

"It's more than Sherpas, I'm afraid. Nepal charges a permit fee, too. But you're right. Everything depends on the Sherpas. We'd be dead before Base Camp if it weren't for them, and we'll need as many as eight."

"Okay, so …"

"It's going to cost a mint, Joe, and the amount Patrick and Renata will pay is only twenty-five percent of the true cost."

Dr. Joe had never been so primed. "Spit it out, Nigel, how much?"

"Three thousand apiece. I'm speaking with sponsors now to cover the remaining nine per person."

"It costs twelve grand to climb Everest? Good Lord, I know people who paid that for their house!"

"I know, old friend, but don't forget, only twenty-eight people in the history of humanity have ever made it to the top. It will be worth it if they summit. They'll get it all back in spades. I'm assuming Patrick is all set in the pocketbook, but what about Renata? Any rich relatives back in …"

"No. Renata's not even here legally, Nigel. She came here running from something and doesn't talk about it. Did you talk money with Angus yet?"

"He's next on the list," said Nigel.

"Well, how about you let me break the news? Angus loves Renata. He sees her as a star. Maybe he'll pay her way."

"Okay, but don't count your chickens. McKinley is six thousand feet higher than Rainier and no joke."

***

As soon as Dr. Joe finished his conversation with Nigel, he picked up the phone and dialed Angus. The businessman was ecstatic. "Everest? *Sweet goddess mother of the world,* ha! Talk about an opportunity! Renata has that twinkle in her eye, Joe. I'm telling you! Count me in for the $3k. The only thing that bugs me is Renata's aversion to publicity. If I knew who she was afraid of, it might be cheaper to fly to Brazil and pay them off like we did in Greece."

"Hold on, Angus, it's not a done deal yet. They must do well on McKinley or Everest may never happen."

"She's going to make it. Just make sure your boy can keep up."

Chapter 81

Sonoyta, Mexico

Urso wiped his brow. As expected, the wife, Aparecida, was the most difficult because she was so out of shape. Even the little girl, Vilma, fared better. The jungle was, of course, the worst of the trip, but Aparecida's nagging continued to the U.S. border. Thankfully, the three weeks passed, and Urso delivered The Farmer and his family to Sonoyta.

Dr. Zé confirmed Urso's report. "She went to Phoenix first, and then a bus to Boston?"

"All I know is they were in a light blue Ford van with Massachusetts plates, but Boston has the most bus routes."

Zé sensed the tingle, and the room turned the color of rosé wine. Allemand had settled in Massachusetts, and so had *Renata,* as she had come to call herself. *Two birds with one stone*, he thought, although he'd begun to wonder why he still cared about Juliana. The farm was gone, so there was no place she could send police. But to forget about Juliana was foolish. He'd already sensed her once. In his vision, she was riding a bicycle. What if she inherited his ESP? Perhaps, one day, she would feel *him*, and that was dangerous. It was best to tie up loose ends.

Forty hours later, Zé, Aparecida, and Vilma arrived in Boston. Tired but ever motivated, Zé rented a hotel room, hoping to get a few hours of rest. There was so much work to do.

CHAPTER 82

MT. MCKINLEY, ALASKA

Like Rainier, Mount McKinley was entirely different from anything they'd experienced. There was a lot more blue ice, which was more challenging to cross, and the conditions were downright severe. It reminded Renata of the weather at the summit of Rainier, yet they were only at base camp. On Rainier, they spent thirty minutes at fourteen thousand feet. Here, they would spend the night. Renata didn't want to admit it, but halfway up, she felt pain behind her eyes. She pinched the bridge of her nose and wished it away but only got two hours of sleep, even after a full day of exertion. The headache was understandable—everyone got one now and then, but deep down, it bothered her. She'd never been this high before; would it go away?

Patrick and the others, oblivious to her pain, were busy setting up their tents. She pitched in at half-speed, hoping hot tea, aspirin, and sleep were the remedy she needed.

Thirty minutes later, Patrick noticed. "Hey, are you okay?"

"Get me in the tent," Renata replied.

"Wait, let's talk to Keely." Luckily, they caught up to the camp doctor as she was getting into her sleeping bag.

"How long have you felt this way?" asked Keely.

"Since we arrived at High Camp. I didn't sleep much. I might be dehydrated. I hope I'm all right in the morning."

"How are your lungs? Does it feel like there might be fluid in them?"

"No. I can breathe fine."

Keely looked at Patrick. "Keep an eye on her. Set an alarm for 2 am and check her breathing. Make sure she wakes up. Sorry, but we don't want to mess around. If Renata is sick, she'll have to turn back, but if she's okay, it's only three thousand feet to the summit."

Patrick and Renata stared at each other. "Turn back" were two words they didn't want to hear.

***

The wind whipped and battered the tent, yet they both fell asleep. At 2 am, Patrick's alarm chimed for an eternity before Renata woke. As if she were made of lead, Renata crawled across the tent, head throbbing, and shut it off. Renata dug through Patrick's toiletries until she found the pills. He used them for more than just pain. It was habit. The meds fell into her palm. Grabbing her canteen, she washed them down and settled, all the while praying to her gods to take the pain away.

***

The next day, they summited, and although others cheered as they touched the pinnacle, there were no smiles as they snapped the photo with Angus's banner. This trip had been about limitations. Although they made it, it felt like a failure. Rather than stay at the summit and enjoy the view, they turned around and headed straight down the mountain.

CHAPTER 83

BEVERLY, MASSACHUSETTS

Angus's car was waiting in the driveway as they arrived home in Beverly. "He must be here to pay up!" Patrick exclaimed. "What are you going to do with your share? You need a car, right? Yours is quite the beater."

"No," she said, not caring to remind him of what she had already told him. Sarah greeted them at the doorway and ushered them in. Dr. Joe, Angus Addison, and a third man were sitting in the living room drinking scotch. Patrick recognized the stranger from his childhood. It was Nigel Fletcher, the one who had once attempted to climb Everest. Patrick's heart pounded.

Angus spoke first. "Look at you two. Well done! How was it, Renata? As easy as Rainier?"

"This one was tougher."

Angus's eyes bored into hers. "Tell me what happened."

Renata felt like a racehorse being evaluated. "I got a headache at seventeen thousand feet, and it didn't go away until we were halfway down the mountain."

"It happens," Nigel interrupted. "It happens to the best of us. Some people are prone, but most often, it's because you didn't acclimatize. Don't let it sap your confidence. Oh, and since no one will introduce me, my name is Nigel Fletcher."

"Pleased to meet you, Mr. Fletcher," said Renata. "I've heard of you."

"Nice to meet you as well, my dear. I should also add that the use of oxygen helps on the bigger mountains."

"Oxygen?"

"Yes, climbers wear oxygen tanks over eight thousand meters. It would be a fool's errand without it. Sometimes, we begin even earlier. Sorry, I interrupted. Please go on. I'd love to hear." Electricity was in the air, and Nigel's visit added a measure of mystery. All eyes returned to Renata.

"Other than the headache, I loved it. It was beautiful, and Patrick had a solid climb. He did well up there."

"Renata did well despite the headache." Said Patrick. "It lasted for three solid days, but she never quit. I believe she can do anything she puts her mind to."

"Well, I suppose you'll want your money then!" Angus said, and reached into his breast pocket, pulling out two business checks with the *Airventix* logo emblazoned in the upper left-hand corner. Renata, who'd been hoping for cash, hid her disappointment. "Three thousand for Renata and two thousand for Patrick. That's how you wanted it split, correct?"

The check was made out to Renata Johnson, which wouldn't work. She couldn't have a bank account without a Social Security number, and using a fake one was too risky. She could lose everything if the bank figured it out. Now, however, was not the time to bring this up. She would talk with Patrick after dinner. "Thank you."

"You are most welcome, Renata. It is a pleasure knowing and doing business with you. Your picture on top of McKinley will be on the cover of our annual report. But don't worry. We only have about a thousand of those mailed directly to our investors. It's a pretty boring read unless you're into P&L statements. I don't think you'll have to worry about any exposure in Brazil." Renata nodded politely and let the conversation die. "Well, I think we've let them wait long enough, don't you, Nigel? Do you have any pressing questions?" said Angus.

Nigel played coy, then started in. "I might. I'm here to invite the two of you to climb Everest with me next spring. Would you like to go?"

"Hell, yes!" barked Patrick. Sarah's eyes bugged wide. Renata was stunned. Things were happening so fast. They'd climbed Rainier in September, McKinley in May, and now Everest was on the table. Three significant challenges in less than two years, each one increasingly more dangerous.

Angus continued, "I have some ideas on how to hide your identity even though you would be the first woman to climb Everest. Imagine that! This, folks, is the reason I'm sponsoring these two. The *first woman* bit is a big deal, and I almost forgot: if you hold up my banner, it's worth twenty thousand this time. You can split it as you like. What do you think?"

All eyes turned to Renata. "I'm sorry, but I need to think about it." The money was a dream come true, but if she died on the mountain, Vilma would not be saved. There were other hurdles, too, that Angus hadn't considered.

CHAPTER 84

It was a quiet car ride home. Both Renata and Patrick were upset. Patrick boiled, wondering how Renata could pass on such an opportunity, yet held his tongue, waiting for her to speak first. When she hadn't said anything by the time they entered the house, he grabbed a beer and drained the can. When the alcohol found his bloodstream, he couldn't hold back any longer.

"Do you realize what you're giving up? This opportunity is important for everyone, not just you." The words fell selfishly, and Renata scowled. "Aren't you going to say anything? If it becomes dangerous, turn around! And if you make it, you save your sister!"

"You haven't thought it through, and neither has Angus," said Renata.

Patrick opened the fridge and grabbed another beer. "Please, fill me in."

"First, I can't cash a check that says Renata Johnson on it. Please ask Angus to write you a new check and pay me the cash. Second, there are things I haven't told you—and won't—unless you promise to keep them secret."

Patrick stared, dumbstruck.

"Promise you won't tell anyone. Not your father, not Angus Addison, and not Nigel Fletcher. Your mother, either. Absolutely nobody."

"Why? Don't you trust us?"

"You all have money, and everyone, including you, thinks that gives you the right to make the plans."

Patrick was stunned. "What haven't you told me?"

"I told you that I have a sister and am saving my money to hire someone to smuggle her out of Brazil."

"I know all that! So, climb Everest, and that should do it, right? Are you sure about the smuggling part, though? That sounds shady, Renata. Who is responsible for that? I promise you, Angus gets things done. I've seen him in action. He can help."

"No. Angus knows nothing about this situation."

"How is your sister in danger?"

Renata shook her head, about to be second-guessed by someone who had never visited a third-world country. Patrick was a rich boy who had never strayed far from mommy and daddy's checkbook. He knew nothing yet felt qualified to preach. Unfortunately for Renata, however, this Everest plan was better than her house-cleaning plan. In order to save Vilma in time, she might have to compromise.

"Promise me you won't let them interfere."

"Seriously? Have you even—"

"Promise me, or I'm not going."

"Okay, okay, I promise. Jeez—"

"My father has her."

It took Patrick a moment, and then, finally, his eyes widened. "Is he—abusing her?"

"Not exactly. I ran away because—" Renata hesitated. It was the first time Patrick had ever seen her emotional. "… he's involved in organized crime, and he's looking for me. If I climb Everest, I believe he will find out."

Patrick stared. "How much money do you need to save your sister?"

"My passage was ten thousand dollars, but that coyote is dead. I must find a new one, someone that can transport a child and be trusted."

"Ten thousand? My God—just to cross the border? That's more than my college tuition. All four years!"

"It's not one border, Patrick, it's ten. And I said *my* passage was ten thousand dollars. Vilma's will be double that."

"Twenty thousand?" Patrick shook his head. "Ironically, the same amount Angus is offering. Look, I—" Patrick held his tongue.

"It could even be more. And if I'm going to climb, we'll have to get married. Then I have to find someone crazy enough to kidnap Vilma."

"Excuse me?" said Patrick as he dropped his beer.

Renata shook her head. "See? You don't know everything. I don't have a passport."

Finally, Patrick understood. Renata couldn't fly legally to Nepal. Or if she could, she wouldn't be allowed back into the United States.

"I don't want to get married this way, Patrick. So, if you like, we can divorce when my immigration process is over. That way, I can raise Vilma here legally when it's over."

"Wait, slow down. You can't hit me over the head with marriage and then go right into divorce. Let's get married to save your sister and hope for the best. We don't even have to tell anybody. How's that sound?"

"Fine—but Patrick—"

"What?"

"I still think my father will find out. We can't have anything about Brazil on the mountain: no yellow parkas, no flags. If anyone asks, I'm American. And if they detect my accent, I'll say I'm from Chile or something."

"All right, you're from Chile. Problem solved." Patrick started to smile when she grabbed him hard by both arms and pulled him close, but it wasn't for a kiss. Her face was gaunt, her eyes as dark as onyx.

Renata lowered her voice and spoke slowly. "Don't let me die. If I die, I can't help Vilma." Patrick blinked as her grip tightened. She wouldn't let him go. "Promise me, or I'm not going."

"All right, I promise."

Chapter 85

———————

"Three months? Are you kidding me?"

"All right, Sarah, calm down. This climb has a lot of upsides that you aren't considering."

"For God's sake, Joe, he owes us a small fortune! You're spoiling him. You always have. Don't you want to retire?"

"Think positive, Sarah. What if he makes it? He can hang a sign in front of the office in the shape of a mountain: *Patrick Brennan, DMD*. He'll be the most popular dentist in town, never mind the endorsements. But don't count your chickens because Renata hasn't agreed and the whole deal rides on her decision."

CHAPTER 86

It was very late, so Patrick waited until the following day to phone in the good news. First, he called his father, who called Angus Addison, and there was much laughter and congratulations for the next ten minutes as Renata sat alone, listening from the living room. She'd called in sick. There was too much to think about. Everest was now on the schedule, and she should start to look for Vilma's savior coyote, but she needed someone to point her in the right direction. Maybe someone from the Pombal could help? Or someone in Phoenix?

Renata's next call was to Beverly City Hall to arrange their private wedding, which turned out to be easy. It would be this coming Thursday night in Patrick's living room. Three people, and three only: Patrick, Renata, and the Justice of the Peace.

Head swimming, Renata left the townhouse for the public library to educate herself on the world's tallest mountain. The floorboards creaked as she reached the second floor. It was an old building but quiet, as most people were at school or work. Renata found an empty conference table in the corner and claimed it. The entire room was, for now, hers and hers alone. Within an hour, she had three tall stacks of books to peruse.

At first, she wasn't captivated. The reading was a bunch of statistics and very dry. Everest was 29,029 feet tall—nine thousand feet taller than McKinley. There were two main passages up the mountain: one from the south through Nepal and one from the north through Tibet. Since she knew they were flying to Kathmandu, Renata concentrated on the southern route. Edmund Hillary and Tensing Norgay were the first ever to summit in 1953, although it couldn't be proven that George Mallory and Andrew Irvine hadn't reached the pinnacle before they went missing in 1924.

Renata also learned that other mountains on the planet could claim, via a technicality, that they were the highest in the world. If you measured

Mauna Kea in Hawaii, it was indeed taller, yet over 29,000 feet of it—an entire Everest—was beneath the surface of the Pacific. McKinley was also taller if you measured base to summit, but all these tidbits bypassed the real point. The crucial statistic that separated the wheat from the chaff was the *distance above sea level.* Altitude was king, and Everest had that in spades.

Renata shivered, having found what she was looking for. The great mountain rose so high it penetrated the stratosphere. At times, the jet stream pummeled it. Winds could reach two hundred miles per hour, enough to blow climbers off the slope. If that wasn't enough, there were spontaneous thunderstorms and the constant threat of avalanches.

Renata flipped another page and realized her fears. On page 346 of the "E" volume of the *Encyclopedia Britannica* was a list of all the climbers who had died, and it read like an epitaph. Renata lifted her hands from the page as if the book itself were a corpse. Seeing the names haunted her. Each of these people had set out with the best of intentions yet wound up a cautionary tale.

The first seven men died in a single avalanche. Renata closed her eyes and imagined the horror of something so large, heavy, and inescapable. *What would it be like to be entombed under the ice and snow, immobilized, upside down, and backward?* The claustrophobia alone chilled her. *Would I hear them searching for me? Would I be able to cry out? Is it dark down there, or does the light make its way through?*

Three climbers had died from something called *falling serac.* Renata had no idea what that meant, so she looked it up. It turned out that a serac was a massive block of ice found between crevasses or attached to the sides of mountains. Seracs formed wherever ice was moving. The Khumbu glacier was in continuous motion, constantly cracking. The chunks between the cracks were seracs, akin to a frozen loaf of sliced bread, slowly expanding. Seracs could be house-sized or bigger and were, by definition, unstable. Direct sunlight made them significantly more so, and they made noises as they shifted in the midday heat.

There were several other ways to die, one of which was the term *sickness,* which came in many forms: altitude sickness, pneumonia, cerebral edema, and brain hemorrhages. Some climbers fell off the mountain or into crevasses. *Exposure* was a killer—the result of people getting lost, not being able to find their tents, and being forced to bivouac in the elements.

The last category, and the most unsettling, were the people that went missing. George Mallory and Andrew Irvine were two of the most famous. Somehow, they'd managed to vanish on the tallest rock in the sky, and Renata didn't yet understand how that was even possible.

CHAPTER 87

When Patrick arrived at work the next day, the office erupted in applause. It was exciting to work for someone who might summit Everest, but not every employee was happy; in fact, several could be heard whispering under their breath.

"Now we know they should be paying us more," said Sharon, a hygienist.

"I can't stand it. You know I'm not a big fan of Junior," said Olivia, the admin.

"Daddy's going to give him three months off. Can you believe it?"

"Yeah, three whole months, and I get two weeks holiday unpaid. Must be nice."

Just then, Dr. Joe entered the room and silenced the clapping. He had a speech prepared, but the whispering continued.

"Here comes daddy to pump up his boy. Wake me up when it's over."

"Everyone—everyone, I'd like to say a few words! Please, quiet down." Dr. Joe could have started yet waited for complete silence for dramatic effect. "Thank you all. As you may have heard, Dr. Pat here is going to have to leave us for a bit."

A smattering of fake boos followed. "Yes, it's true! Dr. Pat, my only son, will have to leave us for a truly higher calling, and I can't say I blame him. Patrick is to climb Mount Everest!" Everyone clapped, and Dr. Joe pretended it was hard to get a word in. "Wait, wait, hold on, he'll be back, and he's not going anywhere for a while, so you'll have plenty of time to wish him well."

"I think I'm going to throw up," whispered Sharon.

"Me too," said Olivia, as Patrick ate up the attention, promising to hold a *Brennan Dental Care* banner on the summit if they signed one for him.

"Oh, dear Lord, who cares?" asked Sharon.

"Not me," said Olivia. "

"Me neither," said Sharon. "I think they're paying the girlfriend's way too."

"Is she going?"

"Of course she is! She's the whole reason for this. I overheard Dr. Joe telling Mrs. Watkins. Without her, Junior doesn't go. They want her to be the first woman to summit Everest."

"Cut it out. How much does it cost to climb Everest? Or how much is this costing *us*, should I say?"

"Hold on, hold on, I have one more announcement," said Dr. Joe. "I've been at this for forty-five years. It's been a good run, but I'm ready to hand over the reins. I'll be retiring next June after Patrick gets back, and I believe I'm leaving you in good hands."

"Oh, shit," said Alicia.

"I'm calling Nichi Tiffin," said Olivia.

CHAPTER 88

BOSTON, MASSACHUSETTS

Zé handed over the money and grabbed the keys. He'd forgotten what freedom was like. He missed the connections he had in Brazil. It had taken longer than he'd thought to get fake papers and to set the family up somewhere so he could go back to work. He looked forward to a new adventure with Aparecida and Vilma out of his hair.

"But the television is all in English," said Aparecida.

"Then find a park and take Vilma." Vilma was watching the TV with the sound turned down and didn't look up when her name was mentioned. Zé didn't like that, but he had more important things on the agenda. The migration had been tough on all of them, the little girl especially. She would come out of her funk—eventually.

***

Zé's first stop was a gas station, where he bought a map that included Boston and Salem, his only lead for the time being. Next, he hoped to find something in the local library, even though it would undoubtedly be written in English.

Boston was bigger than Codó, and the suburbs were even more sprawling. The number of businesses was astounding, each one competing for attention. At one point, he passed a restaurant with an elaborate cactus-shaped sign nearly twenty meters high. As he turned off the highway, the architecture, too, was utterly foreign. Like the barn in his dream, the houses here were made of wood, entirely different from Brazil's concrete and brick.

Every so often, he noticed flags of various nationalities hanging in windows of homes and businesses, predominantly Greek, Irish, or Italian. He looked for Brazilian flags but found none. A *Welcome to Peabody* sign came and went as highway traffic became city streets, and the businesses here were smaller and less flashy than those on Route One. Then suddenly, Zé saw a sign with a word he recognized: *padaria*, Portuguese for bakery. He had to stop.

Within seconds of entering the shop, Zé felt like he was back in Brazil. The aroma of padarias back home was the same, and a Portugal flag sticker decorated the cash register.

A middle-aged shopkeeper noticed Zé and greeted him, "Hello, friend. What can I get for you?"

Zé struggled to understand. The man spoke so fast that it was impossible to split the sentence into individual words. "Fala Português?"

"Of course I do," the man responded in Portuguese. "You're Brazilian? We don't have too many of you around yet. Welcome to Adalberto's Bakery. What can I get for you?"

"Are you Adalberto?"

"Yes, I am."

"I have a few questions if you can spare a moment. I am new in town and will be looking for a place to live. There are three in my family. Where should I start?"

"If you're looking in Peabody there are three apartment buildings around here with Portuguese owners, so I'd start there."

"Would you have their phone numbers?"

"I can get them if you like, but come back tomorrow. I won't see Rodrigo until then. He's the one I know best."

"And what of the witches of Salem? World-famous, I hear?"

"Sort of. Some innocent women were hanged, but I don't pay much attention to the whole thing, except around Halloween when Salem gets crowded with tourists. I remember to steer clear of downtown."

"Adalberto, you don't know anyone named Renata, do you?"

"No. I don't know a Renata."

"How about Juliana?"

"Yes, I know three Julianas. One comes here all the time."

"Is she about twenty-two years old, tall, with dark hair?"

Adalberto laughed. "No, sorry. She's eighty years old and loves my Queijada. The other two are a little girl and my mother. Do you know someone in town?"

"I'm not sure. A friend's daughter came to Massachusetts a few years back, and I thought it might be nice to connect."

"Sorry, but I can't help you there, but bring your family to dinner tonight, my treat. A night on the town as a welcome to Peabody gift from my wife and me. There's a great Portuguese restaurant you'll want to try."

Before leaving, Zé bought a pastel and ate it in the car. It was the best thing he'd eaten in months.

CHAPTER 89

Although their City Hall wedding was little more than a business deal, Patrick insisted on a honeymoon. They settled on a weekend at the historic Mount Washington Hotel in Bretton Woods, New Hampshire. As their Mount Everest climb approached, Renata found herself getting excited.

"Do you think we'll climb something this weekend, or will the heated pool and hot tubs keep us here?" Patrick asked. They'd been on the road for an hour on 93 North, with an overall sense of relaxation in the car. They'd been training for months, and with no concrete plans, a weekend free of climbing sounded nice.

"A nice hotel with good food? I'm taking the weekend off. I can't remember the last time I did absolutely nothing," said Renata, staring out the window as she reclined in the passenger seat with one foot on the dashboard. Suddenly, the sky went from blue to pink, and she sat up, eyes wide. Something was out there in the woods, just off the highway. It was the same feeling she had had on the bike ride through Beverly Farms. "Oh, meu deus!"

Patrick yelled, startled. "Ah! What? What is it?"

Renata continued to search the trees, feeling for whatever it was, attempting to open her mind and understand.

"Babe? You okay?"

A mile later, the feeling faded. Whatever it was was gone.

"Where are we?" she asked.

"The sign said Sanborn, but what the hell! I'm driving! Don't do that!"

"I—felt something."

"Felt something? Like what?"

"Like something strange was back there."

Patrick looked at her sideways. "Are you okay?"

Once again, Renata found herself having to share intimate details with Patrick, but she didn't want to. She slept with him, for crying out loud.

They were even *married*. He was going to get into her business from time to time, but he wasn't ready for the whole truth. To fill him in on Macumba and her newfound sixth sense was too much to explain, at least until she had things under control.

Chapter 90

Zé sat up in his Boston hotel bed, suddenly wide awake.

"What is it?" asked Aparecida.

"Don't touch me!" His body spasmed, and the bed shook.

"Zé, you're scaring me!" Aparecida whispered. "You'll wake Vilma!"

"Stop, stop. I'm fine," said Zé, attempting to catch his breath. "Let me clear my head."

"Did you see something again?" asked Aparecida.

Zé ignored her and continued to process his thoughts. He'd seen Juliana in a car. The image was so vivid and yet so fleeting. She was in the passenger seat, with her foot up on the dashboard. "It was so quick. I saw Juliana in a car."

"And then what happened?" said Aparecida.

"I don't know. Go back to sleep."

Chapter 91

The House on Varney Road, Sanborn, NH

The honeymooners enjoyed a gourmet dinner of red wine, filet mignon, and scalloped potatoes, followed by a soak in the hot tub. For the first time in as long as she could remember, Renata allowed herself to do nothing. Thirty-six hours later, it was time to drive back to Massachusetts. Doing her best to savor the relaxation, Renata put on her slippers and sat back for the long ride home.

"It's selfish, isn't it?" she said.

Patrick looked over at her, wondering what she was talking about. "Babe, you have to include me from the beginning. What's selfish?"

"Risking one's life to climb a mountain."

Patrick frowned. "Well, I suppose it could be, but you could say that about almost anything. What do you mean?"

"When a husband leaves his wife and kids to climb Everest, he's thinking of himself and the glory if he makes it to the top. But if he dies, they've lost a husband and a father."

"No. It doesn't mean he's selfish."

"I don't see it this way."

"What if he's climbing for charity? Raising money for a good cause? You're climbing for that reason, aren't you?"

"I am, but how many hide behind a cause for selfish reasons?"

"Yeah, that's why I said it depends—"

Suddenly, Renata sat bolt upright. "Take this exit! Take it! Take it!"

Startled, Patrick obeyed, wrenching the wheel and cutting off another car before sailing off the highway to the blaring of horns.

"What the hell! I told you not to do that!"

"What color is the sky right now, Patrick?"

"What?"

"Answer me. What do you see?"

"It's blue, like every other day!"

"Pull over at that gas station. Let me drive."

"Do you want to tell me what's going on? Oh, I see: this is the Sanborn exit. Don't tell me you felt something again."

"Yes. I felt it again. I want to drive."

Exasperated, Patrick kept his mouth shut, pulled over, and got out as Renata took the wheel. They were quiet for several minutes as Renata turned left on Rural Route 42/Lancaster Hill Road, and pebbles clattered underneath Patrick's Porsche.

"Hey, this is a dirt road! Slow down! You're killing my car!"

Renata slowed, but only to shut him up. Her eyes never left the tunnel of trees, darting left and right, searching for whatever had called her here. In less than a minute, they had gone from a busy road into deep woods. A mile in, Renata slowed to a crawl to check out the first house they'd seen. The house was dark, and there was a lot of junk in the yard. "What a dump," said Patrick.

Renata drove on. Whatever she was feeling, that wasn't it. Another two hundred yards of trees passed before the woods opened to a meadow on the right, followed by another house, this one in much better shape. It was beautiful, in fact: an old farmhouse in remarkable condition with a pond in the front yard, but again, Renata felt nothing, so she drove on.

"Do you know what you're looking for?" Patrick asked.

"No, but I have to see where this takes me."

Patrick looked on with concern. "What do you expect to find? You never told me about these—feelings or whatever they are."

"They're new. The first one was a year ago, on Mother's Day. I went for a bike ride near your parents' house, and this feels just like that."

"Maybe we should go back and buy a map. I think it would—"

Suddenly, Renata saw a sign that said Varney Road. She yanked the wheel one more time, causing Patrick to crash into her shoulder.

"Babe, give me a warning! Miss the turn, for God's sake! We can always turn around!"

"Quiet!"

Patrick did as he was told, baffled by her behavior. The sooner this was over, the better. It was getting dark, and they were driving further and further into the woods. Six minutes later, she jammed on the brakes again, and Patrick bit his lip. There was nothing but forest around them.

Renata looked up. The sky was blood red. "We're close."

"To what? The end of Varney Road? The end of the world?"

"I don't know."

Renata took her foot off the brake and let the car ease forward. Nearly a hundred yards passed, and finally, a driveway appeared on the right. Renata coasted past, eyes searching. Nestled in a tiny yard was a small farmhouse with a large, broken-down barn. The roof had caved in, seemingly decades ago. Both buildings were dark. Whoever owned it didn't have the time or money to tear it down.

"It's in there," she said.

"What's in where?" asked Patrick.

Renata couldn't take her eyes off the old building. Without a doubt, this was the same feeling she'd had while biking by the smoldering house in Beverly Farms, and once again, she had to wonder if it was any of her business.

"Babe?"

"Wait." Renata tried to see into the barn but couldn't. It was almost dusk, and there were too many shadows.

"I don't think anyone's home," said Patrick, looking at the wrong building. "We've seen three houses in five miles, and nobody's out here. If we were criminals, we could rob them all blind."

Renata stared into the dark barn until the hairs stood on the back of her neck. "I can't do it!" she said. Suddenly afraid, She put the Porsche in gear and sped away as fast as the shoddy roads would allow. Whatever was in there had nothing to do with saving Vilma.

Thankfully, the feeling diminished the closer they got to Route 93. Patrick was frustrated but remained silent as Renata held back tears. Even though she felt she'd done the right thing, she couldn't help but wonder if whatever it was back there might come looking for her.

CHAPTER 92

PEABODY, MASSACHUSETTS

Zé, Aparecida, and Vilma all showed up for dinner at a restaurant called *O Fado* with Adalberto and his wife, Iliana. Vilma was still coming out of her haze with the reintroduction of ordinary foods. Her conversation was coming back, and the programming was nearly complete. She was down to one cup of tea per day.

Soon, Vilma would lose the desire to question, and Zé and Aparecida could begin to talk business in front of her. As time went by and they continued her home-schooling, the bond would strengthen. When she was old enough, she would join the family business.

"If you like bacalhau, you will love this place," said Iliana.

Aparecida put on her best public face. "Adoro bacalhau," she chirped.

Drinks were ordered, and the appetizers came and went. It was a hint of Brazil for Zé and his family until the waiter came with the entrees.

Suddenly, Zé's eyes began to pulse as the waiter delivered the food.

"Who had the Carne Alentejana?"

Zé closed his eyes. He saw Juliana again, this time driving. She was tense—nervous.

"Uh—"

"Zé, that was your order, wasn't it?" asked Aparecida.

"I don't—I'm not—"

"Zé, are you all right?" Aparecida went into caregiver mode.

Zé loathed caregiver mode.

"I'm all right, yes, just a headache. One second—"

Juliana drove by a house very slowly, and Zé could feel the energy of wherever she was and what she was doing. *She was afraid of something, but what was it?*

"He needs to eat something. Zé, darling, you haven't eaten all day. He's light-headed, that's all. The hotel room doesn't have a kitchen, but it'll just be another day or two."

"Wait," said Zé.

"Just take a bite and get your blood sugar back up. You'll feel—"

"No. Wait."

Adalberto and Iliana looked up, and Aparecida withdrew. Zé stood and ran to the bathroom, anywhere away from their talking. As soon as the stall was locked, the vision of Juliana faded. He'd missed something important.

Chapter 93

Zé entered the Salem Public Library and set out to find out all he could about the legend of Claude Allemand, but reading in English would be a challenge. The nonfiction section was easy to find without help, but finding religion and occult took longer. As he combed the shelves, a librarian poked her head around the corner.

"Can I help you find anything?"

Zé guessed what she was after, but answering was the tricky part. "Não sank you."

The librarian's eyes narrowed as she detected his accent. "All right, well, if you need anything, I'll be at the desk."

Zé nodded with absolutely no idea what she'd said.

***

Thirty minutes later, Zé found a biography called *Claude Allemand and the Dead Men of Salem* by Ronald Desjardins. His heart leaped. Even though he couldn't understand what the title meant, he clutched the book, wondering the best way to unlock its secrets.

"Need help? Or still browsing?" the librarian interrupted once again. "Oh, I see you've found something. Take your time." She disappeared again.

Zé found himself an English-Portuguese dictionary and took a stab at self-translation. It occurred to him that simply stealing the book might be the best way to spend time alone with it, but ultimately decided it was too early to burn that bridge. Perhaps he could ask Adalberto for help, but that would invite a third party into his business. Was there another way?

After a frustrating hour with the dictionary, Zé hid the Allemand book in the fiction section and returned to Peabody.

Chapter 94

As soon as Patrick left for work, Renata jumped into her car and drove to Beverly Farms. She had to know. Patrick was too wrapped up in his own world to grasp what happened on their way home from the Mount Washington Hotel. Sharing her plans with him would invite his unknowing opinion.

Retracing her Mother's Day bike ride wasn't easy. It took her almost a half hour to find the house. Of course, the fire was long since extinguished and all that remained was the stone foundation. But Renata knew a mile before she arrived that she wouldn't find anything. The sky was as blue here as it was in Salem.

Her eyes were clear. No rose-colored hues or blood-red skies. Not a twinge of a pulse behind her eyeballs. Whatever was here on Mother's Day had moved to New Hampshire.

CHAPTER 95

With a month to go before Everest, Patrick walked into his townhouse to the phone ringing. It was Nigel Fletcher.

"Just wanted to sync up, mate. How're you feeling?"

"I feel great! I can't believe we're a month out. What's happening?"

"I just wanted to let you know that we secured the permits, so we're all green in that regard. However, I did hear that there's a bit of a mess at Base Camp. The Sherpas are having a helluva time setting up the proper facilities if you know what I mean. Shit is literally piling up, as well as empty oxygen bottles, trash, you name it. Those poor bastards don't get paid enough, and we all know it, but don't repeat that on the mountain.

"Keeping the place clean is becoming an issue, unfortunately. Nepal doesn't quite realize that they've got a business to run up there and that people will only keep coming as long as they're not bloody *sick*. I just wanted to remind you to pack wet naps, that sort of thing. Cleanliness is an issue."

"I will, Nigel, thanks. You don't have to worry about us. We'll be ready. We're both extremely excited."

"All right, then. Cheers mate. See you shortly!"

***

As Patrick hung up the phone, Renata walked in the door, surprised to see Patrick already home. "Was it an early day?"

"My last patient canceled. I got home a half-hour ago. Guess what? Nigel called. He said all the permits are in order, and it's all systems go!"

Renata took off her coat and shook off some snow. "That's good. Did he say anything else? Everything I know about Mt. Everest, I looked up myself. Did he have an itinerary, maybe? Something?"

Patrick didn't budge from his reclined position on the couch. "Uh, no. It was a quick call, and he sounded busy. He'll have us ready, don't worry. How was your day?"

Renata walked from the front door and through the living room to the kitchen. "I got Miriam to cover me and I went to the bank to open an account. What are we doing for dinner?"

Patrick sat up, surprised. "Another account? What for?"

Renata turned. She knew he would balk at the idea, and that's why she went alone. "I want to keep Vilma's money separate. I also opened a safe deposit box with some instructions in case something happens."

"Which bank? Essex?"

"No. I told you I want to keep it separate."

"Well, that would be why you opened a new account, right?"

"I want the money out of sight and out of mind. I want to forget it exists until it is time to use it."

"Are you not going to tell me which bank?"

Renata rolled her eyes. "I was about to! Before that, however, I want to say something." Patrick exhaled as Renata reached into her pocketbook and pulled out a brass key with the number 518 engraved on it. "This is for my safe deposit box. If something happens and I don't make it, open the box. There are instructions inside. I'm trusting you to help Vilma if I can't, and the bank needs you to sign something so you'll be on the account."

"Babe, think positive. You'll be back."

Renata ignored him. "I found someone in Phoenix, a coyote. He knows everything. All the coyote's contact information is in the box. All you have to do is call him and pay him. If Angus doesn't pay because I don't make it, you have my permission to fundraise through your family if you want to. Patrick, consider this my *testamento*. Promise me you will save Vilma if I cannot."

Patrick stared, uncomfortable with the heavy mood. "Okay, I still promise."

Chapter 96

Adalberto, the baker, was busy and couldn't leave his shop until almost 3 pm. As soon as Zé led him to the spot in the library where he'd hidden the Allemand book, the clerk, who was helping a gentleman, spoke up.

"Excuse me, sir? I couldn't find the book you were looking at the last time you were here. Could you explain, please?"

Adalberto translated. When their conversation was over, Zé shook his head and led the librarian to the book's hiding place. "He put it here so it couldn't be checked out," Adalberto explained.

"Please tell him that's not necessary. I can hold it temporarily at the front desk."

"He doesn't speak English, but he's very sorry. I'm here to help him and check the book out. Then we'll be on our way."

"Certainly, but first, I'd like to introduce you to someone. This gentleman is the author of the book your friend wants to borrow. Meet Mr. Ronald Desjardins."

Surprised, Adalberto translated, and Zé became immediately suspicious. Was this the actual author, or had Detective Freitas alerted the authorities?

"Hello, gentlemen. I know this may seem like a coincidence, but I live locally. Margaret and I have been friends for years, and I asked her to let me know the next time a copy of my book went missing. Between the Salem, Danvers, Peabody, and Beverly libraries, we've lost eight copies in a little over a year. I'm working on writing a sequel, and I'd love to speak anonymously with any present-day followers if you two are, uh, indeed involved?"

Adalberto and Zé conferred. "My friend, uh, says he was not going to steal the book, and he is not a follower of anything. What does that mean?"

"To be clear, we're not accusing him of stealing the book. We'd like to know why the books are going missing and what it means to today's movement," said Desjardins. Margaret excused herself to help someone check out a book.

"My friend's name is Miguel," said Adalberto, gesturing to Zé. "He wonders who you think is stealing the books."

Desjardins continued. "Good question. Some of this is covered in the text, but three years ago, a house burned down in Beverly Farms. I believe that house was the headquarters for the disciples of Claude Allemand. My father was found dead there. He'd been missing since I was a boy. I believe he was part of the cult, and it pains me to know he was right under our noses. I'm determined to get to the bottom of it."

Adalberto translated for Zé. "Miguel says he isn't aware of what happened in Beverly. All he's heard of is Allemand and that he was killed many years ago."

"Miguel, may I ask what sparks your interest in Claude Allemand?" asked Desjardins.

Adalberto translated, during which time he wondered what horrors his new friend was involved with. At one point, he took a step back.

"Miguel is a college professor from Brazil, and part of his curriculum focuses on black magick. He's come to the United States to learn more about Voodoo, Allemand, and the like."

Zé looked the author up and down, trying to determine whether or not Desjardins believed his story.

"Brazil! Wow, that's so far away."

"Miguel hasn't read your book and wants to know if your father ever met Allemand."

"I don't believe so. Allemand died in the twenties, and my father went missing in 1936, but as I mentioned, they found his body when their house burned down."

"Where is this house?" said Adalberto.

"About ten miles from here, just over the bridge. Do you know Beverly Farms?"

Adalberto and Zé huddled. "Would it be possible to give us the address?"

Desjardins smiled. "If you have the time, I'd be happy to show you."

***

Zé rode in the back of Desjardins' car. Hopefully, this visit would lead to something meaningful. Desjardins narrated as if the men were on a guided tour. "Allemand never lived here. After he died, a man named

Gideon Walker became the leader and moved to this location, where they lived in obscurity for almost fifty years."

The car slowed and turned down a gravel driveway where Desjardins parked. Zé looked out at the torched foundation and an acre of overgrown field ringed by woods. The three men got out of the car, and Zé immersed himself in the atmosphere. He felt—something, but his vision was clear, and the sky was still blue.

"This is where the house was," said Desjardins. "As I was saying, Gideon Walker ran his cult from here. Several women and children were kept on these grounds while he studied black magick and the writings of Allemand. There used to be a shed in that corner, but they bulldozed it. The house burned to the ground, but no one knows what started the fire.

"My father's body was found in the woods in that direction. He'd been murdered, along with several others guarding the compound. No one claimed responsibility, but the good news is people stopped going missing." The three men walked the grounds, but there wasn't much left to inspect. Still, Zé felt residual energy. Something or someone magickal had been here.

"Why did they bulldoze the shed but leave the foundations of the house?" asked Zé, and Adalberto translated.

"There were some bones of people who had been missing found in the shed. They wanted to be respectful of the surviving family members and it was attracting unwanted attention from the dark side of Salem. They're still deciding what to do with the property."

"How did you learn all this?" asked Zé.

Desjardins sighed. "I had one source: the great-granddaughter of one of the cult members who escaped the night of the fire. But unfortunately, she died before I was done interviewing her."

"Wait a second!" exclaimed Adalberto. "I remember this place! From that stupid TV show my wife used to watch. Wow, it's just a meadow, not at all like they made it look on TV."

"If you'll excuse my language, that TV show was garbage," said Desjardins.

"It was!" said Adalberto. "What was the name? It was a poor man's *In Search Of.*"

"*Only If You Dare.*"

"That's it! What a waste of life, watching that."

"They didn't even finish the story—just started re-runs, and then it was canceled. I investigated everything they reported. Most of it was pure fiction."

Zé interrupted, desperate to catch up, and Adalberto filled him in.

"Miguel wants to hear the whole story," said Adalberto.

"Well, first of all, I never understood where they were going with it. It was as if they had two different stories and mashed them together."

"Yeah, and they liked to show the same clips over and over," added Adalberto.

"Exactly. They tried to tie this place to a house in New Hampshire, and I wasted a week up there searching. I found the house, but it was empty. The owner sold it off because of the TV show, and whoever bought it never moved in. I asked around, and people laughed. The *legend* was fiction. Nobody had ever heard of Claude Allemand or Gideon Walker."

Zé smiled to himself. "Adalberto, ask him if he remembers the address of that house."

Chapter 97

The Trek to Everest Base Camp

March came fast, and it was nearly time to fly to Kathmandu, yet Nigel still had not provided so much as an itinerary. Dr. Joe threw an office Bon Voyage party, and when it was over, Patrick and Renata went straight to the airport. The flight lasted nearly two days, with stops in London and Cairo. Nigel greeted them in Kathmandu, where they took a taxi to their hotel, tired but excited; it was finally happening.

"Where is Everest? Can we see it from here?" asked Renata.

Nigel chuckled. "No, my dear. There's still a way to go, so get some rest, and we'll take our next plane first thing in the morning."

"Next plane?"

"Right. Don't worry. This flight is only thirty-five minutes to a small town called Lukla."

***

The following day, Renata was distressed to see a twelve-seat-twin-propeller sitting on the runway. "We're going in that?" she asked. "Is it safe?"

"Close your eyes one minute before landing, and you'll be fine, love," was all Nigel said.

Renata stewed as she was herded into the tiny cabin. Ten minutes later, the plane lurched down the runway, and they were off. As it soared higher and higher, Renata forgot her anger, and the panoramic view exploded before her. Green mountains in the foreground gave way to snowcapped giants—but Everest was still nowhere in sight.

Propellers buzzed as the twelve passengers rocked and bucked with the ever-shifting crosswinds. Renata and Patrick were seated directly behind the cockpit, and as they descended, they could see the approaching airfield over the pilot's shoulder. All that was visible was a green cliff, a sliver of runway, and a wall of granite. Lukla was built on a ledge, and it looked like they were about to land on an area the size of a postage stamp.

How many times had it been misjudged, and who had been crazy enough to be the first to try? The plane dropped fast, and Renata knew there must be a point of no return when the pilot would have to forego the option to pull up. The mountain engulfed their entire field of vision as they entered its shadow. They were merely ants here, a million miles away from the relatively tiny mountains of New Hampshire.

Renata's palms dripped. A gust of wind rocked the plane, and several passengers cried out in surprise. Mountain gales jolted the fuselage, swaying it from side to side. The pilots held tight to handles built into the cockpit ceiling and braced for landing. Renata dug her fingers into the armrests and looked at Patrick, who stared wide-eyed, watching the two men who held their lives in their hands.

"How long is the runway?" she shouted. Patrick, meanwhile, stiffened and dug his heels into the floor as if it might slow the plane.

"Five hundred meters," the pilot replied, without looking back.

Fantastic, she thought—*five hundred meters between either falling down a cliff or smashing into a wall.* For a moment, Renata felt the pilot had undershot. They were nearly at runway level, but beneath them was nothing but air. Suddenly the wheels exploded in a spray of pebbles as they caught the first few feet of runway, and the damned thing wasn't even paved. Immediately, the pilots began flicking switches and pulling levers in an all-out effort to slow the plane as the cliff wall approached. They used the entire runway, ending with a last-second designed right turn. Renata caught her breath. They made it.

"Welcome to Lukla," said the pilot, and Renata breathed, surprised by how thin the air was.

"How many people live here?" she asked.

"Not many." Less than a hundred, I'd guess. You're lucky this airport is here. It's only nine years old. Before that, you'd have hiked this too."

The altitude was 9,300 feet, the same as halfway up Mt. McKinley. A strong mountain breeze that never let up reminded them where they were and what they had to do.

Twenty thousand feet to go, she said to herself.

When they were away from the roar of propellers and inside the airport, Patrick spoke up. "Damn, Nigel, you didn't tell us about that plane ride! That took a year off my life!"

"Oh, there's lots more fun to come, mate. Sorry, we haven't had much time to chat. It's been a hell of a month. Arranging the Sherpas and their yaks isn't easy, you know. By the way, let me introduce you to the lead Sherpa here. His name is Pemba. If you need anything, you can talk to either of us." Pemba, a smiling man only three-quarters of Patrick's build, reached out to shake his hand.

"Nice to meet you! Keep us safe! Thank you!" The volume of Patrick's voice was abnormally high as if it might help Pemba understand English better. Renata locked eyes with the Sherpa and smiled, and Pemba acknowledged with a head nod.

Patrick continued. "Now that we're here, Nigel, give us the rundown. What's happening today and tomorrow? Oh, and where do we catch the bus?"

Nigel bowed his head, grinning. "There's no bus, mate. Even if the trail could *fit* buses, you'd arrive at Base Camp far too quickly and get sick. We're going to take a hike. How does eighty miles sound?"

"Eight miles? No problem. What's for lunch?" The propellers' noise was still ringing in Patrick's ears.

"No, mate, not eight. *Eighty*. We're eighty miles from Base Camp."

"We're going to hike eighty miles in two days?" asked Patrick.

"Who said anything about two days? It's a week to nine days, depending on how you feel. It's not a race. We've got to get you acclimatized. You don't want altitude sickness, trust me." Renata frowned. She'd been asking for an itinerary for months. It was Day One, and they'd already suffered their first unpleasant surprise.

"All right, that's two heart attacks you've given me in five minutes," said Patrick.

"I'm giving *you* a heart attack? Mate, we're talking about hiking. We've not even got to the climbing yet!"

"How far today, Nigel?" Renata asked through pursed lips.

"Thirteen kilometers. We'll sleep in a settlement called Monjo, just enough to get your blood flowing. You'll breathe the air, feel the altitude, and say a proper hello to the Himalayas. But don't worry, you're only going to carry thirty pounds on your back. The Sherpas are responsible for the rest. Pemba, you're good, right?" Pemba nodded and headed to the plane to claim the luggage. Three men followed to help.

Nigel continued. "Remember to drink plenty of water. Not just any water, either, or you'll get the backdoor trots. You don't want to be dehydrated in this air. Use a water filter. Everybody acclimatizes at a different pace, so we don't have to stay together. In fact, we'll likely pass each other dozens of times before we get to Base Camp. So, take your time, and we'll meet at the end of each day. It's a beautiful hike. Enjoy it, but don't force it."

***

The village of Monjo consisted of four buildings and was slightly lower in elevation than Lukla. It was an easy hike to break the ice. The change of scenery was mentally refreshing, full of long suspension bridges spanning the Dudh Kosi River, which they crossed and recrossed several times as the path wound up the mountain. There was no snow on the ground, and the sun was bright above a beautiful mountain forest. Occasionally, they caught a glimpse of a snowy peak over the trees.

The trail suffered occasional traffic jams: Sherpas and their yaks lugging supplies up or down the mountain from village to village. Boulders lining the path were adorned beautifully with Hindu symbols, and occasionally, they came upon prayer wheels: large drum-like cylinders that rang like bells when spun. Patrick spun every prayer wheel he found while Renata abstained, remaining faithful to her gods.

Houses were nowhere to be seen along the trail. What few locals lived this high lived in the villages, which consisted of clusters of uninsulated buildings. The group spread out as Nigel said they would, and Patrick and Renata couldn't believe their eyes as the Sherpas moved backbreaking loads of equipment up the mountain faster than the two of them could manage without.

Sharing a suspension bridge with the yaks was a horrible, wobbling experience. Renata learned to wait until they were off the shaky spans before she took her turn. Finally, they arrived at their hotel, which was as no-frills as either had ever experienced. The shower was hot, but they had to share the bathroom with Nigel and the rest of the party. Thankfully, they slept well.

***

Renata and Patrick woke to a few degrees below zero. Today, they would hike to a town called Namche Bazaar, a regional trading post that resembled a European village. Once again, the yaks and donkeys were out in force. They would gain almost two thousand feet of elevation today, which meant that tomorrow would be a planned acclimatization day.

"How high is Namche Bazaar again?" Patrick asked.

"11,300 feet. Eighty percent up Mt. Rainier."

"That seems like five years ago," said Patrick, and Renata nodded, too winded to speak.

***

Namche Bazaar sat nestled in a green valley surrounded by snowcapped mountains. One magnificent rock stood out: the double-peaked Ama Dablam, one summit towering over the other. Renata turned her head to hide her tears. It looked like two sisters.

The rooms in the "hotel" were not heated, except by a central stove in the common area. They woke before sunrise to a freezing room, making it difficult to crawl out of bed. Today was their first designated acclimatization day, which meant all they had to do was explore the immediate area. The theory was to *climb high and sleep low*, testing the limits of what their bodies could handle, then retreat to more oxygen-rich altitudes.

That afternoon, after a good hike around the town, they arrived back at the hotel's common room to find Nigel and Pemba in full winter gear, enjoying hot Sherpa tea. They exchanged pleasantries when Patrick unzipped his jacket and released a cloud of steam, fuming like a snuffed candle.

Pemba couldn't help but laugh. "Good hike today! Big hike!"

"Cripes, you look like a heap of mashed potatoes, Patrick! Shall I order you some gravy?"

Renata, despite her disappointment in Nigel, burst out laughing. Patrick looked down at his torso and understood.

"Why aren't you steaming, too?" he asked Renata.

"Because I'm in good shape."

Pemba and Nigel roared even louder.

Chapter 98

Day five was more of the same: wobbly, prayer-flag-adorned suspension bridges and hole-in-the-ground toilets. It was getting colder. At no time did they take their jackets off, as they had further down the mountain. Renata wisely put herself on a fried-rice-only diet for fear of getting sick.

Ama Dablam, Renata's *two sisters* mountain, was always in view: a constant reminder of her goal. They checked in that night in a village called Tengboche, which consisted of three buildings. The 'villages' were getting smaller the higher they went. There were fewer people up here and for good reason. It was getting harder to breathe.

Renata went to sleep thinking about what they'd seen. Today, they'd caught their first glimpse of Everest, far away, barely visible over the surrounding Himalayas. It was so insignificant that Renata didn't even consider it a first sighting. In fact, it felt like the mountain was spying on them.

***

Renata woke the following day with a headache.

"My temples are pounding. I didn't sleep," said Patrick.

It came as some relief for Renata to hear that he was suffering, too. He had fared better than she did on McKinley. "I don't feel good either," she admitted. Renata looked out their frosty window. There was nothing around but rocks and shrubs. The air was too dry up here. "The trees are gone."

"It's getting serious. We need to drink more water. Pemba told me he drinks twenty-two cups a day."

"Twenty-two? That sounds like a chore."

"It was something like that. I can't think straight, let's have breakfast. Maybe food will help."

A stove in the hotel center provided some heat, but from it came an odd stink. Instead of wood, they burned the only flammable resource available: yak dung. Renata curled her nose. Coughing was regular this high up, but burning shit was a catalyst.

"Looks like we'll probably be breathing that smoke from here on up. Has Nigel set us up for failure?"

"Of course not! He's been here before. He knows what he's doing."

"You didn't know about this eighty-mile hike. You were as surprised as I was."

Patrick looked away. "Yes, I was surprised, but it's not like we didn't train for it. When we need to know something, Nigel will tell us."

Renata, too nauseous to argue, let the conversation die. Later, with food in their fragile bellies, they lumbered their way out of Tengboche, feeling twice their weight.

***

The village of Dingboche appeared in the distance, like an oasis in a frozen desert, yet it offered little relief. There was no running water. Instead, the only hotel/teahouse employee on duty filled their sink with potable water from a jug and let it sit, leaving the washbowl unusable. Tomorrow was another rest day, and they wouldn't have to climb any further for forty-eight hours.

***

On the second morning in Dingboche, Renata and Patrick woke with intense headaches and found both the sink and toilet frozen solid. Neither had eaten much the previous day, but despite their nausea, they headed for the breakfast room to try again. Nigel and the Sherpas were staying nearby, and they hoped to see them, but as soon as they sat, Renata realized the place was empty. When no one appeared, Patrick got up and went looking, eventually finding a disgruntled man in the kitchen. The man nodded as Patrick ordered the food.

As they waited, Nigel entered. "There you are. We're moving out. See you in Lobuche. Stay on the trail. Don't get lost."

Patrick was surprised. "You're leaving already?"

"Right. I've been up since four. We've already eaten. It's good that you slept—a rarity this high up. Don't take too long. That cook is as slow as death."

"We barely ate yesterday. Felt nauseous. Where were you?"

"Same thing, mate. I rested. See what I mean about acclimatization?" Nigel turned to Renata, "How's Angus's star climber?"

"A little better," said Renata.

"Nigel, we will get used to the altitude, won't we?" asked Patrick.

"No promises, mate. Everyone hits their limit sooner or later. Some get bacteria-sick because their body doesn't have the energy to fight, so be really careful from here on. Get your rest and be clean. It's impossible to fight the altitude if you're sick."

"Right," said Patrick, confidence shaken. Nausea alone could end a climb, never mind infection. He wanted to hear Nigel say that they'd be all right, but the words never came. "Travel safe. We'll see you in Lobuche."

***

Nigel was right about the slow chef. Patrick and Renata waited forty-five minutes for their food, and the order came out wrong.

"Excuse me," said Patrick. "I ordered momos. What's this?" On the table before them were two bowls of fried rice.

"No momos," was the response. Patrick wanted to argue, but the language barrier was insurmountable, given his energy level.

"Hon, we're not getting our momos. Are you okay with the fried rice?"

Renata picked through the bowl. Mixed throughout the rice were vegetables and a trace of egg. They'd done their best to stay safe, but Nigel was already up-mountain, and their bellies were growling. "I'm starving."

"Okay, thank you," said Patrick and waved the cook away. They finished eating in less than ten minutes and headed up the trail.

***

Halfway to Lobuche, Renata and Patrick arrived at the beginning of the Khumbu Glacier, a twelve-kilometer chunk of dirty ice snaking its way down the valley. It was a sign that Base Camp was close.

As they arrived in Lobuche, Patrick spotted Nigel sitting outside talking with Pemba, but neither had the energy to be social, so he and Renata checked in and went straight to bed. Three hours later, they woke with stomach cramps.

"That cook poisoned us," said Renata.

"The yak smoke is killing me," added Patrick, who began to cough. They realized they were both sick. An hour later, they could barely pick themselves up to go to the bathroom. Helpless, they went to bed, sorrows flowing from both ends. Finally, at noon, a person from the hotel knocked on the door and recognized their condition. The maid fetched water and medicine and took care of them for the rest of the day.

"Where is Nigel?" Patrick managed to ask. The woman didn't understand but returned a half-hour later with the manager, who spoke some English.

Patrick repeated the question, and the man pointed, "Chomolungma." Patrick rolled his eyes but lacked the energy to feel angry. Completely debilitated, they were forced to stay on an extra day.

***

Halfway through the second day, Nigel came knocking. "What'd you eat? I told you to stay away from the meat and eggs, didn't I?"

"That's not helping," said Patrick. "I've had two plates of mashed potatoes in two days, and I threw the first one up. Renata has had even less. The hotel manager put a heater on the toilet so it wouldn't freeze, and it smells like death in here."

Nigel looked long and hard at Renata, who had yet to acknowledge his presence. Angus would not be pleased. "The good news is we don't go any higher than Base Camp for two weeks unless you count practice climbs. You aren't missing out yet, but your health worries me. I spoke with the hotel, told them what to feed you, and left some meds. You should be okay in a day or two. Another eleven hundred vertical feet, and you've arrived. Hike up when you're ready, and don't rush it. And for God's sake, don't forget to hydrate."

***

Twenty-four hours and two plates of mashed potatoes later, Renata and Patrick checked out. The medicine had worked, but their stomachs were still subject to flipping at any given moment. Renata vomited as the wind blew a wisp of dung smoke her way. Patrick, too, caught it and coughed until blood came up, but at least they were on their way to Base Camp.

It was bitterly cold. Having suffered food poisoning chills for three straight days, Renata donned every article of clothing she'd brought. The altitude swelled her hands and face. Patrick complained of dizziness and had to stop several times to rest. A front blew in an hour later, and it began to snow. The only positive at this altitude—the majestic panorama—

disappeared as the clouds closed in around them, and visibility fell to less than fifty feet.

Snow pelted them as they stepped onto the Khumbu Glacier and weaved their way through the rocks and ice. Great boulders, cast aside by the glacier, seemed oddly out of place. By 4 pm, they arrived at Base Camp weak, although feeling better than forty-eight hours before.

Pemba greeted them with a smile and helped them to their tent. As soon as the door was zipped, each collapsed on their sleeping bags, out of breath. Another Sherpa named Norbu brought hot tea and soup. Nigel showed up ten minutes later. "How's everyone feeling?"

"I feel like a gutted fish, but better than last time we saw you," said Patrick. Renata nodded but held back until she had the strength to speak her mind.

"Welcome to 17,600 feet," said Nigel. "Listen to this, and let it sink in. We are higher here than at any point in Europe. We're above the Alps, and yet we haven't begun to climb. That spells it out quite nicely, doesn't it? We'll be here forty days. It's all about acclimatization and weather. Stay hydrated! Headaches, nausea, and such are normal, but you must be diligent, especially since you two are already sick. There's less oxygen up here, and that makes it hard to heal. Speaking of which, how are your feet? Eighty miles in eight days can take a toll if you're not careful."

"Just one blister," said Patrick.

"I'm fine," said Renata.

"Good," Nigel continued. "Our group is eleven now that you've arrived—the three of us, seven Sherpas, and a doctor. We might see other teams, too, I'm not sure. Norbu's going to fetch you two an oxygen cylinder because you're sick. We usually wait until we're higher to start on the Os, but I'll bill Angus because he likes you. Enjoy it though, because it's expensive. One hundred and fifty dollars, a month's rent back home."

Patrick's eyes bugged at the cost. Just then, Norbu arrived with the tank and handed the mask to Renata, who fitted it over her face and twisted the valve open. Her eyes sparked to life as her body feasted. She'd only taken three breaths, but the headache was already fading.

"Give her fifteen minutes, Patrick, and then you take a turn. Keep swapping until it's gone."

"And what if I come up with another hundred and fifty bucks? Will you put it on my tab?"

"Sorry mate, it's not about the money. We don't have a post office up here, you know? Everything you see was carried up here by the Sherpas. Given what you've been through, can you imagine carrying even one?"

***

When Renata's fifteen minutes were up, she handed the mask to Patrick and went to find the bathroom. Norbu, still getting used to having a woman on the mountain, cheerfully directed her to a tent fifty yards away. Inside was a bucket and not much else. As the smell wafted, her stomach flipped again, and she vomited in the snow.

Eventually, Renata did her business but felt the lethargy return without the supplemental oxygen. Dizzy, she made her way back to the tent and flopped, out of breath. Patrick had fallen asleep, snoring within the mask. She looked at her watch and let him finish his time, but as soon as it was over, she took it back and sucked in the healing vapors until she fell asleep.

***

Renata dreamed she was drowning. The mask was still on her face, but the tank had run dry. Desperately, she tore it off, gulping for the type of air that didn't exist this high. She checked her watch: 3:39 am. Sleepless nights were the norm now. Suddenly, something groaned in the distance. Renata looked over to Patrick, who lay still. With some effort, she sat up but heard only the wind. A minute later, a loud crash echoed through camp, but Patrick still didn't move.

Renata began to pray, thanking the Orixás and Exus for allowing her safe passage and asking for their continued guidance up the mountain. For the second time in her life, she was a stranger in a strange land, but she knew her faith would see her through.

The groaning repeated itself, and Renata heard others outside. She rose to put on her boots and glanced at the thermometer. It read twenty-three degrees below zero. Fully bundled, Renata exited the tent and bumped into Tashi and Pasang as they carried food to the cooking tent. The two men stared at the first woman ever at Everest Base Camp.

"What was that noise? Did you hear it?" she asked.

The two men looked at each other, and Tashi replied. "Ice, moving. Khumbu. Never stop."

Renata was perplexed. "Thank you." The two men nodded and continued on their way. *Moving ice. That can't be good,* she thought. Nearby was a four-foot-high stack of climbing rope. She'd never seen so much in one place. Just then, she heard the ice groan again. This place was as foreign as could be for a Brazilian woman. She might as well be on another planet. Nigel touched her elbow, and she jumped.

"Sorry, love. You're up early. Feeling better?"

"I fell asleep with the oxygen on. It helped. I feel better."

"Fantastic. You're the star of this show. If you make it, we'll all look good. There's no pressure, though. I want you to be safe. By the way, if you need more oxygen, stop by my tent, but don't bring Patrick. He's a friend of the family and all, but there aren't enough Os to go around, and I don't get a bonus if he summits—but let's keep that between us, shall we?"

Renata nodded. "Did you hear the glacier?"

"Oh, yes. Haunting. I'd forgotten the sound, you know, since my first climb, but as soon as we arrived, it brought me straight back."

"What was the other noise? About an hour ago? The big crash?"

Nigel nodded his head, understanding. "That, my dear, was an avalanche. You see that cliff?"

"Is that Everest?"

"Technically, yes, but that's only the foundation. That section is called the Western Shoulder. I forget the real name because we don't climb it. La Lho, or Lho La, something. It's an avalanche factory, and unfortunately, we must pass beneath it."

Renata gazed at the high cliff, taking special note of the millions of pounds of snow freeze-blasted onto it. Nigel continued. "It's gigantic, right? Believe it or not, that's only nineteen or twenty thousand feet. Sounds crazy, doesn't it? *Only 20k.* That shoulder is as high as Mount McKinley. It dominates our field of vision, but then again, these Himalayas are all giants. The scale here is mind-blowing.

"A quick little anecdote: Years back, I visited St. Peter's Basilica at the Vatican in Rome. It's an enormous building. While I was there, I learned that Notre Dame in Paris could fit inside it. As I walked down the nave toward the altar, I stared at the ceiling four hundred feet above, every inch covered in mosaic tiles, and realized I couldn't tell I was bloody moving. I'd walked fifty yards yet had to look down to assure myself I wasn't on a treadmill. Everest makes St. Peter's feel like a dollhouse. I've learned not to trust my eyes here. One hundred yards could mean five hours when you're tired, and here, you're always tired."

"If that's not really *the* Everest, then where is it?" she asked.

"It can't be seen from this angle. It is, in effect, blocking itself. The one right here closest to us is Nuptse, the twentieth-highest mountain in the world. It's super dangerous, with lots of avalanches, and it's connected to Lhotse way up in that valley, the fourth-highest mountain, but you can't see that from here either.

"The three mountains together form a gigantic bowl that's spilling ice between them daily. We're going to climb through that Icefall beneath that Shoulder and into that bowl, then climb half of Lhotse before crossing over to Everest.

A terrible avalanche in the Icefall three years ago killed seven Sherpas. I don't mean to scare you, but I'm not joking when I say it's the most dangerous part of the climb. That and the Death Zone, of course."

Renata looked where Nigel was pointing. Both Nuptse and the western shoulder of Everest were on her right. The two giants pinched what looked like a frozen river of ice between them: the Khumbu Icefall.

Renata remembered reading about it in the library, the "loaf of bread slowly opening," full of ever-moving crevasses and leaning seracs. Renata wanted to walk to the Icefall and look into it to see if she could get her first real glimpse of Everest, but after Nigel's speech, she wondered how long it would take to get there.

"What are we doing today?" Renata asked.

"We're going to hike to the Khumbu Icefall and back. That's enough. You'll be knackered by the end. Believe it or not, love, what you're looking at is over an hour away."

Renata, having held her tongue thus far, decided now was the time to speak her mind. "Nigel, why didn't we hear all this months ago? I would have done more research on the difficult parts. I would have brought medicine for nausea, too. Who knows what else I wish I'd known."

"I do apologize, but I was swamped, and in the end, those things don't matter much. It's all about three things: acclimatizing, weather, and luck. If those three things turn in your favor, you'll summit, and it's as simple as that." Renata pondered his words as Nigel continued. "If I had to sum it up, I'd say, be prepared for the toughest test of your life. Not only will you be in danger of frostbite, but there will be times you'll take your parka off because the sun is so intense. But, hot or cold, there's never enough air to breathe."

"What's the Death Zone?" Renata asked, still peeved.

"Anything above 26,000 feet. The body doesn't get enough oxygen up there and begins to self-consume. An invisible timer starts, and you'll die if you don't get down in time."

"How much time do you have?"

"That depends on a lot of things."

"What else should I already know?" asked Renata, and Nigel could see in her eyes that she was still upset.

"There's a reason I didn't tell you, you know, but here it is: Don't think you're going to march straight up the mountain and back down, and then you're done. The first thing we do is march to Camp One on the other side of the Icefall, and then we come back here. Next, we march all the way to Camp Two at the base of Lhotse, sleep, and come back here again. Then we go to Camp Two again and sleep, then go to Camp Three, and sleep, then Camp Two, and sleep again. Shall I go on?"

Renata's eyes never left Nigel's. "Go on."

"You're feeling right shitty by then after three nights on the mountain, but the good news is, we return to Base Camp again. Feeling like a yo-yo?" Renata wished she hadn't asked but couldn't back down. "Sure, but it still would have been nice to kn—"

"Well then, next, we hike all the way to Camp Two and sleep. Then we go to Camp Three and sleep. Then Camp Four for the first time, where you'll lie awake staring at the ceiling of your tent for a few hours before getting up one more time to try and find the strength to summit."

"Is that all there is?" asked Renata, fuming.

"Of course not. After that, you must get yourself down, and that's even harder."

CHAPTER 99

THE HOUSE WITH THE POND, SANBORN, NH

Following the author Desjardins' instructions, Zé started his day alone on the road after buying three New Hampshire maps and heading north on Route 93. Aparecida and Vilma were not permitted to ride along. They'd only ruin his concentration. The Sanborn exit was an hour and a half from Boston.

As soon as Zé left the highway, his eyes relaxed, and everything took on a reddish tinge. As he turned onto Lancaster Hill Road, the feeling overtook him. Zé realized right away he was driving too fast and slowed. The dirt road was pocked with potholes, and grass grew between the tire tracks. He passed only two houses in the next two miles, his pupils dilating more and more the further he drove.

Then, there it was: the house with the pond that Desjardins had mentioned. It was painted white, with a red barn and a tower that resembled a lighthouse. For the first time since taking the turn, he could see the sky through the trees, and it was pink.

No cars were coming, so he pulled over, feeling for direction. Zé closed his eyes and focused, trying to discern whether or not this was his destination. After a moment of nothing, he put the car in gear and drove on.

Any frustration he might have felt vanished a hundred yards later when he saw a sign for Varney Road, and the sky turned maroon. He'd been right, despite Aparecida's protests. There was more magick in the world than just Macumba. Zé pressed the gas pedal. Whatever he sensed was near. With eyes pulsing and car bouncing, he clipped a tree as he rounded the final bend.

CHAPTER 100

SALEM, MASSACHUSETTS

As she arrived at work Nichi Tiffin checked the wire for any news from Mount Everest. It was far too early for anything scandalous, but it was good practice, and if there were to be a story up there, she would be first to pounce.

CHAPTER 101

THE HOUSE ON VARNEY ROAD, SANBORN, NH

Zé pulled his car over and got out. The barn was in bad shape, but whatever was calling him was inside it. Zé ran to the broken structure, his heart pounding with excitement. Once inside, the outside world was muted. The air was musty with a hint of rot, and he closed his eyes, feeling for his reason for being here. The collapsed roof made for a multitude of dark nooks, and he had to stoop to continue his search. Crawling, he found a hole disguised by shadows and fell into the crawlspace beneath.

He was blind, but his nose told him something had come here to die. Spoiled hay lay in clumps as he crept through an abandoned bed, hoping he wouldn't find whatever had once owned it foul and putrid. All the while, the energy called, pressing him forward. Webs from a century of spiders coated his face and hair. Finally, his knuckles scraped the foundation, and his fingers searched the masonry, fumbling, bleeding—arriving.

In a slot between two stones, where the mortar had crumbled, was something smooth. Perhaps it was a board or a tablet; he couldn't tell, but it warmed to his touch, and his heart leaped. Now, whatever it may be was his. With the mystery item clutched in his hand, Zé crawled back through the darkness, searching for the hole he'd fallen through, and as soon as he found it, he heard something.

***

It must be the homeowner. The man was shouting something in English, but it didn't matter. Zé would be leaving with what he had found, and the man would die for discovering him. After hiding his find in the shadows, Zé crept from the crawlspace and searched for a weapon. The barn had long since been emptied of tools, but an old plank would do nicely.

Four minutes passed as Zé hunted his prey, and when the opportunity presented itself, he struck. Within seconds, the man was dead as Zé ran to the house to look for family members. Luckily, the man was alone. Once the house was clear, Zé ran back to the barn, retrieved his find, and brought it into the light.

It was a book. *The* Book. The Book from his vision, when he passed out in the operating room in Boa Vista. Just like the vision, the cover was black, and there was nothing printed on the outside. Language would again be a problem, he knew, but he would figure it out.

CHAPTER 102

Zé knew bringing the Book back to the hotel room would be a disaster, so he found a payphone and told Aparecida he wouldn't be returning that night. He had a mess to clean up and tracks to cover, and, above all, he wanted to be alone with his new find.

Zé put the farmer's body in his rusty pickup truck and drove until he found an even more desolate turnoff. He took it as far as it would go, then gunned the engine and turned off-road as far as it would go. When the truck was hidden, Zé walked back to the house and moved his car behind the barn.

At last, Zé was alone with the Book. Excited, he sat in the living room and opened it, surprised to find that there was only one page. On it was written what looked to be a poem or a recipe. Written in the margins were symbols, and the text was either Latin or Latin-based.

Zé read it to himself, wishing he understood, but nothing happened, so he read it out loud as best he could, but still nothing. Zé looked closer, hoping to find a slit or secret pocket holding something more. He'd murdered a man for this! Frustration set in, so he put the Book down and stepped outside.

Not one car had passed since he'd been here. He wondered how long it would take for the owner to be missed. He needed a place to stay, and preferably not with Aparecida and Vilma every night. Renting an apartment in the country would be tricky, too. Foreign language speakers would be easily remembered.

Chapter 103

Everest Base Camp

Renata dreamed of her father sitting in a chair and holding a black book. She opened her eyes, and the room was red. Her dream had become a vision. Dr. Zé opened the cover to reveal a single page, on which was written *Latin*, best guess. She examined each word, searching for some clue as to where he was or what he was up to. *Where was Vilma? Aparecida?*

Renata sat up. There was no earthly reason her father should be able to invade her thoughts like this. Was he aware he was doing so?

When Zé finished looking at the book, the vision ended, and the tent's ceiling changed from red to yellow. Renata exhaled and lay down. She was shaking, and there was no way she would fall back asleep.

CHAPTER 104

THE HOUSE ON VARNEY ROAD, SANBORN, NH

Zé woke in the dead farmer's house. The first thing he did was check the windows for the police, but there were none. Satisfied, Zé returned to the Book and, much to his delight, found a surprise.

Underneath the Book were three wooden cubes that hadn't been there when he went to bed. Paranoid, Zé rechecked the windows, then picked up the cubes. Some of the faces had symbols carved into them, and some were blank. Bewildered, he opened the Book. Now, there were two pages.

Chapter 105

Everest Base Camp

Patrick slept while Renata dressed quietly, the vision of her father still vivid in her mind. She had to get out of the tent. She couldn't breathe. It was more than the altitude this time. When she was ready, she reached for the exit zipper, and there on the floor of the tent were three wooden dice.

Symbols adorned the cubes, and she knew right away that they didn't belong there. Had Zé found her? Was he coming, or was this a warning from the gods? These runes had nothing to do with Macumba. Dr. Zé was into something new, and here, high in the clouds, there was nothing she could do about it.

Chapter 106

Zé blinked twice to be sure he wasn't imagining things, trying both pages of the Book with his fingers to be sure there weren't more, then sat down to read. Again, he had no idea what the words meant, and reading without understanding was all he could do. When no more dice appeared, he decided to give it a rest and got in the car to drive back to Boston.

Now that he possessed the Book, he was more relaxed. Perhaps some English lessons would help. He'd have to put that on the to-do list. Suddenly, Zé stopped the car. Had he driven in this way? With all the excitement getting here, his memory of the drive to Varney Road was spotty. There was a turn coming up, wasn't there? Zé saw a sign for Lancaster Hill Road and vaguely remembered. All the American names sounded the same.

The more he thought about it, however, the more he remembered. The author, Desjardins, had told him the name of the road. *Yes, that's right. One turn,* if he remembered correctly. Now, where was it? When he reached the bottom of the hill, he made a left. Feeling confident he was on the right track, Zé continued as the car bounced. There had been potholes forcing him to drive slowly. This way was correct.

Through the trees, he saw the crest of a roof. It was the house Desjardins had told him about. The one featured on a TV show. Nothing about it had called to Zé on the way in, but today was different.

As his car approached, he nearly missed the driveway, which was almost entirely hidden by two maples. The asphalt, too, was beginning to sprout weeds. Did anyone live here? Zé checked his rearview mirror. He'd yet to see a car on this road. He turned in.

If he was wrong, he might be seen and remembered. Zé stroked the Book, feeling for a sign. Indeed, if it were magick, might it warn him? The Book swelled under his palm, then fell as if it were breathing.

Finalmente, algo em que posso acreditar.

Finally, something I can believe in.

Chapter 107

Everest Base Camp

Renata picked at her breakfast. Her father had ruined her appetite. The wooden dice were in her pocket, and she hadn't shared their discovery with anyone, including Patrick. Suddenly, Nigel called everyone to a mound of stones draped with prayer flags. The Sherpas were about to perform a ceremony.

"What's this?" whispered Patrick.

"Quiet, mate. It's called a Puja. They're talking to the mountain, praying for a safe climb."

Prayer flags whipped in the wind as they rubbed some flour on their faces. When it was done, the Sherpas threw more of the flour into the air, and then Nigel handed out equipment, including ice axes and climbing helmets. Renata examined hers. The initials RB were painted in white block stencil. Seeing it was surreal. She was born JM and then became RJ, but now the initials RB were her identity—one identity for each country: Brazil, the United States, and Nepal.

The group set out for the Khumbu Icefall toting twenty-pound packs, but the Sherpas carried four times as much. The sun was not quite up as they zig-zagged between ice pinnacles, and Renata again marveled at how different her life had become: as a child, she had a sloth living in her backyard. Renata heard crunching close behind and turned to look. A young Sherpa stopped dead and blushed as if caught red-handed. Suddenly, Pasang shouted something in his native tongue, and two more Sherpas burst out laughing.

"What is it?" she asked Tashi. "Am I slowing him down?"

"No, you surprise him. He want to talk, but no English."

"What does he want?"

The Sherpas spoke amongst themselves, huge smiles on their faces, looking at Patrick. Finally, Pemba broke the silence, "Nahwang is boy. Eighteen years. He thinks you're pretty."

The other three Sherpas roared with laughter. Nahwang, embarrassed, punched Tashi in the shoulder.

Renata smiled. "Tell him I said thank you."

"Patrick, Renata, wait up," Nigel called out. "Walk with me. We've got Sherpas in the Icefall setting ropes and ladders. Do you know why we use ladders?"

"To cross crevasses," said Renata.

"Well done. If I could show you a time-lapse of the Khumbu Icefall, it would look like a bucket of slush getting kicked over. The ice moves thirty to forty inches daily, but you can't see it unless something big falls over. Once we're in, we go without stopping. It's two and a half miles and two thousand vertical feet of sweaty palms.

We'll be susceptible to avalanches the whole time. Patrick, listen close. I already told some of this to Renata. See that packed ice high on the Western Shoulder? That's a hanging serac. From time to time, one of those lets go. I've seen slabs as big as buildings bury the valley. You'd think you could remedy that by hiking on the far side, but no. The spray buries everything. Sometimes, it even reaches Base Camp."

"I heard one last night," said Renata.

"Yes, but that was a small one. The valley-plastering ones, like the killer three years ago, thankfully don't happen very often."

"Are you trying to scare us?" said Patrick.

"Not a chance, lad. I'm only trying to prepare you. I don't want to lead you lambs to slaughter. I want eyes as terrified as mine watching for danger, and I want you to shag-ass through that Icefall."

By noon, everyone was tired. A half-hour later, they were panting like dogs. By two o'clock, they were utterly spent and limped back to camp, sucking wind, where they collapsed in their tents.

***

The following day was for scheduled acclimatization, but only if your last name wasn't Sherpa. Renata and Patrick once again struggled with sleep, which they knew by now was part of the game.

"Good morning, Your Highness," said Patrick, still buried in his sleeping bag. "You're the star of camp. You even have someone crushing on you. How does that make you feel?"

"I don't want the attention. Are you jealous?"

"I'm teasing. I'm so glad this is a free day. I don't even want to get up to pee."

"Me either," said Renata.

They remained motionless until 8 am when Nigel poked his head in. "Everyone all right? Feeling healthy?" Renata nodded, and Patrick gave a thumbs up. "Looks like the living dead in here. Are you coming to breakfast?"

"Ugh," said Patrick, "I'm nauseous."

"Everest without food is impossible," said Renata, taking the lead. She had to pee anyway.

***

That night, Nigel had the Sherpas build a campfire, and everyone gathered around to sip tea. "What's planned for tomorrow, Nigel?" asked Patrick.

"A practice climb on Lobuche. It's the equivalent altitude to Camp One on Everest but saves a trip through the Icefall."

"Lobuche? The town I left my guts in? I don't even want to hear that word."

"Not the town, the mountain the town is named after. The summit is 20,000 feet. It's good practice, and there's a hell of a view, weather permitting."

"Can you see Everest?" asked Renata. Chomolungma had yet to reveal herself.

"On a clear day, you can see the summit behind Nuptse."

Lurking like a shark, thought Renata.

"Drink your tea and lots of water," continued Nigel, "tomorrow will test you."

"Nigel, what do you think happened to George Mallory and Andrew Irvine?" Patrick asked.

"I wish I knew," said Nigel. "For those who don't know, Mallory and Irvine were climbers in 1924, last seen on the Northeast Ridge before clouds moved in, obscuring them from the spotters. They were never seen again."

"Not even a trace?"

"They found Irvine's ax at 28,000 feet, but that's it. There was nothing found at the summit, but Mallory had a camera with him. If it is ever found, it might prove something."

"How is it nobody can find two men on a mountain that is visited every year?" asked Renata.

"Because it's bloody huge, my dear. If you fall up there, you fall a mile-and-a-half. It's a sheer cliff on either side, almost ninety degrees in places."

Renata shuddered. "Has anyone else gone missing?"

"Uh, I'm not sure about 'missing,' per se, but ..."

Patrick cut him off. "Not all of them are missing. They're still up there. You'd have to chip them off with a—"

"That's enough, Patrick. We don't want to be disrespectful to the dead."

"I'm not trying to be disresp—"

"Let's not speak of the dead at all, shall we?" barked Nigel, and Patrick fell silent. "To answer your question, Renata, yes, there are a few souls that have not been recovered, but you have to remember that oxygen systems back then were not what they are now. Modern equipment has streamlined the climb. We've got it down to a science. Some of the first teams didn't even bring a doctor."

"Are we going to—see them?"

Nigel cringed, and Renata noticed. Had they been hiding this information from her? "I'm afraid we might, love, unless they've been buried by other climbers or covered by snow. I distinctly remember three."

"How can they be buried in ice?"

"Well, dear, mountaineers share a gentleman's code that if they can be lowered into a crevasse, then that is the honorable thing to do."

"They drop them in crevasses?

"Sometimes."

"Do they push them off the mountain, too?"

"It is considered more dignified than becoming a trail marker."

"Yet another thing I wish I'd known before I agreed to this trip," Renata barked. "I don't want to be left up there. What else are you hiding, Nigel?"

"Renata, I wasn't hiding anything, and I sincerely apologize. It will be a great thing for all women if we can get you to the top."

Renata stood, turned, and disappeared into the night.

***

Two days later, after a successful summit on Lobuche, it was time for the real deal. Nigel woke them at 4:30 am, and they marched in darkness, headlamps bobbing like fireflies on a mission. House-sized seracs loomed as they clutched fresh, red ropes set by the Sherpas. It wasn't long before they came to their first ladder, spanning a crevasse that appeared bottomless. Renata shined her light down, only to find it was far deeper than the beam would reach. Suddenly, she felt dizzy and wobbled, alerting both Sherpas. Tashi tightened his grip on her rope, but she recovered.

The route led them through shallow grooves and winding hollows, both beautiful and dangerous. At one point, they entered what looked like a frozen arena made of seracs, which the Sherpas had thankfully worked a way around.

The avalanche threat was in the back of everyone's mind, but no one said the word as they moved along, ever mindful of the time. Twilight illuminated the Khumbu, and silhouettes began to appear. Renata looked up at the hanging giants, some as big as ocean liners, frozen to the rock until the day Chomolungma decided to let them go. It was essential to make it through by 9:30 am before the sun warmed the seracs.

They climbed the last wall at 9:45 am, but there was still more than an hour's hike to Camp One. The three-sided valley lay before them, a desert made of snow. Fluctuating temperatures had shattered the ice field, leaving patterns like dried mud. The air was noticeably thinner here, and because of the nervous energy they'd expended, the short walk was torturous.

"Welcome to the Western Cwm," said Nigel.

"The Western boom?" said Patrick.

"No, Cwm. It rhymes with boom. A basin, essentially. The only way out is back the way we came."

Renata was disappointed. They were above the Icefall and still couldn't see the peak.

***

The team spent the night at a cluster of tents known as Camp One. Due to the wind hammering the ever-flapping tents, sleep was even more challenging than at Base Camp. Renata pinched the bridge of her nose, attempting to will her headache away, but it was no use. They tossed and turned, achieving no more than a weak nap when a loud cracking noise got them up for the day.

Patrick lifted his head, attempting to hear what the Sherpas were saying. Renata picked out the word *avalanche* and poked her head out in time to see a cloud of snow settling in the Icefall. A serac had let go, likely covering their way back to Base Camp. Nigel conferred with two Sherpas, who broke from the conversation and grabbed several coils of rope, heading down the mountain at double speed.

"I'm sure you heard," said Nigel. "There's been an avalanche, and they're going back to check. Hopefully, we haven't lost much in terms of rope and ladders, but in any case, be prepared. We're headed back, and it might take longer than expected."

Luckily, things were not as bad as feared. Only one ladder was buried, and about a hundred meters of rope was missing. It took longer than planned, but the team made it back to Base Camp safely.

***

On April 8, they woke for the same trek up through the Icefall, except this time, the goal was a similar cluster of tents at the Lhotse base known as Camp Two. Even with the recovery days, they were exhausted. The thought of surpassing their previous outing was daunting. Renata prayed, reminding herself that Vilma was in an even more dangerous situation.

As they entered the Icefall, they found one of the ladders squeezed by the ice and bowed to the breaking point. After the Sherpas replaced it, a serac the size of a silo cracked like a gunshot as they traveled around it. Shaken, the team pushed forward. When they left the Icefall, there were still occasional walls to scale and ladders to cross, but not nearly as often.

As noontime arrived, the sun bounced off the walls of the Cwm, turning the valley into a microwave oven. Seventy, eighty, ninety degrees; the sun beat down, and the parkas came off. Norbu broke out an industrial-sized container of zinc oxide to lather on their faces before blistering sunburn could be added to their list of ailments.

Renata, all the while, still awaited her first good look at the goddess mother of the sky, and when Chomolungma showed herself, there was no doubt who the Queen of the Valley was. She stood out in every way. Black as onyx and taller than her inferiors, Everest was a marvel. The wind at the summit roared like a jet engine, and a plume of snow ten miles long painted the sky. Renata shivered.

The dead men up there came to mind. Renata wondered how many there were, like frozen flies caught in a web. Angus' offer to save Vilma in exchange for corporate promotion was akin to a deal with the Devil. Suddenly, searing pain behind her eyes dropped her to her knees, and Patrick and Nigel scrambled to help.

"I'm dizzy," she said.

"It's bloody roasting out here," said Nigel. "Get her some water. Move quickly." Patrick did as he was told and produced a canteen. Renata drank slowly, but even the water brought on pain. "You're dehydrated. Have you been drinking like I told you?" asked Nigel.

Renata nodded slowly and continued to sip. Their faces were sunburned despite the zinc, and suddenly, it got cold again. A wind picked up and began to beat the tents into a frenzy. Renata couldn't wait for the trek back to Base Camp, where the air had more oxygen, but to do so, they'd have to get through the Icefall again.

***

Base Camp, where Renata and Patrick had once arrived sick and breathless, was now their healing sanctuary, but despite the therapy, Base Camp was utterly boring. Renata pulled out a deck of cards, and as they played, monotony got the better of her.

"You never talk about your ex-fiancée. What happened between you two?"

Patrick looked up from his cards, suddenly uncomfortable. "Where'd that come from?"

Suddenly, the room went pink, and Renata's eyes began to throb. She sat up straight. "Nothing, I'm just bored," she continued. "I couldn't wait to get down the mountain, but now that I'm here, there isn't enough to do. Tell me about Peggy."

"Ah, let's add mental anguish to my list of miseries. Why not?" Patrick chuckled, hoping to change the subject.

"Oh, come on, it's in the past. You don't have to be upset anymore. Tell me your story." Pink turned to red, and Renata was captivated.

"You want the dirt? All right, well, Peggy and I probably should never have been together. She was a summer person, and I am a winter person; exact opposites. She also had an annoying habit of bossing me around, and that included choosing where we went on our vacations."

"She liked summer, so she wanted to go to warm places, you mean?"

"Yes, and she hated climbing. I can't tell you what an ordeal it was every time I wanted to go to New Hampshire. What about you? I never get to hear about your former boyfriends."

Renata wasn't ready to let him off the hook. "Give me a break. Men hate to hear about ex-boyfriends. Tell me more about Peggy. She was your fiancée. That's all I know."

"I wish I never popped the question so I wouldn't have to call her that for the rest of my life." Patrick squirmed, put the cards down, and lay flat, staring at the ceiling of the tent. "You want to know about Peggy?" he said as if he'd sucked a lemon. "Well, Peggy would never have come here, I'll tell you that."

"What places did you travel with her?"

"France. She loved France and Europe in general. Cities, too. Almost anything that didn't have mountains. Do you know how I got to see Switzerland? From a train. It was like she was doing it to torture me."

"What about Italy? I've always wanted to see Italy."

"Yes, but another thing I disliked about Peggy was we only went to restaurants with the menus posted in English—tourist traps near all the popular attractions like the Vatican or the Colosseum. We'd wander the streets, see a menu at the door, and if she couldn't read it, she'd pass. The problem is when you see a restaurant with ten flags on the menu, the food isn't great."

"Ah, you like the authentic places where Italians eat."

"Exactly."

"Well, your way sounds better than hers." Renata's vision pulsed, and Greece came to mind. "What about Greece?"

"Yeah, we went to Greece—another hot vacation. I was not too fond of it. Not the food, the people, nothing."

"Really? I met some Greeks in Peabody, and they're very friendly."

"Not the ones I met. I mean, the people on the street were good, but ..." Patrick stopped talking.

"Who? The hotel people?"

"Renata, I never told you because it hurts to talk about, but Peggy died in Greece."

Renata dropped her cards. "But—how come you never told me?"

"Because it was the worst day of my life."

"Wow. What happened?" Renata felt a twinge of anger. He'd hidden this from her, and she was sick and tired of men and their half-truths and omissions.

"We were hiking on the edge of a caldera, a cliff, a thousand feet above the ocean. She wanted me to take a picture, and—" Patrick paused, "she slipped. Don't make me go into detail."

"She fell to her death?"

Patrick said nothing.

"Patrick, the Greeks you disliked: were they the authorities?"

Patrick nodded. "Yeah, pretty much."

"Explain it to me completely, Patrick. Peggy wanted you to take her picture, and you're holding the camera. What happened next?"

"She slipped on the gravel because she wouldn't wear the damned hiking boots I told her to, and she fell. She never listened to me! I think that's why it bothers me so much. If she'd listened, she might still be alive.

We probably wouldn't be together, but at least I wouldn't carry all this grief."

Renata thought of Patrick's Porche and all of the climbing toys he'd purchased from the ads in *Rock Climber* magazine. *What grief, Patrick?* "Is there anything else you haven't told me?"

"No. And don't act like I was hiding that from you." Patrick tossed his cards and rolled over, facing the wall of the tent.

Renata stared at his back, sickened. For a moment, she considered getting dressed and walking down the mountain, but the money was so close now. In four weeks, Oxalá willing, they'd be home, and she could pay the coyote. For now, nothing else mattered.

Chapter 108

The House with the Pond, Sanborn, NH

At first, Zé couldn't believe his good fortune. Someone had put some money into the house, as Desjardins said. It was almost too good to be true, but his nerves would not settle. Blind faith was not in his blood, yet he found himself stroking the Book's cover, finding the texture comforting. It spoke to him, or at least he thought it did.

The house with the pond seemed perfect: secluded and quiet. The front yard was three acres of hayfield surrounded by trees with a pond in the middle. As he inched up the driveway, he kept his eyes on the windows, still in disbelief that this property might be available for his use. His car was almost to the far end of the house when he looked up at the small tower that resembled a lighthouse. The first time he saw it, he mistook it as circular. Now that he was beneath it, it was clearly octagonal. It was the room from his vision.

***

Zé drove to Boston to appease Aparecida. The Book came with him, of course, but the downside to this was he'd have to share it with her. She was losing patience caring for Vilma alone. The downside was there would be no alone time with the Book, which was unbearable. Aparecida hit him up as soon as he stepped through the door.

"Where is it?" she asked.

"It's right here, but you'll have to wait."

"Why? I want to see."

"I'll show you later."

"Never in all my days did I think I'd be jealous of a book."

Zé ignored her and placed it on a shelf in the closet. "Hello, Vilma! I missed you. What have you been up to?"

"I'm bored, Pai. All we do is go to the park, but I can't speak English, so I can't talk to anybody."

"I have a friend that can get us some books from the library, and you can start learning. I think we're going to love it here once things settle down."

"When?"

"Soon, I promise."

"Why can't we come with you?"

"There's no electricity or water at the house."

"Why don't we get an apartment then?"

"It's not like the city. There's more to do here, and there are more people like us."

"Well, I haven't met anybody like us."

"It takes time, Vilma, trust me. How about we get some lunch?"

"Okay."

"Right after I shower. Give me ten minutes."

As soon as she heard the water, Aparecida opened the closet door and took out the Book. It was thin, and the text was illegible. She couldn't understand why it was so special. After five minutes, Vilma saw it too. "What's that?"

"This is the reason we're stuck in this hotel room."

Vilma looked puzzled. "Can I see?"

"Go ahead," said Aparecida.

Vilma opened it, and ran her hand over the cover. "It feels cool."

"I didn't feel anything," Aparecida replied.

Suddenly, Zé charged from the bathroom. "What do you think you're doing?" Zé grabbed Vilma by the arm and squeezed. "Don't ever touch this! You hear me? Never!" Zé pushed her aside, and Vilma fell against the wall, sobbing. Zé turned to Aparecida, "Did you take it out of the closet? Do I have to tell you again?"

Aparecida hesitated, then fired back. "Why don't you just go? Get out! Come back when you can act like a husband and father!"

***

Zé slammed the hotel room door and drove the hour-plus back to Sanborn. After a guarded approach, he parked around the side and went in. Paranoid, he searched the house, but everything was as he'd left it. As he returned to the kitchen, something caught his eye; a drinking glass full of liquid was sitting atop the Book. He picked it up and sniffed. It was drinking water.

CHAPTER 109

FIRST TREK TO CAMP THREE

On April 14, Renata and Patrick left Base Camp again, this time for Camp Three, a niche carved out of the ice of the Lhotse face at 24,000 feet. The Cwm wasn't hot today, but Renata was uneasy. Clouds obscured Everest like a monster in fog. The air was white with snow as more than a foot fell. As a result, the night at Camp Two was miserable. She didn't sleep at all.

***

Stepping from the Cwm onto the Lhotse face was like crossing a football field and continuing up into the stands. At times, the pitch was as much as fifty degrees and consisted of glare ice covered by fresh snow. The climbers had to clip to a fixed line or risk sliding to their death.

Sleep was hard to come by at Camp Three, too, and the following day, dizzy with fatigue, Renata crawled out of the tent to relieve herself. Once outside, she realized she had the view of the valley below to herself. She couldn't recall how many times they'd been through it. Was it only twice? Could that be right? It seemed like a dozen. The clouds were gone, and Everest was there as clear as day, although, from this angle, she still couldn't see the summit.

Men had the luxury of staying in the tent and urinating into a bottle, but Renata did not care to practice that trick in front of Patrick. Clipping onto a line, she maneuvered behind the tents in search of privacy. There was a pile of snow back here, remnants of the original camp carve-out, so she found a spot and did her business.

As she was zipping back up, something caught her eye: a small piece of fabric beckoning like a finger. At first, she thought it was a prayer flag buried by a storm, but upon closer inspection, she realized she was looking at a dead body.

Renata pulled her hand back as if she'd been bitten. It took a minute to decipher the dead man's position. She was looking at his leg. He'd died on his side, and as she followed it down, she found the top of his boot. The once-red snow pants had faded to pink, the result of a decade of overexposure. He looked as if the mountain was absorbing him.

A snowdrift over his leg was sobering proof. No film crew could dress a set so perfectly as time and blowing snow. The man was part of the rock, frozen yet battered by the elements, like an uncovered steak in a freezer. It would take hours to chip him out and days to carry him down. Renata thanked Oxalá for burying his face.

***

With the night at Camp Three over, the climbers trudged cautiously back down to Base Camp. Renata never mentioned the dead body to anyone, mainly because she was exhausted, and it hurt too much to talk, but the image was forever burned into her memory.

The team got some excellent news when Nigel announced they'd be taking a break from the mountain for a body-rejuvenating retreat down in Dingboche (14,500 feet) for six whole days. Despite her many aches and pains, Renata couldn't help but smile. Patrick grabbed her face and kissed her.

Once they reached Base Camp, they kept right on going, and it was strange to see the color green appear. The food was decent, and the air was oxygen-rich compared to what they were used to. Sleep, too, was a forgotten luxury. "Feeling better?" asked Patrick.

"It was nice to bathe," Renata replied, "even though it was only a sponge bath."

"This was the place we ate the bad eggs, wasn't it?"

"It was. We thought that was the end of the world."

"Wouldn't it be great if it was all over? The whole trip, I mean?"

Renata's smile faded. "Of course, it would."

"We've got five more days of rejuvenation. We'll feel better after that. Then, we'll start the summit push, and all this will be over in less than a month. Hang in there."

***

On day four of the retreat to Dingboche, Renata woke up coughing. Patrick was coughing, too, but not as severely. As always, the room smelled of charred yak dung, but this time was different. Someone had forgotten to open the flue in the common room, and more coughing could be heard throughout the hotel. With little choice, they got dressed and headed outside.

***

On the morning of April 23, the vacation in Dingboche was over. Renata packed her things and suited up. The smoky hotel had done a number on her lungs. Without thinking about dinner, she went to her tent.

"She'll be fine," said Patrick.

"That's a nasty cough," said Nigel. "Hacking all day?" Patrick nodded. "That's not good, said Nigel. "Was it the yak shite again?"

"Yes, they smoked us out of our teahouse—forgot to open the flue."

Nigel couldn't believe his ears. "The son of a bitch wanted to save a little money, and they buggered the stove. That's a new one."

"Son of a bitch? Who do you mean, Angus?" said Patrick.

"Yeah, I told him we needed better infrastructure up here, and he didn't listen. We're hoteling in unheated plywood shacks, for God's sake. Sodding millionaires. How much would it cost to get us to Base Camp healthy? Pennies, I kid you not, don't ever wonder how they got to be rich. They're the cheapest assholes on the planet."

***

Thankfully for Renata, the first day back in Base Camp was a designated rest day, and she needed it. The following day was April 25, and it was time to climb through the Icefall again. No matter how many times and how well she knew it, the fear never went away.

A third of their way through, a horrific roar echoed through the valley, and there was no way to ready themselves for what the Western Shoulder released. A bus-sized serac had detached, obliterating the trail ahead.

The Sherpas shouted, having gone into emergency mode. Nigel rushed to Pemba, whose eyes were wide with fear. The two men disappeared behind a serac for ten minutes. When Nigel reappeared, he was hanging his head. "It's Norbu. He was leading the pack, and it got him. Turn around, we're going back to Base Camp."

"Norbu is dead?" Patrick asked in disbelief. Renata couldn't comprehend the words. The man who made her last cup of tea was buried beneath tons of ice and snow.

"The other Sherpas are staying to look," said Nigel. "They found one of his boots, and it wasn't empty. Trust me, you don't want to be here." No one said a word as they marched back to Base Camp.

***

The Sherpas spent the rest of the day attempting to recover Norbu's body, so Nigel took over cooking duties and made fried potatoes with yak meat and onions. Renata managed a few bites but stuck mainly to drinking tea. By dusk, the Sherpas returned, heads hung low. The mountain had been fierce this day, and it was more than an hour before they touched their food, but when they did, they finished the whole pot. After that, no one spoke of Norbu.

The next day, Nahwang left to notify Norbu's next of kin. Aside from the lost day, the schedule called for two days of rest, so everyone hung out in their tents, mourning and drinking tea. At 4 pm, twenty-four hours after Nigel's dinner, Renata felt her first cramp and made a beeline to the toilet. As she sat, she heard retching from the next tent and soon after, voices congregating outside.

"Renata, are you almost done?" It was Patrick.

"I don't know. I'm sick again."

"I think we all are. Tashi couldn't wait and ran to the glacier. If you can, come out. If not, I may have to follow him."

Renata unzipped the door to find three pacing men. "Where's Nigel?"

"He's sick, too."

CHAPTER 110

THE HOUSE WITH THE POND, SANBORN, NH

Zé spent the afternoon in the turret reading the Book's third page. As usual, nothing happened immediately, but for the first time, he was confident something would. Only one car passed the house all day. Staring out at the field, waiting for something to happen, was relaxing, monotonous, and hypnotic at the same time.

Eventually, he fell asleep with the Book in his lap. An hour later Zé opened his eyes to realize he was dressed in different clothing: blue jeans and a plaid button-up shirt. He'd never owned such attire. *Why?* Was his sense of fashion calling attention?

Chapter 111

Everest Base Camp

Renata went to bed, but Patrick had to move closer to the toilets. With the tent all to herself, she settled in a way she hadn't been able to the entire trip. She and Patrick had been joined at the hip since the journey began, and ever since the Peggy revelation, she couldn't help but see him in a different light.

Life on Everest was as bad, if not worse than the Colombian jungle, and she despised being Angus Addison's guinea pig. Nevertheless, the summit push was coming, and the pressure was palpable—so she prayed. Renata unzipped her backpack and pulled out a small red tablecloth and several candles. She also set out snacks and two airplane bottles of whiskey as offerings. When the makeshift altar was finished, she paused, looked down at her despacho, and began to pray.

"Orixás, hear me, that I may overcome these obstacles, both human and rock. Do not allow me to die before I can help my sister. If I should die, do not leave me on this mountain. Grant that Patrick will see my plan through, but if he betrays me, I want vengeance. I pray you make this true."

***

As soon as her prayer was over, Renata unzipped her bag for a pair of fresh, long underwear to sleep in. There was no shower in her future for quite some time. Choosing the driest pair of undergarments was crucial.

But she was already dressed. *How?* Suddenly, the tent went red, and she saw her father again reading the black book. Outside his window was a sprawling field with a pond. He was not in Brazil anymore. The architecture was pure New England. Zé stood, inspecting his clothing. Renata had never seen him in such clothes. He looked like an American.

CHAPTER 112

Renata woke the following morning wondering if there would be more surprises. She felt better than most everyone in camp, Patrick for sure. It was a good thing she didn't indulge in Nigel's cooking, but her nasty cough remained. Something by her feet caught her eye. The despacho was still set up with all the candles and offerings as she'd left them. Before anyone checked on her, she packed it all away and finished getting dressed.

The sun was up, and the day was clear. Pasang was the only person outside his tent, and he didn't look well. "Good morning, Pasang. Are you sick?"

"Bad yak," he said, wagging his finger in the air. Renata offered him a Diamox pill and moved on, stopping next at Nigel's tent, where she listened in and heard him snoring. Since this was another off day, she let him rest. Finally, Renata arrived at Patrick's tent, which he shared with Phurba. Very quietly, she unzipped the doorway and peered in. Both men were awake, staring back at her like zombies.

"Did you sleep?" she asked. Patrick shook his head. "Do either of you need water or tea?" Both shook their heads and Phurba, too sick to speak, blinked his eyes that she understood as a thank you.

Patrick had eaten an entire plate of yak the night before and was so ill that Nigel ended up adding a third recovery day. They were not only missing practice but were weaker than they should be, just five days from the summit push.

***

On April 30, a New Zealand team of climbers arrived at Base Camp, wondering why everyone looked so sick. Renata had fared better than most, but Patrick resembled death warmed over. Nigel, too, had dark circles under his eyes and described himself as questionable. The Sherpas, who were also sick, had zero time to fix the route through the Icefall. Weak stomachs or not, it was time for one last up-and-down to Camp Two, no small feat even in perfect health.

"All right, everyone, gather around," said Nigel. "Pemba tells me that since I poisoned you all, we'll have to climb the route we're accustomed to, and that's not good news." He paused, searching for words. "This means

we have to walk past Norbu. There is—more than a little blood, I'm told, and it is my heartfelt recommendation that you look away as much as possible."

***

No one said a word during the hour-plus climb to the Icefall. As they made their way through, the path took a right between two seracs and continued through a fifty-meter hallway made of ice. Renata could tell things had changed. Five days meant five meters of movement, and the passage had taken on a noticeable lean.

They had to do some ducking near the end, and as they emerged, there was no mistaking the spot where Norbu died. It was evident that the Sherpas had worked hard to conceal the gruesome smear, but there was no time to complete the job. Blood was everywhere as if the missing body still fed the ever-blooming stain.

They made it to Camp Two and slept. The next day, they headed back to Base Camp, forced to pass Norbu's grave one more time.

CHAPTER 113

THE HOUSE WITH THE POND, SANBORN, NH

In the end, the incident with Vilma at the hotel made things easier. Leaving the two of them in Boston bought him time. Aparecida wanted to complain, but she started the whole thing. Despite his time away, however, Zé knew he would have to revisit the family situation soon.

Aparecida had an attitude about the Book. She wasn't ready to abandon Macumba. Zé wondered for a moment if he should bring them to see the house and kill them, but instinct told him to wait.

A glass of water and some dried beef waited for him on the kitchen counter, but he let them sit, too agitated to eat. After climbing to the turret, Zé was delighted to find a fourth page in the Book. Something must be going right, shouldn't it? His mind raced as he recited more words he couldn't understand.

Except this time, he didn't have to wait. The moment Zé finished the page, the words moved, translating themselves into Portuguese. What had once been illegible was now familiar, and he sat up straight to reread them.

"This spell, when read, will enable the believer to see the sacred writings as though written in their native tongue."

Zé flipped back to page three, the spell that had changed his clothes, and read again:

"One who reads this spell aloud will have the power to change their attire. This skill has proven valuable in instances such as shaking followers and deceiving victims. It is also used by the dead, who, on occasion, outlast their clothing. The Believer's taste in clothing comes with time."

Giddily, Zé revisited the first and second pages. He could read the whole Book now, and after a long month in the United States, it was like coming home. Now, he understood the first four pages but wondered why the decoder was on the fourth page. Perhaps it was a test of some sort. Everything had been a test up to this point. The Book was the teacher, and he was the student.

***

Programmed for survival, The Book of Shadows retooled itself as it had twice before. After fifty years in Beverly Farms, the Book was stolen and stashed beneath the barn on Varney Road. For two years, it called out, seeking a new courier, and finally, someone answered.

Claude Allemand's Book had a new apprentice, and its future depended on him. Dr. José Machado of Brazil was worthy of restarting the clan, but twelve were needed. There had been a time when Zé would be required to wait ten years for such an invitation, but desperate times called for desperate measures.

Chapter 114

Everest Base Camp

Renata grabbed Patrick's arm before he could leave the tent. "I'm nervous," she said. "My stomach feels a little better, but I don't know if it will last. And I'm going to repeat something. Tomorrow begins the most dangerous part of the trip. Do you remember our discussion about the bank account and the safe deposit box?"

Patrick nodded. "I do. Merchants Bank. But you'll be fine. You're doing better than I am."

"This is very important, Patrick. Don't take this lightly."

"I'm not! I just don't want to think about you dying, all right?"

"Tell me what you must do in case I die," said Renata, her eyes boring into his.

Patrick sighed. "Open the safe deposit box and follow the instructions."

"And what are the instructions?"

"Call the coyote and pay him so your sister can come to America. I know what you want, but do you know this guy? I mean, couldn't he take your money and run?"

Renata glared, and her adrenalin took over. "Don't even think of changing the plans. You call the coyote, and you pay him. That's all."

"I call the coyote, and I pay the money. Done."

"One more thing: where is the key to the safe deposit box?" Renata watched as the look on Patrick's face changed from frustration to embarrassment.

"I don't remember."

"It's on a small hook inside the bedroom closet above the door. Don't let me down, Patrick."

***

They woke the following day to windy darkness, tents flapping wildly, as the six climbers left Base Camp for the final ascent. The group consisted of Nigel, Renata, and Patrick, along with Pemba, Nahwang, and Pasang. The weather wasn't great but was supposed to improve, which sounded promising. Renata chose to numb her mind on this seemingly umpteenth trip through the Khumbu Icefall. She occupied her mind by pretending the sun was up, but the illusion was shattered when the spot Norbu had been crushed surprised her one more time.

It was worse than before. Everywhere Renata's headlight shone was glistening red as if a crimson avalanche had soaked the valley. When Patrick didn't flinch, she realized she was the only one witnessing the bloodbath. Her sixth sense was firing warning shots, but this trip was their only shot at the summit. Renata trudged on for Vilma's sake.

***

Renata coughed, and it hurt the center of her chest. Patrick joined in, and they hacked their lungs to Camp Two together. Nigel spoke up. "You two sound terrible! Drink some tea and get some moisture in there. Soothe those throats!" Despite the tea, the two stared at the ceiling until midnight when high winds kicked up, bending their tent poles, and they were forced to hold the walls steady until sunrise.

As the sun rose, Everest revealed itself, and Renata was spellbound. This massive obstacle was all that stood between her and Vilma's salvation. *It's a race, not just to the summit but back down the mountain,* she thought. *But I'm sick, and this air is too dry to heal me.*

The group stayed two nights at Camp Two, acclimatizing. Renata managed to nap once or twice, and Patrick drifted in and out between coughing fits. Nigel pumped them full of food and tea and let them rest, but he, too, was nursing a headache by nightfall.

***

Nigel woke the next day with a crippling migraine and was no longer able to shepherd Renata and Patrick up the mountain, so he assigned Pemba to Renata and Nahwang to Patrick, hanging back to fend for himself. Per Nigel's orders, the couple was given water breaks every fifteen minutes, whether they wanted them or not. Keeping their coughs in check was of the utmost importance.

Three-quarters of the way up the Lhotse Face, Nigel stumbled, only to be saved by the rope he'd clipped onto. Shaken, the party climbed on, but the same thing happened twenty minutes later. Pemba took custody of the senior climber, and it wasn't long before Nigel complained of poor vision. The Sherpas convened.

"Nigel, you done. Go down," said Pemba.

Nigel was in shock but didn't argue. There was no argument, for he couldn't see and was even slurring his words. "Dammit, Pemba, make sure she summits, and it's her before him if push comes to shove." Nigel threw up as the words left his lips. Everest had beaten him again.

With Nigel and Pasang out of the picture, Pemba turned up the mountain, troubled. He'd thought the excursion was all but over when the entire camp was food-poisoned, but the pressure to get Renata to the summit was becoming reckless. Pemba was young, with a family, and wanted to see them again very badly. Renata and Patrick were coughing. With any luck, they would turn back soon. What Pemba didn't know, however, was that Renata would never quit because her sister's life depended on it.

Once at Camp Three, Renata insisted on sleeping far away from the corpse she'd seen on the previous trip. Pemba consented but called to mind at least three more bodies further up the mountain. Chomolungma didn't get any easier from here on up.

***

A stiff wind howled as they left Camp Three, and it took Renata nearly twenty minutes of climbing to get warm. Pemba turned on their oxygen tanks as they continued over the blue ice, holding fast to clamps fixed to the rope.

The four continued across the Lhotse face before heading over a strip of exposed rock called the Yellow Band. Hours later, they climbed over a darker buttress called the Geneva Spur and onto the South Col of Mount Everest. For the first time, Renata stepped foot on the great mountain. Momentarily, her stomach turned, and she felt like a fly landing in a spider's web.

They arrived at Camp Four late in the afternoon on a windswept saddle-shaped strip of land that marked the beginning of the final ascent. Three tents were prepped and ready, but they used only two because Nigel and Pasang had turned back. The altitude was 26,000 feet—the beginning of the Death Zone. Their bodies would not last without supplemental oxygen from here on up.

Pemba knew the Sherpas hadn't had time to run ropes and silently prayed this would spell the end, for if they continued, he and Nahwang would be pressed into double duty, a near-impossible feat. "You cough. Is bad. No more. Tomorrow, we go down," he said.

Patrick shook his head. Pemba looked to Renata, but she, too, shook her head. He then turned to Nahwang, who, much to his surprise, looked worse than anyone. Something had happened to Nahwang in the second half of the day, and he had begun to lag. Now, it appeared he was a victim of mountain sickness.

Patrick and Renata went to their tent and began boiling snow. As they did, they shared a bottle of Robitussin, which did little to settle their diaphragms. Finally, after the sun went down, Patrick turned out the light. In three hours, they would begin the final push to the summit. The wind, as always, wailed like a banshee.

***

The alarm went off at 11 pm, the start of an eighteen-hour climbing day. Renata had once cleaned houses for sixteen hours at sea level and found that exhausting. Painfully, she rose to all fours and immediately started hacking. Patrick passed her the last swig of cough syrup, but it was several minutes before she could catch her breath. Finally, Patrick pulled out another package, this time his codeine tablets. Renata stared, wondering if it was a good idea.

"Take it," said Patrick.

Renata grabbed two pills and said a quick prayer. Forty minutes later, they were ready but wondered where Pemba and Nahwang were. The answer came when they unzipped the Sherpa tent and found Pemba tending to his fellow countryman. Nahwang's eyes bulged as he lay in his sleeping bag, his tongue lolling from his mouth.

"We go down," said Pemba. "No more. Nahwang sick."

"Get better, Nahwang! We love you, and we'll see you at camp!" said Patrick. "Should I just follow the ropes, Pemba?"

"No. You too," replied Pemba. "Down."

"Can he walk?" Renata asked.

Pemba looked to Nahwang, who nodded his head.

"Then, no. We're going up."

Pemba shook his head. "Lines not set. Not safe."

"There's plenty of rope up there," said Patrick. "We're not going down, Pemba. We're going to take our shot. Hand me the camera."

Pemba started to argue, but Patrick cut him off. "There's no way you can drag three of us, Pemba. Get Nahwang down. We're heading up." Patrick took the camera and closed the tent flap. "Good luck."

***

The stars were out, and the sky was outer space blue. A stiff wind blew over the South Col, and Renata felt she was on the moon. A wave of dizziness hit her, and she wondered if it was the pills or the altitude. It was too dark to see how high they were or how majestic the valley below was, so they took it one step at a time, not talking, scared, following their headlamps, hoping to keep the coughing at bay.

It was dark for six more hours. Patrick followed the ropes the Sherpas had set. Everything up to this point had been prepped for them. If the equipment failed now, they would have to fix it themselves. They would also have to calculate their oxygen usage in a mind-bending atmosphere. Worried, Renata tapped Patrick on the back and pulled her mask down so he could hear her. "Do you know how much oxygen we're using?"

"Four liters per minute."

"Is that too much? We have to budget, or we won't make it back down." Depriving herself of oxygen for any amount of time made it feel as if a plastic bag had been thrown over her head.

"I heard Pemba say they left some tanks at 28,000 feet," said Patrick. "Keep an eye out. While we're at it, let's dial down to three liters per minute." Patrick adjusted her regulator, then did the same for his own.

"If we get this wrong, we're in trouble. We have to be careful," said Renata, coughing. She saw stars and not the shimmering beauties of the Himalayan troposphere. She felt dizzy.

"Are you all right?"

"Let me sit for a minute."

Patrick stood over her, clearly displeased. "Things will get better when the sun rises. Let's move. Stopping in the dark is no good."

Renata knew he was right. She remembered the nights in the Darien Gap. Hope hid like a frightened child when the sun was down. The saying *it's always darkest before the dawn* was the absolute truth.

Patrick grabbed her arm, and she stood. "Are you good?" Renata nodded, and he turned up the mountain. Fifteen minutes later, Patrick grunted inside his mask.

"What is it?" she asked.

"Another body. We'll have to squeeze by." Renata's heart skipped a beat. "Look left. He's on your right."

Patrick resumed, shining his headlamp to the left, leaving the body in the dark. Renata sensed the presence as if someone was staring from a darkened room. As her turn to pass approached, she realized the body had to be crawled over.

The dead man wore a red parka and one missing glove, revealing a bone-white hand, snow drifting over and around him. His head was turned away. All Renata could make out was the eroded profile of his nose. If he weren't frozen solid, it looked as if he could stand up and join them. For reasons unknown, Renata touched him.

"What are you doing?" asked Patrick, surprised.

"I'm not sure."

"We need to continue if we don't want to join him." Renata stood, and Patrick steadied her.

***

At 3:45 am, twilight warmed the sky. Sunrise was still an hour and a half away, but they could begin to make out silhouettes and shapes below. Mountains, clouds, and slopes appeared, and it was beautiful, except for the pile of vomit Renata left behind. It felt as if she'd drunk three beers. Her worries had dissolved, even though she knew she was in danger.

When the sun peeked over the horizon, they were joined by Everest's triangular shadow over the Himalayas. The dark presence chilled Renata. *You won't intimidate me*, she thought. "Where are we?" she screamed to Patrick.

"I'm pretty sure this is The Balcony," yelled Patrick, winded.

"Is that the top?" Renata pointed to the last visible section of the pinnacle, and Patrick followed her gaze.

"I don't think so. I think that's the South Summit."

Renata wished she hadn't asked. Her plug had been pulled, and she began to doubt she'd make it. "How long until we reach the South Summit, then?" It looked close, but Renata had learned a hundred times that distance on Everest was an optical illusion. She guessed the climb would be two hours but kept it to herself.

"Nigel said it's three to five hours from Balcony to South Summit, but damned if that doesn't sound wrong. At least the sun is up."

Renata wanted to sit but knew she shouldn't. Instead, she stuck her ice ax in the snow and leaned on it like a cane. Her dizziness was more intense whenever they stopped. Even though they breathed oxygen from a tank, it was nothing like being at Base Camp. Renata tried to calculate how many hours before they were on their way back down but couldn't concentrate. "How long from here to the summit and back down to Camp Four? I'm light-headed."

"You have hypoxia. We should open your valve more. Do you need to rest?"

"No, I want to get this over with. What time will we be done?"

Patrick drew numbers in the snow with his ax. It seemed like an eternity before he arrived at an answer. "If we get to the South Summit in four hours, we should reach the true summit in five and a half, but then we have to get down, which takes three-quarters as long. Ten to thirteen hours, maybe?"

"Let's go. Ten hours is bad, but I won't make thirteen," said Renata.

***

A half-hour later, the rope they were following came to an end. "Oh, shit," said Patrick.

"What is it?" said Renata, senses dulled.

"There's no more rope. The Sherpas stopped here."

Renata's heart sank. She wasn't ready for further complications. Ropes on Everest were intended for single use, but old rope littered the mountain. There were literally miles of it, rotting in the conditions because no one had the energy to dispose of it.

Patrick spent precious time looking for a worthy replacement. Eventually, he found a blue one under the snow and pulled it to the surface. Some segments were completely encased in ice, and they sometimes had to rely solely on their ice axes, but neither was willing to quit. The going got slower the higher they went. Taking a short break, Patrick looked down. Anvil-shaped clouds had filled the valley, leaving only the tops of the surrounding mountains visible. It was, without a doubt, the most beautiful view of the trip thus far.

"Looks like carpet," said Patrick.

Renata nodded, holding her ax tight. She wanted to enjoy the view but couldn't think beyond breathing and walking. Patrick noticed and upped her oxygen to five liters per minute. That helped for a short while, but soon, she was back to feeling sick. The good news was the South Summit was within reach, so they pressed on. The bad news was they both forgot to look for Pemba's oxygen stash at 28,000 feet.

***

Renata and Patrick reached the South Summit in just over five hours. It looked, at first, to be the top of the world, but as soon as they rounded the apex, the actual summit showed itself high and behind a windy chasm.

Despite her nausea, Renata wanted to be there. The ultimate goal was 150 yards away, as the crow flies.

Between here and there was a dangerous, four-hundred-foot knife edge with giant hanging cornices carved by the wind. Some chunks were as big as motor homes and could let go at any moment. It was the worst place in the world to feel drunk, and Renata was three sheets to the wind.

The knife edge was a foot wide with a mile-plus drop on either side, and the valleys on either side were filled with the same clouds they'd seen earlier. Renata didn't know how she'd find the strength to make it across, but she'd come this far, and Vilma's salvation was within reach. On the other side of the Cornice Traverse was the Hillary Step, a forty-foot rock wall and the last obstacle before the summit.

Renata looked away, needing to take things minute by minute. *Vilma,* she repeated over and over. "Are the clouds rising?" she yelled, but not loud enough to be heard. Her head swam, followed by a feeling of euphoria. Her toes warmed, and the headache faded. It was the best she'd felt since Dingboche, yet she wasn't supposed to feel this good right now. Patrick stepped off the Second Summit and onto the knife-edge Cornice Traverse. Renata followed, for better or for worse.

***

Ninety minutes later, the Cornice Traverse and the Hillary Step were in the rearview, but Renata couldn't move her right leg. If she could only reach the summit and take the picture with Angus's banner, it would be okay to die. At least then, Patrick could pay the coyote.

"Don't sit! We're almost there, look!" said Patrick, but Renata didn't move. He grabbed her shoulders. "Get up!" She mumbled behind her oxygen mask. "Give me … a minute. I need a minute."

The wind roared, but Patrick couldn't hear. He looked to the summit. It was right there. "Let's get you clipped in," he said, but she didn't respond. "Renata!" Patrick touched her shoulder, but she didn't move. Suddenly, Patrick realized the clouds had risen to their level.

Patrick cursed out loud. Another dead lover would not play well back home, but Renata wouldn't survive whether he tried to help or not. He checked their oxygen levels. His tank was too low for his liking. Patrick cursed himself for forgetting to look for Pemba's stash.

***

Renata knew she was in trouble. To summit, she would need all her strength and all the Orixás and Exus blessings. Closing her eyes, she let her thoughts drift, searching for the part of her mind with the special gift. She remembered the last time she'd seen Vilma, right after Fernanda's disappearance.

"Juliana. Juliana, are you sleeping?"

"Almost, Vilma. I'm sorry, honey. I'm so tired." Renata said out loud inside her oxygen mask.

"Please get up, Renata. I don't like it when you're down."

"It's only for a little while, Vilma. I just need to gather my thoughts. Then, I'm going to pray, and after that, I'll feel stronger, and I can be happy again."

"I still think you should get up. You know I need you." Vilma bent and kissed Renata's cheek while stroking her hair, and it felt good. Vilma was the only thing in her life that reminded her of happy times. As she dreamt, a tear dripped from Renata's cheek and froze to the inside of her goggles.

***

With clouds surrounding them, Patrick justified his decision. *Nature makes the decisions up here, not me.* Reaching behind Renata's head, he twisted her valve closed. He was practically doing her a favor.

Patrick rolled Renata over and pulled Angus's banner from her backpack. Maybe when things settled down, it would be worth something for the millionaire to see his banner flying on top of the world's highest mountain. "Thirty minutes, Renata, and we'll see if you have the energy to help me get you down the mountain. I'll be right back."

***

Renata opened her eyes. Where was Patrick? It felt as though the energy she'd prayed for was lost in the wind. She tried to pick herself up but couldn't move. "Patrick," she gasped, but there was no air. The line between life and death was blurring. The last thing she heard was Patrick's footsteps crunching away. With her thoughts dimming, Renata decided to spend her last moment with Vilma, who stroked her hair until the candle burned out.

"It won't hurt much longer," said Vilma. "You'll be back stronger than ever."

***

The winds howled as Patrick marched the final approach to the summit. As with every stretch, the distance was deceiving and took more time than anticipated. Thoughts bounced like popcorn in his hypoxic mind. Two hundred feet should be twenty minutes: twenty up, five for pictures, and fifteen back to Renata's oxygen. Despite his delusion, a knot tightened in the pit of his stomach. Sooner or later, he'd have to answer for this.

There would be hell to pay, especially if he had pictures and she wasn't in them. Another dead sweetheart would call negative attention. Even though Everest was a thousand times deadlier than Santorini, people would talk. Would summiting and keeping it a secret be enough? *No.* He'd never be able to hold his tongue. He'd have to tell everybody she'd fallen and had given her full blessing. It was only two hundred feet, after all.

But there was no time for thinking. It was time to become the twenty-ninth person to summit Mount Everest. As long as he lived to prove it, his name would be in the record books forever. Patrick coughed hard and stumbled seventy feet from the summit, panting out of control. He pulled off his mask, which was clogged with ice, and prepared to clear it.

The winds were increasing, and the sky darkened. The clouds had enclosed the summit. Patrick had misread the weather. Those anvil-shaped clouds were beautiful from a distance but murderous in person. The absence of the Sherpas and their guidance had turned the climb into a suicide mission.

But it was too late for regrets. Ten more minutes up or down would not save his life, so Patrick pressed on. Before setting his mask, he noticed a mass of ice had formed between the hose and regulator, and his gloved hand was too bulky to knock it away. Working fast, he removed his glove, and as he did, a gust of wind caught it, hurling it over the Southwest face.

Patrick knew he was in big trouble and screamed as the cold went to work on his fingertips. It was thirty below zero: fifty below with the wind. His hand would be rock-solid in no time. The snow swirled, stinging his face. If Patrick had a chance at surviving, he'd have to turn back now. He looked up at the summit, the prayer flags flapping, so close and so untouchable.

There were no pockets in his snowsuit. Patrick tried unzipping the front to shield the hand, but it froze his neck. Thunder cracked, and Patrick knew he was powerless to the elements, shaking with fear, hand stiffening, unable to hold the rope. Visibility was near zero, but Renata and her gloves should be close.

Suddenly, the footsteps in the snow came to an end. Patrick had reached the Hillary Step, but where was Renata? He turned back, but the storm shrouded the summit. *Where was she?* He needed that glove. Come to think of it, he needed her oxygen, too.

***

Somehow, Patrick found his way to the bottom of the Hillary Step, but Renata wasn't down there either. Not only would he lose his hand, but without her oxygen, he might not survive. His hand had frozen into a club, and he was delirious.

Seven hours after descending the Hillary Step, Patrick stumbled into Camp Four and collapsed outside the tents. Luckily the New Zealanders had arrived that afternoon. One of the Kiwis heard him outside and scrambled to find oxygen. As they hooked him up, Patrick's frozen hand hit the oxygen tank, making it clang like a bell.

"He'll be losing that paw," said one climber.

Chapter 115

The House with the Pond, Sanborn, NH

Zé stared at the Book, wondering what he had just read. What he hoped would be six pages of revelation turned out to be disappointing. Once again, some of the spells seemed outdated. The ability to spot a virgin or be immune from other witchcraft might have been helpful in years gone by, but there was no use for that now, was there? Additionally, the ability to detect weapons on someone's person was something he couldn't practice on his own.

However, he did enjoy creating diversions with sounds: finally, something useful. At one point, he made it sound as if someone was hammering on the barn's roof. Growing bored, Zé killed more small animals with his mind and watched them rot in quadruple time. Why this was useful, he had no idea, and unfortunately, there was no one to ask.

As he tired, Zé drove to a payphone to call Aparecida and asked to speak with Vilma.

"Hello?" said Vilma.

"Hello, Vilma. I'm calling to apologize for our little fight the other day. The Book is old and fragile, and I lost my temper. I'm sorry."

"That's okay, Papai. When are you coming? It's boring here, and I need library books."

"Soon. I'm busy learning some new things, but I will be back shortly."

Suddenly, Aparecida stole the phone back. "When, Zé? Make it soon, or I will lose my mind!"

"I'm onto something. I can read the Book now and practice as new pages become available, so I can't leave now. Perhaps this weekend."

As Aparecida began to complain, Zé hung up, growing ever-tired of their relationship. When he arrived back at the house, a light dinner awaited him on the counter. Finally, Zé went to bed, hoping for a productive day.

CHAPTER 116

SALEM, MASSACHUSETTS

Nichi Tiffin choked on her coffee as she read the newswire. A woman named Renata Brennan had gone missing on Everest. With her editor's permission, she put her work-in-progress aside and spent the rest of the day searching for more information.

Chapter 117

Nepal

Renata's body was missing, so Nigel alerted Base Camp: every team on the mountain was to be on the lookout. Despite Nigel's urgency, however, expectations were low. Anyone who had ever set foot on Everest knew how easy it would be to lose a body. There were thousands of couloirs she could have fallen into. Like Mallory and Irvine, who had been missing for fifty years, the chances of finding her were slim and none.

***

Patrick spent a painful week in a Kathmandu hospital before flying home. His world was upside-down. His dental career was ruined, not to mention the questions he would have to answer. Despite his fatigue, Patrick couldn't sleep. The Everest experience was the opposite of what he'd imagined, and, worst of all, he didn't summit. The only silver lining was Renata had no next of kin he had to notify.

The Brennans held a dinner upon Patrick's arrival, but what had been planned as a celebration was now about damage control. Sarah gave the maid the night off, and Angus flew in, as did Nigel, to round out the party.

"All right," said Sarah. "No bullshit. What happened?"

Patrick laid his bandaged stump on the table for any sympathy it might garner. "Well, it's Everest. People die there all the time. I'm lucky to be here."

"Patrick, I'm at my wit's end! You lost your hand! You can't take over the practice! We'll have to find a buyer, which doesn't happen overnight! Your father is too old, and he should be retired. But, first and foremost, we need to get your story straight. If we don't have the right answers, we'll lose our clientele. Have you seen this? Nichi Tiffin's been busy." Sarah tossed the Tuesday edition of the *Salem Evening News* on the table: *Salem Woman Lost on Everest: Local Dentist Last to See Her*. Nobody touched the newspaper on the table as if it were poisonous.

"Two of our hygienists quit as soon as they heard, and it goes much deeper than that. We stand to lose everything." Despite his dead wife and missing hand, hearing his mother's words hit home.

"Mom, I couldn't help it. I'm disabled for crying out loud! Renata's death was a disaster for the entire team. Nigel didn't finish either!"

"Oh, please, Patrick, you made your bed. Now lie in it. We spoiled you. You don't even know right from wrong." Sarah shot a glance in Joe's direction. "You'll find something else. You're young. Maybe you can sell insurance."

"What the hell are you talking about?" grumbled Patrick.

Angus interrupted. "Patrick, take a breath. Tell us what happened up there. We need to hear it from the horse's mouth, and then we can tweak it and make it sound perfect. This story has to go away."

"What happened after Pemba and Nahwang left you at Camp Four?" asked Nigel.

"We set off on our own, and I led the way. I felt good about it, but we knew the ropes weren't fixed all the way up, so we had to make do after the Balcony." Dr. Joe nodded approval.

"That's dangerous. You shouldn't have done that," said Nigel.

"Well, that's not what went wrong. Renata didn't die because of the ropes," said Patrick.

"How can you be sure if you don't know where the body is?" asked Nigel.

Patrick wanted to answer, but no words came.

"All right, well, we've learned something already," said Nigel. "We must never mention *old ropes* in public. I'll talk to the Sherpas, and we'll have to hope the Kiwis didn't notice."

"Okay," said Angus, "we're learning. Don't mention the ropes. We don't want to spark an investigation, because those cost big money, as we all know. What happened next?"

"We were both coughing blood. Renata complained of dizziness, too, but up there, that's normal." Patrick anticipated more questions, but no one spoke. "When we made it to the top of the Hillary Step, she sat down."

"You had a right case of summit lust, didn't you?" said Nigel.

"Nigel, let him talk," said Sarah. "Patrick, stay on track. You say Renata sat down? That, to me, sounds like a warning, but finish the story. Tell us what happened, minute for minute, and don't leave out one detail."

Patrick took a deep breath. "I could see the summit like it was right there—from here to across the backyard. Renata said she'd be okay, and I figured I could take fifteen minutes to finish the climb and I could take a picture with Angus's banner and head straight back."

"Renata gave her blessing?" Sarah continued.

"Yes. Renata said she wanted to rest."

"Rest? Good Lord, Patrick, you know damned well—"

"Wait, Nigel!" said Sarah. "Go on, Patrick. Then what?"

"I opened her oxygen up a little more, then took my shot at the summit."

Nigel could no longer hold his tongue. "You damned well know the distance from the Hillary Step to the Summit and back is *not* fifteen minutes. That's forty minutes to an hour, depending on how long you linger. Plus, there was a storm brewing, am I right?"

"Nigel, it's hard to think up there. You wouldn't know."

Nigel's face turned beet red. "I swear, Patrick, the only reason you aren't laid out on that floor behind you is I don't punch the handicapped."

"Hey, hey, let's not go there," Dr. Joe interjected. "The boy had her blessing, and—"

Sarah cut him off. "Patrick, how could you be so wrong again?" A hush fell over the room. "First, there was Peggy, and we came to your rescue. Now, you get careless again because you needed to summit that mountain." Sarah's tone changed mid-sentence from angry to furious. "I can't take anymore! I'll tell you what's going to happen: any legal bills that come up will be added to what you owe."

Patrick was upset. "Good luck collecting! How much money do you think I'll make selling insurance?"

CHAPTER 118

EVEREST BASE CAMP

Pemba cooked for a Japanese group who had recently arrived at Base Camp. It was May 21, about two weeks since Renata went missing, and several teams were on the mountain in different phases of the journey. Pemba and his squad were on rotating duty, and it was his day to remain in Base Camp.

The sun went down, and Pemba was thankful to be in the kitchen. Base Camp was the easy part. It was easier to breathe, relax, and forget the recent misfortunes swirling around the mountain. However, the calm was shattered when Tashi and Phurba came huffing up to him at double speed, eyes wide.

Tashi tried to speak but couldn't. As soon as he caught his breath, the words spilled out. "We were coming back from Camp One and kept hearing footsteps and false avalanches. I said earlier that I thought the valley had a strange echo, and Phurba agreed. By the time we entered the Icefall, we were both shaking. The shadows were as black as night, even though the sun was still up."

Pemba felt the hairs stand up on the back of his neck. Superstition was a part of his heritage, even though he'd never witnessed his entire life. When the chill passed, he gave his orders. "You boys are delirious. Grab some tea, get some rest, and don't scare the other climbers with your story."

CHAPTER 119

SALEM, MASSACHUSETTS

On the Friday after the emergency meeting, Patrick caught himself daydreaming about Renata's safety deposit box. Although it conjured bad memories, he owed it to her to fulfill her final wishes—even though there wasn't enough money to pay for them.

Patrick wondered if his mother was exaggerating about the negative buzz in town. Nobody read the *Salem Evening News*, did they? He'd always been a *Boston Globe* reader, himself. Would people recognize him at Renata's bank? He'd been there once, but the population of Salem, Peabody, Beverly, and Danvers combined was nearly one hundred thousand.

Thankfully, nobody batted an eyelash when he walked through the lobby. Signing in was easy, and he produced the key without hesitation. Before opening the box, he settled into the private room and reflected.

Whatever was in there was the product of Renata's sweat and elbow grease. She'd done it the hard way, the honest way, and was to be commended. *God rest her soul.* Patrick removed the plastic cover and gasped. It took him ten minutes to count one-handed. Renata had saved more than seven thousand dollars.

Along with the cash was a handwritten note dated February 28, just before their trip to Kathmandu. Staring at her handwriting was surreal.

'Patrick here is $7,255 toward saving Vilma. If you're reading this, things went as I'd feared, and I am unable to do this work. If I failed, I imagine Angus would not pay. If this is the case, I leave it to you to make up the difference somehow, some way. Use your influence and friendship with Angus or your parents to save Vilma, but only borrow the money! If they do it their way, Vilma will die.

The coyote's name is Lobo, and his phone number is 011 55 (56) 5209 4711. The price is twenty-thousand dollars, but that fee is only valid until July 1. Call him as soon as you have the money. My friend Ana and her husband, Paulo, live in Peabody and have agreed to take custody of Vilma. Ana's phone number is written below. Don't do anything but wire Lobo the money. Angus should at least loan it to you. I know you can do it. Please, save my sister's life."

Patrick sat back, feeling the codeine kick in, and let the note fall to the table. He needed thirteen thousand to help her, but his career was over. Angus would never pay, knowing, as he did, all about the Brennan Dental crisis. Patrick stared at the cash in a daze and began to rationalize. Renata didn't know he lost his hand. Things were different now, and this new set of circumstances changed everything.

Patrick savored the dulling of the pain as the codeine coursed through his veins, and he realized he was in no position to make a decision. With his good hand, he put the money back in the box and signed out.

Chapter 120

Beverly, Massachusetts

Two more Brennan Dental employees quit the following week. The *Salem Evening News* ran another Nichi Tiffin article entitled "Is Mountain Climbing a Selfish Sport?" and revisited Renata's ordeal. Patrick's name was all over the story, albeit cleverly enough to sidestep a libel suit.

Dr. Joe did his best to settle things at work by setting his retirement date back indefinitely while Patrick healed in private, temporarily living with his parents, waiting for the story to die. One night, Patrick had a nightmare. He dreamed he was back on the mountain, climbing down into one of the valleys where he found Renata's body. He tried to pick her up by the leg, but the whole corpse came with it, frozen and unbending.

Patrick woke with a start, sweating. His stump hurt. Hopefully, it was time for another pill, not that he was following the doctor's orders anyway. At 8 am, Sarah came in to wake him.

"Get up! Your father needs you. We have another quitter: no-call, no-show. They're jumping ship! It's just him and the new girl right now. Two patients are waiting."

"Mom, no! I had a dream—about Renata. Besides, how can I?"

"The business needs you. You'll work in the back. Your one hand will have to buy your father some time. Go through the back door."

Groggy, Patrick got up and showered. As soon as he got to the office, he let himself in the back door and changed clothes. Then, he found his father working in the first treatment room. Dr. Joe, noticing him at the door, excused himself and met Patrick in the hallway.

"I'm going to send you Mr. Watkins. You worked on him last time, and he's been coming here forever. So, get him started, and I'll be with you in ten minutes. Go ahead to Room Two and wait. I'll bring him in."

"But Dad, what—"

"Just get him prepped and talk to him. I'm running ragged!"

Patrick rubbed his stump and re-familiarized himself with the set-up. He hadn't been in this room in over three months. A minute later, the door opened again, and he heard his father in the hallway, making small talk.

"All right, we've got you in Room Two today, Mel, and I think you'll be in good hands with this fine young gentleman. You remember Patrick, correct?"

"Mr. Watkins! Good to see you again," said Patrick. "Have a seat right here. Has anything changed since your last visit?" Melvin Watkins stood in the doorway, staring at Patrick's stump. "Mr. Watkins?"

Another second passed before the older man spoke. "Oh, hell ... I can't do this. I'm sorry, Joe, but it's just not right." Neither of the Brennans had time to react before Mel Watkins left the building for the last time.

Chapter 121

Everest Base Camp

The day after Tashi and Phurba shared their superstitions with Pemba, the Italian team made its way down the mountain and into Base Camp. All anyone could talk about was the bad luck they'd had. Three climbers suffered altitude sickness, and all hands were needed to carry their fellow countrymen down the mountain. Three years of fundraising and training went down the drain.

Suddenly, Phurba began speaking rapidly, and Pemba spoke in his native tongue. "Stop! Do not share your superstitions. We'll talk later."

"I don't want to talk later. I want to go home," said Phurba.

"You won't get your bonus. And don't forget, the Japanese are coming. You won't see any of their money either."

"I'm sorry, Pemba, I can't stay." Phurba marched off, and the Italian team wondered what happened. Now, Pemba had a staffing problem. Thinking fast, he ran to catch up with Phurba.

"Send Lobsang when you get to Dingboche. And don't say a word about what you think might be happening. Some of us still want to work."

Chapter 122

The House with the Pond, Sanborn, NH

Zé stayed in Sanborn that night without calling Aparecida. He wanted to be on the scene when the next page in the Book appeared, and it was risky to be seen at a payphone. He shuddered to think how different things would be without this miraculous house, a true gift from the Book.

No additional pages appeared for the rest of the day, so he practiced changing clothes and making wooden runes until he could do it with his eyes closed. Then, when it was time to sleep, he went upstairs and chose the sunniest bedroom so he would wake early.

Much to his delight, six new pages waited for him the following day. Zé could barely contain himself. He would not be returning to Boston any time soon.

Chapter 123

Salem, Massachusetts

Patrick moved back to his townhouse, preferring the unpleasant memories of Renata to another minute of his mother's nagging. He'd been there only once since the Everest trip, but now that his mother was on the rampage, it was the only choice. As soon as he stepped inside, the atmosphere enveloped him. The apartment smelled of Renata and her collection of perfumes and soaps.

Patrick grabbed a beer from the fridge, opened it, and sat down, hoping to settle his nerves, flipping the beer cap over and over in his remaining hand. At least he wasn't heartbroken. He'd thought he'd miss her more, but there was so much going on. Maybe he would if everyone would just leave him alone.

When the beer started working, his thoughts turned to Everest. When he got right down to it, he was miserable he hadn't summited. Patrick took another swig and thought about watching television, then quit on the idea. Getting up to change channels was too tedious, and the silence, for now, agreed with him. Finding no comfort, he pulled Renata's lace throw over him and closed his eyes.

Sometime later, he heard a sound. *Knock—knock—knock—* Patrick opened his eyes and sat up, trying to remember why he was on the couch. The lights were off, and he couldn't recall getting up to flick the switch. As he shook the cobwebs, the knocking started again, and he turned his head.

There was a woman by the door. Or was he seeing things? Patrick could make out the shape of a dress in the ambient light. Whoever wore it lurched forward, and Patrick's heart began to pound. Every time her right foot hit the floor, it made a noise like bone on wood. Patrick squinted. Her face was in the shadows. Her eye sockets were dark, and she had concave cheeks. She was morbidly gaunt.

Like a puppet on strings, she hobbled her way to the living room and found a seat on the opposite couch in front of Patrick, who was trying to convince himself he had taken too much codeine and couldn't remember doing so. Testing his sanity, Patrick spoke. "Who are you?"

"My name is Fernanda. I'm your reminder."

Patrick jumped, not expecting to hear a voice at all, never mind one with a Brazilian accent. "Reminder?" Patrick leaned forward and stared. *Her eyes were missing.* "You're not real," he whispered.

Fernanda smirked, but the skin didn't stretch correctly, and the corner of her mouth wouldn't close. "You remember your promise, don't you?"

"Did Renata send you? There isn't any money. I'm not a dentist anymore!" Patrick held up his stump as if it were a good excuse.

Fernanda leaned in, and a drop of blood squeezed itself from the stitches in her eye socket. "You can find the money. You promised." Fernanda stood up and limped to the front door. "Don't make me come back."

"Tell Renata I'll work on it," said Patrick. Fernanda turned and disappeared into the darkness. Patrick didn't hear the door open and spent the rest of the night wondering if she ever left.

***

The phone rang early. It was Patrick's mother. "We're covered at the practice today, so stay home, but there's bad news. Your damned story is in the newspaper again. The tenants at the apartment Renata lived in have started a candlelight vigil, and an *Evening News* reporter noticed them while driving by. At this rate, the Boston TV stations will pick it up, and our goose will be cooked. Come over tonight. We need to talk."

Patrick's eyes searched the room, praying they wouldn't find the ghastly woman that haunted his evening. Thankfully, he was alone. "Can't we just talk on the phone? I was just—"

"No. Face-to-face is better," said Sarah. "Be here by seven."

Patrick rolled his eyes, dreading the occasion. They hung up, and he rubbed his temples, wondering how everything had gone bad so fast.

Knock—knock—knock—

Patrick wasn't sure if he'd heard the sound again or just imagined it. With great hesitation, he got out of bed to check the living room. Thankfully, Fernanda wasn't there. Overwhelmed, Patrick collapsed against the wall and began to cry, wondering if there was any way out of his mess.

If last night really happened, he'd have to find thirteen thousand dollars. The way his mother was talking, he would owe them for the rest of his life. He'd have to beg a bank for money, and they would secure his savings account if he were even deemed worthy of a loan. Maybe he should wait one more day to call the coyote to see what his mother was going to say first.

***

"The money's not coming in, Patrick. People who owe us aren't paying, and appointments are canceling left and right. We wouldn't need you, even if we wanted you, so here's what's going to happen. I'm sixty-two, and I'm tired. Your father is tired too. He's making mistakes on the job. We built up this practice with the hope of one day selling it to you, but all we got in return are your damned newspaper articles."

"I didn't kill Renata, Mom! She's not the first to die up there, and she won't be the last!"

"Oh, Patrick. Don't talk to me like I'm stupid. You left an unconscious girl on the highest point on Earth. Obviously, she fell, and where were you? You were trying to reach the summit! The party is over. We're getting out." Dr. Joe said nothing.

"What do you mean you're getting out?" asked Patrick.

"We're selling the practice. We wanted to sell it to you, but that ship has sailed. Angus is right. If we wait, there won't be anything left to sell. I'm calling around tomorrow."

"But, I won't have a job. What am I going to do?"

"You'll get a loan. We'll help if we can, but it depends if we find a buyer. You'll live off the loan until you transition your career. Teaching. Administration. Sales. Take your pick."

Patrick's jaw dropped. None of those jobs paid even close to being a dentist. This meeting was harsher than he'd expected. Boiling mad, he stood up and walked out. On the way home, he bloodied his knuckles on his dashboard.

***

Patrick almost stopped at a bar but thought better of it. The Fernanda *dream,* for lack of a better term, was still vivid, and it wouldn't be wise to go home drunk. Still, his anger made it impossible to close his eyes. His mother was the bad guy, but his father had pissed him off too.

251

Dr. Joe hadn't said a word during her rant. Another loan? Patrick was still paying for college—and Greece. He'd better talk to the bank while there was still a practice to attach his name to. Before that, however, he'd better call the coyote, and he'd better do it soon.

***

Patrick stared at the phone while arranging Renata's notes and making a few of his own. Twenty thousand dollars was a ton of money. He could have bought almost three Porsches with that kind of cash, not that he would now.

It couldn't be twenty thousand bucks to smuggle a kid across the border. *No way.* Renata had said something about special circumstances and her father, and it was life-threatening, but Patrick couldn't recall hearing one great reason why it was so pricy. Special circumstances or not, twenty thousand was ten times the going coyote rate, or at least according to the redneck he struck up a conversation with at the bar.

When Patrick bought his first convertible, he talked the salesman down a thousand bucks. The trick was to make the other guy blink first. Then, if need be, increase the offer in small increments, letting them know you're still open to deal. Patrick dialed, and someone picked up on the other end.

"Hello?" said Patrick, unsure if he was connected.

"What's the code?"

"Uh, 'Lobo'?"

"Okay, gringo, are you ready for transfer instructions? I will have them mailed."

"You have my address?"

"We have your address. We have everything but the money. You do your thing, and we go to work."

"And where will the package be delivered?" Patrick asked.

"That's not your problem."

Good, thought Patrick. "Uh, one more question. Since I won't know if you've lived up to your end of the bargain, how about we say fifteen in cash and call it a day?"

Patrick heard a *click,* and when the line went dead, his heart almost stopped. In shock, Patrick redialed, but it was busy. He tried for the rest of the day with the same result. The following day, he tried again, but the line was disconnected.

***

For the next two days, Patrick kept to himself, drinking. He drank for his failures on the mountain and for self-pity, disguised as sympathy for Vilma. Lobo's line was dead, and he had no Plan B. Sarah called on Monday morning to see what he was up to and reminded him that he should be securing a loan.

Patrick sat on the couch with a beer close by, twirling the safe deposit box key on his index finger. There was no home for Renata's money anymore, and the way things were going, he might need it. Patrick ran to the bathroom, gargled away the taste of alcohol, and grabbed his keys. It was time to go to the bank.

***

As Patrick returned to his parking lot with Renata's money, Nichi Tiffin stepped out of her car. "Hello, Patrick. I'm here to give you a shot at clearing your name. Give me an interview. Tell Salem your side of the story. You're taking a beating, and so are your parents."

Patrick looked up, shocked to see his ex in his parking lot. He was glad he'd stopped at McDonald's on his way home, not only for the hamburger but also for the brown paper bag to hide the money in. Patrick stiffened.

"I guess your restraining order expired? Maybe it's time I got one," he said.

"I'm not here to break your windshield, Patrick. I'm here to offer you a chance to explain what happened. Maybe it'll make those candlelight vigils go away."

"Oh, I'm sure you'd portray me in a good light, Nichi. Leave me alone. I'm not walking into your ambush."

***

The phone rang, and Patrick knew he'd better answer it. The world was burning in his mother's eyes, and she would show up at his door if he didn't pick up.

"Patrick, those vigil people from the Peabody apartment complex showed up at our office today. They've moved to in front of the practice! We've had three of them outside all day, just off-property. The police said they weren't doing anything illegal and couldn't get rid of them."

"You're kidding me," said Patrick, unwilling to share the news of his parking lot encounter with Nichi Tiffin.

Sarah continued. "That's going to scare buyers away!"

"How about the appointments?"

"Not good. One dead girl was bad enough. Two, and people want nothing to do with us."

Chapter 124

Everest Base Camp

Despite Pemba's attempts to calm things down, the Sherpas' superstitions had gone wild. The mountain was alive with rumors. Frustrated, Pemba went to bed but was awakened after midnight by a glow on the ceiling. He blinked twice, to be sure, before sitting up.

At his feet were two burning candles sitting on a handkerchief. Pemba drew back. Between the candles was something that should not be there, but was. He recognized it by the initials he had spray-painted nearly two months ago: *R.B.*

It was Renata's climbing helmet.

***

Pemba kept Renata's climbing helmet to himself, but somehow, the other Sherpas knew something happened. The Japanese, however, didn't care. They'd paid big money to be there, and their only worry was the support staff's frame of mind. On the morning of May 26, four Japanese climbers, along with Tensing and Pasang, set off for the Khumbu Icefall, leaving Pemba, a Swiss group, and their Sherpas in Base Camp.

Eight hours later, another deathly rumble came from the direction of the Icefall. A powder cloud rose high in the sky, blotting out the sun, and for a moment, Pemba thought the runout would reach their tents, but thankfully, it stopped short.

Pemba's first concern was whether the climbers were safe, but the timing didn't look promising. Pemba continued to pray as he suited up, expecting the worst. Four hours later, they found a ladder missing. The sun was low, and shadows had lengthened. They would run out of daylight very soon.

As darkness fell, the group turned back, and Pemba sent one of the Swiss team's Sherpas down to Dingboche for more help. Tomorrow, they would return to look for bodies. Seracs groaned in chorus as Pemba, last in line, left the Icefall, and a chill ran down his spine. Pemba turned, expecting to see Renata, but there were only shadows. In fear, he backed the rest of the way down.

CHAPTER 125

SALEM, MASSACHUSETTS

Patrick picked up a bottle of bourbon on the way home, in a state of shock at how fast his life was unraveling. In despair, he drank straight from the bottle and cursed himself for flushing the codeine. Quitting cold turkey had never worked for him and he should have remembered that. When the pizza arrived, Patrick fumbled in his wallet for far too long and dropped the cash, causing the delivery driver to pick up the bills off the floor.

"Sorry, man, keep the changsh," Patrick slurred before closing the door.

"Wait, you didn't give me enough," complained the driver.

"Oh, yeah, I thought the five was a ten. Waitaminnit." Patrick handed over the correct amount sans tip.

The delivery man had had enough. "Enjoy the rest of your Tuesday."

Patrick closed the door, oblivious to the man's dig. Two hours later, the whiskey was gone, as well as two beers from the fridge, so Patrick went to bed. At 1 am, he woke up with a full bladder but procrastinated getting up to pee. As soon as he opened his eyes, he could feel the first hint of tomorrow's hangover.

Despite the head pain, his bladder hurt more, and his first step was shaky. Righting himself with an awkward lurch, he stumbled toward the glow of the bathroom night light. On the way there, something squished between his toes.

Blood trickled down Fernanda's torso to a puddle by her foot, and a band of light from between the curtains drew a line down one of her eye sockets. She'd been watching him sleep. Patrick screamed.

"Ah! Leave me alone!"

"There's still time. Renata doesn't know yet."

"What are you talking about?"

"She's still sleeping, but she'll wake soon. Do as you promised, and then give her a proper funeral."

"Funeral? Nobody knows where she is!"

"People are dying."

"Who's dying?"

"Lots of people, including your parents. But you can still save some of your Sherpa friends."

"My parents? I just saw my parents. What are you talking about?"

Fernanda grinned. "I just saw them, too."

"What did you do?" Patrick asked, eyes wide.

"It looks like a murder-suicide. You'll still be able to travel."

***

Patrick, nauseous, gripped the steering wheel as he drove to Beverly. He hadn't called the police. Instead, he spent seven hours in his apartment, vomiting and attempting to sober up. Now, on his way to discover their bodies, this trip over the bridge felt like it might be his last.

Mr. Bloomstein, the neighbor, noticed him drive up, and that was a good thing. Now, the man could vouch that Patrick's car wasn't there all night. Patrick forced a smile as he waved, knowing he would have to show a markedly different mood two minutes later when he came running from the house.

Patrick turned the key, wondering what he might be walking into. The living room and kitchen were empty. *Pills,* he thought. Hopefully, they'd overdosed, and one had strangled the other. *Fingers crossed for an overdose and a strangling, the most demented best-case scenario in history.* He found them in the bedroom.

It appeared Sarah had been sitting up in bed, but now her body was slumped to her left, with the path between the buckshot holes and her bloody corpse connected by an arching, crimson smear. Dr. Joe was much closer to the door and twice as messy. Ironically, the gun had fallen—or had been placed—perfectly upright against the bed. Patrick lurched, vomiting next to his father's remains, an unintended touch of realism for the police.

Patrick dialed, practicing surprise in his voice. Then, when the performance was over and the police were on their way, he called Nigel.

"Nigel, it's Patrick. I ..."

"Patrick! How are—?"

"Not good, Nigel. Not good at all. My parents are dead!" "The police are on their way. It looks bad. It looks—"

"Dead?! Good lord, what's happened?"

"I came to visit this morning and found—my father's shotgun."

"Shotgun?!"

"Can you come, Nigel? And tell Angus. There will be a funeral. Two funerals. I don't know how this works ..."

"My God. I'm so sorry, Patrick. Let me get off. I've got bookings to make. I'll be there by morning."

They hung up, and Patrick burst into tears again, but not for his parents.

***

After a long, noisy day full of police and news vehicles parked along the street, Patrick went back to his Salem apartment and pulled the shades, half-expecting Nichi Tiffin to show up. But she wouldn't, would she? Surely, there was a grace period for mourning, especially since he wasn't a suspect.

Patrick wanted a drink, but his stomach wasn't having it. Instead, he turned on the television, and then the phone rang. *Please don't be another reporter.*

"Patrick," the voice was distant, and he detected an accent.

"Pemba? Is that you?"

"Yes. Patrick, come back. Make peace."

Patrick sighed at the voice of reason halfway around the world. "Make peace with Chomolungma?" Patrick asked, hoping against hope that Pemba's answer would be *yes.*

"No, with Renata. Mountain is unsafe. Norbu, Tensing, four Japanese dead, Tashi and Lobsang missing. Chomolungma is closed now. You come to Base Camp for puja ceremony."

Patrick had never had faith in anything, but his belief system had become as tattered as a prayer flag. "Pemba, have you seen Renata?"

"We talk when you come, but come soon."

CHAPTER 126

THE HOUSE WITH THE POND, SANBORN, NH

As soon as Zé opened his eyes, he picked up the Book and found one new page. He'd already decided that if it were as lackluster as the previous six pages had been, he'd give it just an hour of his time. He had to head back to Boston to appease the family.

It turned out to be a fantastic spell—the ability to call objects to his hand. Zé started with an acorn, placed it on the counter, and willed it to his palm. After several trials, he determined he could not see the acorn move, like a sleight-of-hand trick, so he switched things up and experimented with an old hatchet he'd found in the barn.

Two hours later, Zé realized he didn't have to look at the object for the trick to work. If he knew where the hatchet was, he could call it. With all this excitement, Zé blew off his Boston plans and practiced all day. Before long, he could call objects through walls, doors, and windows without breaking anything.

CHAPTER 127

BEVERLY, MASSACHUSETTS

Both Nigel and Angus were there by noon on June 1, and neither could fathom what had happened.

"I don't know," said Patrick. "Maybe it's because of the business? Dad was supposed to retire, and Mom was extra agitated because of the bad press. Everything they'd built was slipping away. There are even protestors in front of the office. People Renata used to live with." No one said a word, all parties fully aware of the mess Patrick had created.

"Is there anything we can do?" asked Angus.

Patrick thought before answering. "I feel bad for my parents, but I didn't kill Renata—or Peggy. It was all just a ton of bad luck."

Angus considered his words carefully. "Patrick, Renata never wanted to climb Everest, am I right? She needed the money. What was she saving for?"

"She—wanted to bring her sister here, to save her from her father, or something like that. It had cost her ten grand to come here, and she was trying to save double that for the sister."

"Twenty thousand? That's an insane amount of money. Why didn't you tell me?"

"She wouldn't let me! She knew all about Greece and how you got involved. She said the more people involved, the more likely her sister would be killed. Her father was dangerous or something like that."

"Why didn't you loan her the money?"

"Angus, I'm up to my eyeballs in debt. I don't have twenty grand kicking around!"

"We're talking about your wife's sister! I'm upset you didn't think you could trust me with this."

"Yeah, well, sorry, Angus. I'm having trouble pleasing just about everyone."

"Renata was trying to save twenty grand by cleaning houses?"

"Yeah, and she'd saved seven thousand. Three of it was from McKinley, but she was a hard worker."

"Seven thousand! Wow! You could have borrowed it from me and said it was from you! How much money do you have in the bank?"

"I had about four thousand at the time."

"So, you had four thousand, Renata had seven thousand, and—you're driving a Porsche?"

Patrick shrugged his shoulders. "I get what you're saying."

"I offered the both of you twenty thousand. How were you going to split the money?"

"I was going to give it all to her," Patrick lied.

"I was hoping you'd say that. Anyway, what's done is done. What's the next step?"

"I'm pretty sure the practice is going to go bust before I can sell it," said Patrick. "Half the city is going to think I killed my parents, even though the evidence proves otherwise. This town doesn't want me here anymore. Maybe I'll sell everything and move to Colorado, but first, I have to go back to Base Camp. Pemba called me. Nigel, did you give him my number?"

"I did, mate, but it's just the Sherpas and their superstitions. What did Pemba say?"

"He said people are dying, and he wants me to go there and pray to restore peace for him and the Sherpas."

"Everyone knows what they're in for when they set foot on Everest, Sherpas included," said Nigel. "You've had enough death to last a while. Take some time off. Grieve for crying out loud. Get your life in order."

"Actually, I thought it might be cathartic," said Patrick. "My life is upside down. Maybe I could use some religion."

"You're not going to try and climb it, are you? Not one-handed!"

"No climbing. The mountain is closed. I just need to take a walk—for myself, Pemba, and the rest of the Sherpas. I owe them. Nigel, will you look into it for me? Hell, I'll spin all the prayer wheels on the way up."

Angus managed a smirk, and Nigel smiled, but neither man knew how serious Patrick was. "I will look into it. Are the police okay with you leaving town?"

"I think I'll be okay to travel, and I can worry about the estate when I get back. Until then, I'll leave it as collateral if that's what they want. I just need a break from Beverly."

***

The funeral for Patrick's parents was two days later, and, despite the gossip around town, he insisted on burying them together. Many readers of the *Salem Evening News* immediately labeled it as an unintentional admission of guilt on Patrick's part, even though forensic evidence showed otherwise. With no reason to detain him, the police granted his request to leave town.

"Call me when you get to Kathmandu," said Angus. "Let me know you've arrived safely."

Patrick hugged him just as he spotted Nichi Tiffin nearby. "Angus, I have to leave quickly before that reporter gets in my face. I dated her in high school, and she hates my guts."

As Patrick slipped through the crowd, Angus shook his head. Patrick was a bad egg. Hopefully, he wouldn't come asking for any more favors, and their paths would never cross again.

***

Patrick unlocked the office door for the last time. It was early morning, and he'd planned it this way to get things done before the protestors arrived. The first thing he did was find a Magic Marker to scribble "PRACTICE PERMANENTLY CLOSED" on a sheet of paper and taped it to the window.

With a sigh, Patrick turned to look at the office he'd grown up knowing. It was supposed to become his, but now it was gone. Reaching down, he unplugged everything from the walls and drew the shades tight. He did the same in the back office, then paused to wonder if it even mattered.

On his way out, he poked his head into Room Two, perennially the practice's busiest. As he reached for the light switch, something caught his eye: a string of prayer flags bouncing in a phantom breeze. From the opposite side of the dental chair protruded two legs, one footless and wrapped in a bloodstained ball of gauze. Suddenly, the wind exploded.

"Tell her I'm coming!" Patrick yelled and backed away. Cabinets emptied their contents, bouncing off walls and breaking fixtures. Patrick shielded his face and ran, not bothering to lock the back door.

Chapter 128

Bristol, England

Nigel spent his day making phone calls and setting the table for Patrick, which was much easier this time because there was only one person and no permits. When Patrick's plane was in the air, Nigel relaxed in his library.

Ever since the double funeral, he'd suffered insomnia, but it was different this time. It was an uncomfortable, overcaffeinated feeling, which sabotaged not only his nights but his days as well. Nigel took a long sip of tea, hoping this cup might do the trick, but disappointingly, his hands continued to shake.

Frustrated, he set his cup down and browsed the walls for a book. Reading had defeated insomnia countless times, and ten pages of a dull novel might do the trick. Too lazy to stand, Nigel leaned forward and squinted at the blurry spines, but as he did, he heard something.

Knock—knock—knock.

Nigel looked to the doorway. The hallway was dark, and the sound had come from that direction. Fernanda staggered into the room.

"Dear God! Who are you?" exclaimed Nigel. The woman was covered in blood, and her dress was askew, the apparent victim of what must have been a horrible accident. Nigel gasped. Her eyes were missing. Fernanda said nothing but stopped at the fireplace and picked up an andiron.

"Who are you and what are you doing?" The woman wouldn't respond. Thinking fast, Nigel charged, but Fernanda was ready and raised the fire poker, pushing it through his ribcage and into his heart.

As she lowered him to the floor, Fernanda answered his questions. "My name is Fernanda, and I'm here to make sure you never get anyone else killed."

Chapter 129

Kathmandu, Nepal

Patrick touched down in Kathmandu, feeling slightly better. There was a certain peace to having decided one's path. Here, most of his problems were thousands of miles away. He knew he might never return, but there wasn't much to return to. In Salem, he was ruined, a fate worse than death.

As Nigel had promised, Patrick found a large suitcase waiting for him at the hotel, including everything needed to hike to Base Camp. As soon as he saw a telephone, Patrick called Angus. It was late back in the States, and Angus sounded as if he'd been sleeping.

"Sorry, Angus. You told me to call when I landed. I just wanted you to know I'm here, and I'm taking the plane to Lukla tomorrow." Patrick heard a female voice in the background.

"Who's calling?" the voice said.

"It's Patrick," said Angus. "The Everest kid. Sorry, Patrick, go ahead."

"Sorry, I woke your wife."

"Don't worry about it. How are you feeling?"

"I feel numb."

"Well, that sounds about right. I feel the same if that helps. I'm still in shock."

"I know what you mean. There are no words. Well, I'm here, and I'm safe, so I'll let you go. Thanks for everything, Angus."

"Okay, Patrick, thanks for calling, and be careful."

"Will do."

***

Angus hung up, and Stacy draped her arm over his chest, which was a surprise. They'd fought again when he'd got home, and it seemed another divorce was on the horizon. Affection was the last thing he expected after the horrible things they'd said to one another, but sex was better than fighting, so he went with it.

"Hey, sorry about earlier," said Angus. Stacy said nothing but tapped his chest twice. "That was Patrick Brennan, the kid who just lost his parents. He's just landed in Kathmandu. Doing some soul-searching, I suppose. Do you remember?"

"I do. Do you know why his father did that?"

"No. I knew Joe for decades and never saw it coming."

"No, you're supposed to guess."

"What?"

"Do you know why his father killed his mother and then shot himself? See if you can guess."

"Are you messing with me? You're still angry aren't you."

"I am." Suddenly, the knife slipped between his ribs, and Angus gasped. He reached for her hand but found only a nub of bone. As he struggled to comprehend what was happening, Fernanda pulled the knife out and plunged it again.

"The answer is because I made him do it."

CHAPTER 130

EVEREST BASE CAMP

Patrick arrived at Base Camp on June 16, exhausted and coughing. From a distance, Pemba recognized who it was. One look at Patrick's face said it all. It was the stare of a man who had made selfish choices and ruined his life. Pemba rushed to greet Patrick, relieved, but with a heavy heart for all the bad news they had to discuss.

"Thank you for coming back," said Pemba. "Chomolungma will know peace again."

Patrick nodded, catching his breath.

"You're welcome, Pemba. It's good to see you. I'm sorry for everything." Patrick neglected to mention that Fernanda had not given him much of a choice.

"Patrick, I have sad news. Nigel's dead."

Patrick absorbed the words and dropped his head. "Wow," he mumbled. "How'd he die?"

Pemba had heard the news via Sherpa and mule. Nigel was beloved in the climbing community, and word had spread fast. "I don't know," said Pemba.

Patrick nodded. "How about Angus? Oh, wait, never mind."

"What?"

"I was going to ask about Angus Addison, but you never met him. Sorry, I'm tired." Patrick sat down on the edge of a boulder. "Tell me, Pemba, what's going on up here?"

Pemba, too, took a seat. "Very bad. Avalanche in Icefall. Four die, include Tensing. Tensing leaves wife, two children."

"Pemba, have you seen Renata?"

"No. But—" Pemba hesitated. The following would be difficult to convey in words alone.

"But what?" asked Patrick.

Pemba excused himself, ran to his tent, and returned with Renata's climbing helmet.

Patrick's face went white. "Oh, my God. Where'd you find it?"

"I wake up in my tent, candles burning by my feet."

"And that's why you called," said Patrick. After a long pause, he spoke again. "She told me a few things about her religion, but I took it with a grain of salt. I don't—I'm not a spiritual man, in case you haven't noticed."

"You are now," Pemba countered.

"Maybe, but it's too late to find a god who will help me."

"Not too late for next life."

Patrick smiled, unsure.

"We pray later, bring peace for everyone."

"As easy as that?" Patrick asked with skepticism. "I hope you're right."

"Never too late."

"Where are Pasang and Phurba?"

"Pasang in hospital, Kathmandu. Phurba quit."

"Pemba, you know I have to go up there again, right?"

Pemba frowned but nodded. "But too early. You just arrive. The mountain not ready too. Monsoon come soon."

"We'll see. I'm not sure I have a choice."

Pemba nodded again, unsure. Over the next hour, the sun went down, and the temperature began to drop.

"Pemba, give me a day, and we should go. I don't have a permit, so don't say anything. You and me only. We'll sneak out on the eighteenth."

Pemba nodded, then looked away.

***

Patrick dreamed he was on a farm with hundreds of cows in long, white industrial barns. It was a professional slaughterhouse. The sun was too bright, and he felt sick; something was wrong. He was running from someone, trying to escape, when he heard voices with accents, for this was Brazil. Afraid, he doubled back but suddenly saw blood. It was everywhere, all over his hands and body, soaking his hospital gown. He turned to search for the wound and noticed the trail of drops. For sure, his hunters would find him.

Suddenly, he found a gate on the periphery, his first glimpse of freedom in weeks. Patrick threw the latch and opened it but stopped short. There was nothing but red dirt for as far as the eye could see.

Then, voices. *Oi criança, aonde voce vai? Hey kid, where are you going?* Oddly, he understood everything, even the sarcasm. He wasn't going anywhere, and they all knew it. Patrick was a prisoner on a thirty-three-thousand-acre organ farm in the middle of nowhere and losing blood. Heat radiated up from the dirt, and suddenly, he felt faint.

Two ranch hands appeared out of nowhere, each grabbing an arm and dragging him back to the room beneath the barn, where the doctor jabbed yet another needle into the small of his back.

***

Patrick woke in his tent screaming, triggering a coughing jag. Soaked with sweat, he couldn't help but break down. *I understand* he thought, hoping the dream might signify an opportunity to make things right.

Pemba, hearing the commotion, poked his head in and handed Patrick a mug of Sherpa tea. "Drink this. Help your cough. Breakfast thirty minutes."

"Thank you, Pemba," said Patrick, his sweat beginning to cool. It was ten below zero, and he would freeze if he didn't change, but the nightmare lingered, especially the pain in his lower back. Renata had told him bad things were happening in Brazil, and for the most part, Patrick ignored her. After breakfast, he returned to his tent but didn't dare close his eyes. In less than twenty-four hours, he would begin the climb of his life, and there was no telling how things would play out.

***

Pemba and Patrick slept in separate tents, as Base Camp was only half-full. Tashi was safely in the hospital, thankfully, but Pemba couldn't rest, so he reached into his duffle and pulled out his pictures.

The first was his wife, Dawa, seven years his junior and, without question the love of his life. Together, they shared three children, one boy and two girls, and it was Pemba's mission to work hard enough so his son didn't have to follow in his footsteps. Pemba's other pictures were of the individual children: Maya, Lhakpa, and Ananda. In turn, he prayed for each one, then prayed he would live to see them again.

Unfortunately, he would have to doctor a new route through the Icefall, but that was the least of his worries. Pemba held the photos to his chest as his eyelids drooped. The prayers soothed him, and he thought he might even sleep, no small feat with all at stake—but suddenly, he heard something.

***

Patrick woke before the alarm and stared at the tent flap for hours, anticipating Pemba's arrival, but his Sherpa friend was late. The plan was to leave a note for the others saying they'd hiked to Tengboche for supplies, but where was Pemba? Patrick double-checked the time. If they waited much longer, the others would be up and see them heading for the Icefall. Worried, Patrick got dressed and crawled out.

It was still dark, but he could make out the shapes of the tents in the moonlight: thirty canvas domes swaying in the wind. Patrick half-expected to see Pemba on his way, but not a soul stirred. No doubt some climbers were sleepless in their tents, so Patrick sneaked to Pemba's, but something was amiss.

In the poor light, Pemba's tent seemed too short. Had it collapsed in the wind? Yes, the canvas flapped free in the breeze, licking the ground, and as Patrick drew closer, he realized it had been ripped down the middle. Panicked, Patrick ran the final twenty yards and pulled the tatters back to find Pemba, eyes open and still as a stone. A puff of wind scattered photographs from Pemba's hand, and Patrick scrambled to catch them as they spiraled away.

"I need the doctor! Wake up, Pemba needs help! Can I get the doctor?" Patrick stood, continuing to call out. Then, from the darkness, figures appeared out of nowhere, surrounding the tents. As many as thirty men stared.

"Which of you is the doctor? Help Pemba! I think he's—" Not a soul moved, and Patrick noticed that many of the tents were in ribbons like Pemba's, each one shredded. Patrick regarded the circle of phantoms.

"Who are you?" One man was missing an arm. Blood soaked his parka, his face shattered by an avalanche. Patrick took a step back. Another man was frozen solid, and Patrick recognized the parka. "You were above Camp Four." Patrick took another step down the mountain, but three dead men closed the gap.

"Are you going to kill me or let me climb?" After another long silence, Patrick stepped toward the Icefall, and the dead let him pass.

Chapter 131

With eleven thousand feet to climb, Patrick was already spent. Oddly, there was no wind. The mountain was quiet and darker than he'd ever seen it. One headlamp was not enough to illuminate the ghostly seracs, making the start of this trip the most frightening to date.

When the rope disappeared beneath the snow an hour later, Patrick realized he'd have to find a new route. Surrounding him were piles of ice that weren't there a month ago—incalculable tonnage formerly adhered to the cliff above. Somewhere beneath his feet were the bodies of five good men being processed through the Icefall—at least, he hoped they were still there.

The sun rose just as he left the Icefall, and he breathed easier in the wide-open Western Cwm. Two hours later, Patrick thought he heard waves crashing, only to realize it was the high winds scraping the great peak above. Then came crunching footsteps. Patrick turned to see two of the dead climbers from Base Camp following a quarter mile back, and it was all the motivation he needed to press on.

An hour outside Camp Two, the dead men disappeared, and Patrick made camp, hoping they would not return. He felt nauseous but forced himself to eat. After dinner, Patrick lay awake listening. It was impossible not to imagine them outside the tent, about to slice it down the middle and him with it.

***

As Patrick left Camp Two, he spotted the two corpses again. It chilled him to think it could be Mallory and Irvine, but he hoped to never find out. With that thought, he started up the steep ice of the Lhotse Face. Eight hours later, Patrick limped into Camp Three. At 8 pm, Patrick turned down the lantern. A vicious wind whipped the tent, and the stars were bright, giving the tent an ethereal glow.

Patrick drifted, and the nightmare picked up where it had left off, except he wasn't being chased this time. Instead, he was in a cell beneath the barn with two naked boys, showing their scars. Mateus had been there a week, and Luiz, nearly two months.

"Where am I?" asked Patrick.

"You're under the barn. Don't move. You're bleeding, and it will hurt until the Doctor comes with pills."

Patrick looked down. His hand was missing and there was a gauze bandage wrapped around the stump.

"Why would a doctor—?"

"We call him the Witch Doctor, and this is not a hospital. He's bad, and he's killing us piece by piece."

"I don't understand."

"There are only two reasons to be down here: for sale or for sacrifice, and those that are sold are never disfigured like we are."

"So, I'm for sacrifice?! Why?"

"Offerings."

"Offerings to whom?"

"Dark spirits. But the rumor is that he doesn't believe anymore. We pray the rumor is true."

Patrick, panicking, began suggesting ways they might escape. Perhaps they could trick the guard or take turns digging? Mateus and Luiz stared back, their hope long gone. Patrick looked at their hands. Judging by their missing fingers, they'd already tried everything.

"You won't escape," said Luiz. "You were stupid and ignored instructions."

"What do you mean? I tried, I—" said Patrick.

"You could have helped someone."

"You don't know—"

"You are the son of a dentist with money and you've had everything handed to you your entire life. Renata told you her sister was in danger, and then you stole her money. She feared you would let her down. But this isn't Peggy, friend. You messed with a Kiumba."

"Khumbu? Like the icefall?"

"No. Kiumba is a dark spirit. Worse than anything nature can inflict, even on Mount Everest."

Patrick stared, dumbfounded. "She's going to kill me?"

Luiz looked down at his damaged hands and scraped the dirt from one of the remaining nails. "Sometimes Kiumba let you live but ruin your life somehow, but you've already ruined yours."

***

Patrick woke from the nightmare, shaking. *Kiumba. Kiumba. Kiumba.* The word was stuck in his head. An hour before the alarm, he heard the distinct sound of the two ghosts chipping their way up the mountain. It was time to move. Patrick crawled out of the tent and, before clipping into the fixed line, looked down. Even if he jumped and tried to take his own life, the dead men would surely stop his slide. Pained, he turned toward Camp Four and set out on what should be his penultimate day.

In the late afternoon, Patrick arrived on the wind-whipped South Col, climbed into the tent, and began melting snow. He ate what might be his last meal, knowing there would be no sleep tonight.

Chapter 132

The House with the Pond, Sanborn, NH

Zé went to bed, but he was too excited to sleep. Although there had been some boring pages to date, the ability to call up objects was a certified gem. He woke early the next day, opened the Book, and couldn't believe his eyes.

As soon as he finished the first sentence, his life changed. Anything he'd ever coveted, every human desire, was answered. With everlasting life came power, wealth, and experience—and with this new page, the Book provided instructions. It was only a matter of time before he became the most powerful being on the planet.

Zé read, taking notes on how to achieve his goal. Everything seemed feasible except for one tricky part: he would have to be buried at a crucial juncture. The thought of asking Aparecida was unrealistic, as she had no faith in the Book, nor could he imagine her doing it correctly. Even if he did ask her, where would Vilma be? It took hours of contemplation before he had a plan.

***

Zé bought a spade and a hunting knife at a hardware store in Concord, and when he arrived back in Sanborn, went into the woods to search for a brook. Two minutes into the walk and not far from the house, he was surprised to stumble upon a perfect avenue of trees—several hallways, in fact. He'd found an abandoned tree farm. *Vilma would like this*, he thought, surprised to catch himself thinking of his daughter.

Zé continued past the grove and searched for three hours before finding a brook with sufficient flow. After walking it for a quarter mile, he found the proper slope, did some perfunctory landscaping, and began work on what would become a temporary grave. When it was finished, he put the shovel down and read aloud from the Book, reciting every word carefully. Then, he hid the Book under a log and readied the knife. The next part was crucial: he had to divert the stream with a pile of dirt, get in the grave, pull as much dirt over him as possible, slit his wrists, and bleed out. As long as he set it up correctly, the stream would cover him with the rest of the dirt.

***

The brook washed the dirt into the grave, and mud pooled over and around Zé's body, planting him firmly under the stream's new course. He awakened a few hours later, packed tightly with no need to breathe. He was immortal now, and if he played his cards right, today was the first day of eternal life. First, he wiggled a finger, then his whole hand. His arms were noticeably more powerful, the left breaking up through the surface as the right followed. Finally, the legs kicked, and he stood, muck falling off into the babbling waters.

Zé grabbed the Book from under the log and carried it back to the house. He felt different, most notably his strength and lack of everyday aches and pains. For a practice drill, he called up the spade, and it worked. Then, remembering how much fun it could be, he called the hatchet faster than ever.

Chapter 133

Nine thousand feet down the North Face

Renata's eyes opened. The pale glow of daylight was just enough to make it through the snow. She wondered for a moment if the gods had answered her prayers, and in an instant, she knew they had.

There was no pain and no panic, nor was she cold or claustrophobic. The fall killed her, but that didn't matter anymore. She was awake, and all she had to do was dig out from beneath the sloughs that had buried her. Renata balled her hand into a fist, then opened it back up. The snow and ice were no match.

CHAPTER 134

The alarm went off at 11 pm and outside was pitch-black. Patrick rose, coughing as he did, wishing to take back the day he started mountain climbing. Once his eyes adjusted, the Milky Way above made it seem as if he was floating in the cosmos, and the temperature did nothing to dispute the illusion. As soon as he started out, the crunching footsteps returned. This time, they were closer, and there were more of them, but he didn't dare look. At 4 am came twilight and an hour later dawn, but his followers put a damper on the optimistic boost the sun had provided his first time here.

As Patrick closed in on the Second Summit, he realized that his followers had dwindled to one. Without turning, Patrick listened to the pursuer's pace and labored to match it, but it was a losing battle. Finally, he turned, and sure enough, there was one corpse there, ensuring he continued up. In desperate need of a break, Patrick stopped for a drink, but the climber kept coming. As Patrick huffed on his regulator, hypoxia washed over him, and he was drunk in a matter of seconds.

With his fear diminished, Patrick began to wonder who the climber might be. Like everyone who made it to this altitude, goggles and an oxygen mask covered his face.

Patrick shouted down, "Hey! Who are you?"

The man yelled back, but it was unintelligible. Patrick, dizzy and confused, nodded his head. Finally, the mystery climber caught up.

"You and me! Let's do this!" said the climber.

The man's enthusiasm was the last thing he'd expected. Forgetting to ask the essential questions, Patrick turned up the mountain, and together, they climbed down the Second Summit's backside onto the Cornice Traverse.

Halfway across the knife-edge, the stranger called out. "Hold on!"

Patrick stopped and almost lost his balance. Then he looked down, and it was not unlike the view from an airplane window. Aside from the cliff face, there was nothing below but open air. Light-headed, Patrick clung to the rope for dear life.

Suddenly, the mystery climber twisted Patrick's oxygen valve, and he breathed in the rejuvenating vapors.

"How's that?" asked the man.

Patrick wondered for a second if he'd forgotten the man's name or if he'd even asked. *Come to think of it, was this guy alive or dead?* "Much better." Hey, did I ask your name?"

"Joe! But let's get off this damned knife-edge first!" The two men continued as Patrick's mind wandered. Questions mounted but were just as quickly forgotten as they pressed on through heavy crosswinds and past giant cornices that flared off the north side.

When they arrived at the Hillary Step, Joe took the lead, fixing ropes and running the show for the handicapped Patrick. An hour later, they'd beaten the Step, leaving Patrick to wonder how he'd gotten this far. The two men celebrated as Patrick realized he was standing in the exact spot where he'd last seen Renata.

"Where're you from, Patrick?"

"Beverly, Massachusetts. How about you?"

"Get outta town! Me too!" said Joe.

Patrick's intuition cried out. Joe's voice was familiar, after all. "You wouldn't be a dentist, would you, Joe?" Joe stared back, looking like a frozen fighter pilot behind the goggles and mask. "Did you hear me, Joe?" Suddenly, the wind died.

"I heard you. How'd you know I was a dentist?"

Patrick smiled as if he knew a secret. "Because you're not real. It's not *that* small a world." Patrick stood and, for an awkward moment, tried to decide if he should lift his dead father's mask. "I've got one more question."

"What's that?"

"Where's Renata?" said Patrick.

"Renata?" Joe bowed his head as if caught in a lie. "She's waiting. The spell worked."

"What spell?"

"The one she cast while you were shitting your brains out. They told you to stay away from the meat and eggs, son."

Reaching over, Patrick grabbed Joe's goggles and tore them off his face. Dr. Joe stared back, his eyes grayed by death.

Patrick gasped. "Oh my God."

"Never mind me, son. Let's prep you for the final run." Dr. Joe reached over, slowly removed Patrick's goggles, and began clearing ice from around the nosepiece. Patrick felt the cold go to work on his face, stinging his cheeks and nose.

"Do you have anything else you should tell me before I go up?" asked Patrick.

"Just a question, son. Why did you leave her? You made a fool of your mother and me. Most people smarten up sooner or later, but not you. I wish I had it to do all over. I'd kick your ass every time you opened your damned mouth."

Patrick stood aghast, realizing, too late, that his father was backpedaling.

"Wait! Stop! My goggles!"

"Oh, you're not getting these back, son. You know that. I mean, we spoiled you, but you aren't that stupid."

Patrick squinted in the bright sunlight. "You're not my father. Give me the goggles." Patrick lunged and caught Joe's oxygen hose, yanking his mask off and releasing a mask full of congealed blood. All the damage from the shotgun was there, fresh and red. Half the jaw was missing, as was part of his neck. Suddenly, a rogue wind caught Joe full in the chest, throwing him out and over the North Face. He tumbled wildly in the air, down and out of sight, Patrick's goggles still in his hand.

"No!" Patrick screamed. He would go snowblind without the goggles, and he had to see to descend. Patrick sat down hard and closed his eyes to think. He needed Renata now. Maybe he'd get a chance to speak, and he could convince her it wasn't too late to save Vilma. If that didn't work, he could end it all with a running jump.

***

Patrick struggled to his feet, eyes crusting, prepared to climb in the only direction that might save his life. His stump ached, and his lungs felt like leather. He tried alternating eyes, cracking one and then the other, to preserve his vision, but he knew his eyesight was on a timer.

For the first time, he could hear everything but the wind. His crampons crunched, the legs of his snowsuit rubbed together, and the heave of his respirator deteriorated to a screeching whine as the tank ran dry. Instantly, his energy ebbed, dropping him to one knee. Once on the ground, he shed the tank and let it tumble down the mountain.

With only yards to go, Patrick turned, and Renata was there, facing away from him, a blurry silhouette in his watery eyes. Her snowsuit was gone, replaced by a long, white dress that seemed a part of the mountain's ten-mile snow plume. With his remaining strength, Patrick stood up, eyes burning.

He searched for the words he'd practiced on the trek to Base Camp, but at the moment he needed them, he choked. One eye teared up, and he reached to wipe it, sending searing pain through his skull. He dropped to the snow, howling. Facedown and head spinning, Patrick sucked for oxygen that wasn't there.

"Dying," he managed to say.

"Yes," she said, turning to him.

"I can still help Vilma. Give me one more chance. I didn't understand." As he finished the words, Patrick went blind.

"Stand up," she replied.

"I can't see!"

Renata reached out, and Patrick found her hand. Together, they got him to his feet. Encouraged by her helping hand, Patrick couldn't help but wonder if he might make it down the mountain. "I need goggles and oxygen."

"Up here," she said and nudged him in the direction of the summit. Patrick couldn't see her gray skin and frostbitten features.

"Are you saving me?" he asked, speech slurring, legs buckling, but Renata said nothing. Suddenly, they stopped, and Renata let go of his hand.

"Don't leave me here! I can't see where I'm going!"

Renata circled behind.

"Renata! I can't find—"

Patrick felt her foot in the small of his back, and his neck, arms, and legs followed his torso as he lurched toward the edge. There would be no forgiveness, no second chance. He managed two stumbling steps before the mountain ended and the sky began. With nothing beneath him, the Tibetan winds roared to life, whipping him momentarily upward like a discarded candy wrapper.

The impacts he made down the North Face happened in quick succession. Patrick's body caught jagged outcroppings at 28,000, 20,000, and 14,000 feet, feeling every tooth-shaking thud and crack of bone. Death finally came when he smacked the last ledge at one hundred and twenty miles per hour, then skidded through shattered shale before becoming wedged in a rocky couloir. What was left of Patrick froze in less than an hour.

Renata smiled, splitting a frostbitten lip before sending an avalanche after him. Patrick never summited.

Chapter 135

The House with the Pond, Sanborn, NH

Zé smiled as he awaited further instructions with the Book by his side. Magick coursed through every muscle. Becoming immortal was beyond amazing. *What's next, Book? Teach me everything.* Four hours later, a brand-new page appeared. The instructions were more detailed than ever:

Create others just as you were created.

Find eleven more revenants and eleven only.

Do not forewarn the recruits: kill, recite, bury.

Do not attack the heart. Guard the heart.

The reluctant will reconcile with time.

Live in secrecy.

Trust in The Book of Shadows.

The Book of Shadows! It had a name and a sinister one at that. And *Revenant!* That must be what he had become—a *revenant.* He would have to look the word up soon. Aparecida and Vilma would remain in the family after all, and when they were ready, they would search for disciples together.

Now that he had a direction, it was time to drive. Before he stood, however, a fly landed on his arm, and though he waved it away, it wouldn't leave. A second buzzed his head, followed by a third and a fourth.

Before getting in the car, Zé had a thought and called the spade into his hand. Vilma was young and must be distracted when it was her turn. Preparation was essential. Flies buzzed as he dug two graves around the side of the barn.

The lack of running water was becoming a detriment. Drinking water was appreciated, but the flies had discovered his poor hygiene. When he finished digging, he dove into the pond, but stagnant water and frogs' eggs did little to cleanse him.

CHAPTER 136

BOSTON, MASSACHUSETTS

Zé arrived back in Boston a disheveled mess, and Vilma caught the whiff immediately. "Papai, you smell bad."

"It must be the pond. I went for a swim. Perhaps I shouldn't have. Anyway, it's time for you to come to New Hampshire. First, I'll show you where I've been working, and then we'll rent you a place to stay." A fly swarmed Zé's head.

"I hate flies. Kill it!" said Vilma.

Aparecida, meanwhile, was surprised by Zé's change of heart. "You're not too busy with your book?"

"I'm all caught up, love. It's time for me to share what I've learned. The hard part is over. We will be a new family."

"Where are we staying?"

"There are plenty of places to choose from. I figured I'd let you look."

A fly landed on Aparecida's arm, and she brushed it away. "Did you bring these flies? When was the last time you showered—with soap?"

Zé couldn't recall. "I'll take one before we check out."

***

Even after his shower, Vilma continued to complain about the smell. Thankfully, it was a warm enough day to drive with the windows down.

Zé looked to Aparecida. "Do you smell it too?"

Aparecida sat against the passenger door, staring back. "I do," she said in a whisper. "Did the Book do this?"

***

After making sure they weren't followed, Zé turned up the driveway and pulled around to the barn, out of sight. Then, leaving the Book in the trunk, he executed his plan.

"All right, stay out of the yard and the field because you could be seen by a passing car. The house isn't ours yet, and no one knows we're here. Come here first, though. I have something exciting to show you both."

Zé got out and led them up the path through the woods. "I found this the other day when I went for a walk. Someone planted a tree farm years ago, and it went to seed. Now, they look—like—this!" Suddenly, the wild trees gave way to parallel rows, with the canopy blocking most of the sunlight.

"Cool!" said Vilma. "I'm going to sprint to the end!" Off she ran, only to run out of steam far short of her goal.

"Come back, Vilma! Do you want to see a trick?"

"Yeah!"

"All right, watch this. I'm going to call a knife from the house—to my hand."

"No way."

"Watch." Zé snapped his wrist, and his hunting knife appeared in his hand. Both Vilma and Aparecida gasped.

"How'd you do that?" asked Vilma.

"I'll tell you in a little bit. But first, let me show you a few more things. Do you see the last tree in the row down there? On the left?"

"Yes."

"While Aparecida and I walk back to the barn, stick the knife in the ground at the base of that tree. Keep your eye on it because I will call it to my hand from the barn like last time. When you see it disappear before your eyes, come find us, and I'll show you how it's done. Do you remember how to get back to the house?"

"Straight down that path?"

"Exactly. It's going to take us five minutes or so, but come to the barn as soon as you see it disappear."

"Okay!" said Vilma.

✳✳✳

Zé enthusiastically led Aparecida down the path toward the barn, repeating the directions in his head. Like his own burial, he would have to be quick, albeit for different reasons. *Kill. Recite. Bury. Do not attack the heart.*

"How did that happen? Did the Book teach you that?" asked Aparecida.

"Yes! You won't believe what I've learned. I haven't been up here relaxing. I promise you that."

Aparecida smiled. She hadn't seen him this passionate in years. As they passed his car in the driveway, Zé jogged the final steps to the right side of the barn and disappeared around the corner. She lost him temporarily until he stuck his head back out.

"Come here before I call Vilma. The Book is here, and I want to show you something first." Aparecida did as she was told and stepped around the side of the barn, ducking between the building and thick brush. Many of the closest trees had branches that overlapped the barn's roof. Once past the bushes, there was an alleyway running the length of the building, and Zé was there waiting.

***

Vilma waited in the grove, staring at the knife, waiting for it to disappear. It was spooky here all alone, and she was beginning to get antsy. She thought she heard footsteps, like bare feet on pine needles, but from which direction she couldn't tell. The knife hadn't budged, and she didn't want to wait any longer.

Then something flashed in the next row, and Vilma stood, ready to run, when a woman in a white dress stepped through the trees, her arms wide open. Vilma could hardly believe her eyes. "It's *you!*"

***

"Ready? I'm going to call the knife," said Zé.

Aparecida noticed two holes in the ground behind him. "Have you been digging? Where's the Book?"

Zé snapped his fingers, and the knife appeared instantly. Aparecida was about to congratulate him when Zé swung the blade, catching her across the throat. It didn't hurt, but she was in shock. Blood spilled down her front, soaking her blouse. Her throat filled with blood. Aparecida watched in disbelief as Zé stuck the knife into the side of the barn and rushed to her side.

"This is part of the plan. Let's get you in the hole before Vilma arrives. Trust me." Zé seemed nervous as Aparecida's vision dimmed. Finally, Zé jumped into the pit and eased her into the grave. *Vilma should be here any second.*

Flies swarmed as he leaped from the pit and emerged from the hidden passage, holding the knife high over his head like a trophy. He'd cut

Aparecida so fast the blade was dry. Vilma would soon emerge from the shadowy path, and then it would be her turn. Not telling the victims was part of the plan, after all. *Kill. Recite. Bury. Do not attack the heart.*

When they were both in their graves, he'd fetch the Book from the trunk, recite the words, and bury them. But another minute passed. Where was she? Zé wondered if she might have seen what he did and ran, but there was no way.

Suddenly, the sky turned red, and Ze's heart sank. He dropped the knife and ran as fast as he could to the grove, checking row after row, but Vilma was gone. Flies buzzed around his face as he cursed at them, killing four with one slap as he struggled to understand what had happened. As he slapped, a dozen more took their place, and he realized he'd forgotten something.

In a panic, Zé sprinted to the car, grabbed the keys from the ignition, and opened the trunk. The Book was gone. Zé screamed, called the knife, and ran through the field. It didn't matter if someone noticed him now. Did Vilma have the Book? No, she didn't even know where he'd hidden it. Someone was on to him. *The timing was too perfect.*

At a loss, Zé headed back for Aparecida, whose body lay cooling at the bottom of the pit. Zé struggled to recall the written words because he'd read them only once and straight from the text. It was far from memorized. Without The Book of Shadows as a guide, it was a shot in the dark. In desperation, he began shoveling dirt over Aparecida's corpse.

***

As the sun went down, Zé, out of options, waited in desperation. He listened for cars, sirens, and potential threats. He still wasn't sure who was responsible for what had happened but suspected *one*. He'd seen Juliana in some of his visions, but that seemed so long ago. Did she have the skill to craft such a plan? As he stood to walk to the car, it hit him: *If I could see her, then perhaps she could see me.*

One last time, Zé stood over Aparecida's grave. *Climb out*, he willed, desperate for another mind to help him think, but the grave remained still. His words were off, somehow. It was time to say goodbye to the house and, for now, the Book. At least he was immortal. He had all the time in the world to find it again.

***

Shaken, Zé got into the car and reached for the ignition, but the keys weren't there. Remembering he'd used them to open the trunk, he reached for the door handle when something lurched out of the dark barn doorway and into his peripheral vision. Before he could turn his head, the driver's side window exploded, and she was on him, swinging and smashing with abandon.

Zé saw stars, and he passed out. When he came to seconds later, she was still hammering away. Blood was in his eyes, and his shoulder had separated. He tried to raise his arm, but it was too late. His orbital socket was broken, and his arm was useless. Blood flowed as the hatchet connected again and again. As she opened the door, Zé spilled into the driveway.

If he could only stand, but the punishment continued, and Zé never made it to his feet. In less than a minute, both arms and one leg, from the knee down, were amputated and kicked aside. When Zé stopped moving, Fernanda dropped the hatchet. "Remember me?"

Zé nodded.

"No immortality for you," said Fernanda. "Juliana has The Book of Shadows, and I have my instructions. When I'm finished having fun, I'll remove your heart, but first, I'm going to let you know what it feels like to be kept in a dungeon."

Zé wanted to pray, but he had abandoned his gods. If he could, he would pray for the ability to finish himself, but Fernanda—along with Juliana—had robbed him of the ability.

"Sorry for your loss, Dr. Zé. It was a beautiful eulogy but not moving enough for Aparecida. She's around the corner, right? Let's get her up here. I'll be right back."

Chapter 137

Vilma sat in the back seat of Renata's car, excited to have her big sister back in her life. "Where were you, Juliana? I missed you!"

"I've been to so many places, Vilma. I even climbed to the top of the world."

The young girl's eyes lit up. "You climbed a mountain? You never used to climb mountains!"

Renata smiled at Vilma in the rearview mirror, unsure how this conversation would end. "Well, I wouldn't recommend it."

"Then why'd you do it?" said Vilma.

"I thought I had to. It was freezing and hard to breathe, but I thought of you when I was at my worst. You comforted me."

"I did?"

"Of course. I missed you terribly. Vilma, I need to tell you some things that will be hard to hear, and you won't like some of them, but I must be honest. They're things you need to know. Is that all right?"

Vilma sensed the serious nature of Juliana's voice and sat back. "I guess so. What am I not going to like?"

"Probably the changes. Changes can be difficult. But once you're over them, you'll never look back."

"All right, what is it?"

"There's good news and bad news—and truth and lies. One of the good things is that our mother, Beatriz, never left us. She was murdered, and our grandmother was, too. We were lied to by Papai. What I'm telling you now will help you later in life. You shouldn't grow up believing your mother left you.

Vilma took a moment to process the thought. "I didn't know about grandma. Papai said you ran away, too. You ran away because the Monster of Codó took Fernanda."

Juliana nodded, never losing eye contact. "That's what Papai said, but he wasn't telling the truth. I did run away, but it was because I was running from *him*."

"Is Papai the Monster?" Vilma was smart.

"*Was.* Yes, he was, but I took care of that. He's not the Monster anymore."

"Did you take care of Aparecida, too?"

"No. Papai took care of Aparecida. She was bad, too."

"I'm not surprised." Vilma turned her head to look out the window.

"Do you think you're going to miss Papai?" asked Juliana.

Vilma took a minute to think. "Mmm, I don't know. Papai was always working. Juliana, am I going to live with you now?"

"I would love to, Vee, but I can't."

"Why not? Who am I going to live with?"

Juliana heard a twinge of fear in Vilma's voice. "I'm going to be completely honest with you, but first, I want to tell you that I would *love* to live with you, and it breaks my heart that I can't. I set things up for you, though. I know a cute family with a daughter your age. Her name is Janete, and you two are going to be sisters and best friends."

"I don't know those people! I want to live with you!"

Juliana took her hands off the steering wheel and turned around to look at Vilma. "Vilma, I can't stay. Things didn't go well for me on that mountain, and I'm different now."

"Are you *dead?*"

"The way you mean it, yes. But we wouldn't be having this conversation if I weren't alive in some way."

"Is that why you're not really driving this car?"

Juliana smiled. "You're smart. Yes. Would you be more comfortable walking in a park? Or floating in a rowboat? I can make it happen."

"No, that's okay. I think I understand what's happening."

"Vilma, I'll be watching. I may not always be around, but if you light a candle and say my name, I will know. We have a connection that can't be broken."

Tears welled in Vilma's eyes. "When are you leaving?"

"Soon. Do you remember Fernanda? She's going to bring you to see Ana, Paulo, and Janete. They heard about what happened on the mountain and wouldn't understand if they saw me.

"I don't want you to go," said Vilma, and the young girl's face pinched tight as she began to cry.

"I know, little sister. I know," said Juliana. "But it's not for forever."

ABOUT THE AUTHOR

Michael Clark grew up in New Hampshire and met his wife, Josi, in Massachusetts. He now spends a chunk of his summers visiting his in-laws in Brazil and speaks Portuguese like a six-year-old (on a good day).

In addition to *Hell on High*, he is the author of *The Legend of Mildred Wells* (formerly *The Patience of a Dead Man*), also from Brigids Gate Press.

ACKNOWLEDGEMENTS

Brasileiros:

To Janete Velky, for helping me better understand Umbanda, Candomblé, and Quimbanda, three religions commonly lumped together under the term *Macumba*.
To Renata Reveley for suggesting I begin my story in Brazil.
To Mateus Roberts for the fantastic cover art. *Instagram @mateusrobertsart*
To Josilene Clark for sharing her culture with me for twenty-two years and counting.

Estrangeiros:
To Erin Bergin, Sherry Pratt, and Linda Martin, my early team of beta readers: Thanks for keeping it real.
To Ross Jeffrey, Erica Metcalf, and Joshua Marsella: My second wave of constructive criticism.
To Kevin Whitten, aka *Well Read Beard,* for his thorough critique, followed by an intense back-and-forth in which he was the one to nail the book's title. Also, for being instrumental in hooking me up with Brigids Gate Press.
To M.J. Pankey for completing my unfinished thoughts and fixing the broken ones.
To Alyson Faye for her top-notch copy editing and proofreading skills.
To Heather and Steve at Brigids Gate Press for publishing this adventure.

CONTENT WARNINGS

amputation
blood
bodies/corpses
organ trafficking
death
drug use
forced captivity
rape

More from Brigids Gate Press

MELINDA WEST: MONSTER GUNSLINGER

KC Grifant

In an Old West overrun by monsters, a stoic gunslinger must embark on a dangerous quest to save her friends and stop a supernatural war.

Sharpshooter Melinda West, 29, has encountered more than her share of supernatural creatures after a monster infection killed her mother. Now, Melinda and her charismatic partner, Lance, offer their exterminating services to desperate towns, fighting everything from giant flying scorpions to psychic bugs. But when they accidentally release a demon, they must track a dangerous outlaw across treacherous lands and battle a menagerie of creatures—all before an army of soul-devouring monsters descend on Earth.

The Witcher meets Bonnie and Clyde in a re-imagined Old West full of diverse characters, desolate landscapes, and fast-paced adventure.

THIS COLD NIGHT

Erica Schaef

Following the death of a loved one, Rachelle Collins visits Ferguson Estate, an expansive country mansion which holds many fond memories, and one sinister secret, within its walls. Throughout the course of a single, terrifying night, Rachelle must confront horrors, both psychological and tangible, to prove just how far she is willing to go to keep her family together.

EXTINCTION HYMNS

Eric Raglin

A vengeful owl haunts the man who poached her. A desperate entrepreneur holds a ghost hostage for profit. An addict finds hope and terror in an imprisoned angel. A father and son search their dying world for something to eat other than human flesh. Eric Raglin, author of Nightmare Yearnings, returns with his second collection of horror and weird fiction. Strange, terrifying, and tender, these eighteen stories explore what happens when extinction comes for us all.

ENTER THE DARKNESS

Sarah Budd

During the Spring Solstice, four people enter the caves underneath London.

Garth: a shy young man, who seeks to save the girl of his dreams.

Cassie: a beautiful young woman, who seeks to use the dark magic of the caves for her own purposes.

Bill: an older man with a terrible secret, who seeks to find Garth and Cassie before it's too late.

Sienna: a con artist with a dark past, who seeks to escape her fate as a chosen sacrifice.

Four people enter. Each of them must battle their personal demons before facing the White Lady, who rises each year during the Spring Solstice with a hunger for human flesh.

Only one of them will survive.

Visit our website at: www.brigidsgatepress.com